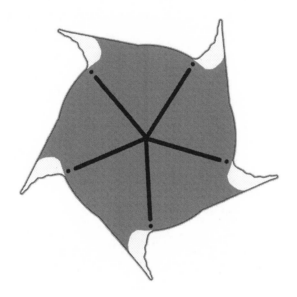

CAPPING S'ERS

Book 1 in the Star Universe

By L. R. Kerns

Published by L. R. Kerns

Cover Design and Interior by Kimmi Kerns.

ISBN-13: 978-1-7327101-0-8

www.lrkerns.com

AUTHOR'S NOTE

Suicide is a serious and growing problem.

This book is not intended to treat the subject lightly. It is the hope of the author that anyone contemplating suicide seek help because death is NOT the answer. That is why the author is contributing 50% of all proceeds from this book to suicide prevention.

The National Suicide Hotline number is: 1-800-273-8255. Call them. They want to hear your story.

DEDICATION

To Joey

A life that ended way too early

Table of Contents

Prologue

I wake up, roll over and look at my clock. 10:23 a.m. Just under twelve hours till show time. I have been waiting for this day, it seems like forever, and now that it is here, I don't know what I am going to do. Am I going to live or am I going to die? Isn't that the question facing all S'ers?

I fold back the covers and get out of bed. I don't bother making it. What does one wear on your last day on earth? I fix a breakfast twice as much as normal and then can't eat it all. I scrape the extra food into the trash and pile the dirty dishes in the sink. As I open the door to leave, the phone rings. I pause for a moment, then close and deadbolt the door.

Season One, Episode One

CAPPING S'ERS
XCAL - 1
10-11 pm
New "Dawn Adams"
S1/EP01, (2017), The premier of a weekly show that highlights one individual who desires to commit suicide. With an assist from thrower Ricky Fordham, the individual may go through with it or not.

I arrive at the cavernous Studio 13 an hour early. My footsteps echo in the emptiness, but I can't sit at home any longer. I've already had dinner, and I am ready to go.

The two stadium-style 100-seat capacity portable bleachers that are arranged on one side of the studio are empty. It is too soon for the audience to be let in, although I hear a crowd gathering outside. There are a few stagehands milling about, but I don't know any of them, so I proceed to my trailer.

Yep. There is my name on the door. Ricky Fordham. I go inside and sit at the table. After a quick glance in the mirror, I put my backpack on the table and pull out the star. I hold it with both my good right hand

and my mangled left hand. I stare down at the disc-shaped object with its five sharpened points.

The disc has an eight-inch diameter with the points sticking out an additional two inches. The body is half of an inch thick in the middle, a quarter of an inch on the edge, and the tips of the points are razor sharp. It is painted silver, and if you look closely you can still see the scars from when it was beaten. The points are white. The disc body has straight line grooves on top that begin with dots beneath each point that flow to and join in the center.

The studio wanted to paint different colors on the body to create a swirly look as it spins through the air. I won't let them because I don't allow anyone else to touch the star. I've never let anyone touch it, and I wasn't giving it up for a week for someone else to play around with. I wouldn't be here if it wasn't for that star.

My mangled left hand aches as it always does when I am anxious. As I stare down at the star, I also see the scar in the web of my right hand from the time the star cut me, and I bled all over it.

After about a half hour, Brian knocks on my trailer door.

"Ricky, you in there?" he calls.

"Yes. Come on in, Brian."

"You're here early."

"Yeah. Anxious, I guess."

"Well, they're almost ready for you in makeup so you can head over whenever you're ready. After that, your assistant will help you get into your costume."

"Okay."

"Now, things are going to go a little different from what we talked about. Everything is still the same, but we added a segment where Phil is going to interview you. Since you are the star of the show, and no one knows anything about you, we figure the audience will be curious and want to know more."

"We haven't rehearsed this. What if I mess up the interview? What questions is he going to ask?"

"Don't worry about that. Phil is only going to ask you background stuff. Besides, there is a five-second delay on the live show, all except for your throw, of course. That way we can bleep out anything awkward you may say. Any questions for me?"

"No."

"Okay, good. I'll see you again before we air. All right? Break a leg, kid. You'll be great."

After patting me on the back, Brian leaves and I think back to when I first met him. I lay the star flat on the table and touch one of the points with my right hand. I found if I hold the star this way while trying to remember something, it is as clear as if it just happened.

I discovered this by accident as I was sitting in a foster home, remembering how I used to brush my twin's long silky hair. I was idly holding the star. This was after I started throwing again. When my hand touched one of the points, my memory became so vivid, I felt like I was time traveling. I tried the other points and it didn't matter which one I picked. They all acted the same. Now, whenever I want to remember something, I touch or hold a point of the star while doing so.

I remember I was still reluctant as I drove onto the studio grounds for the first time bright and early that Monday morning. After parking outside Studio 13 as I had been instructed by phone the previous week, I walked into the building and looked around. Against one wall was a stage. Arranged facing the stage were two sets of metal bleachers on wheels. The back half of the room was empty except for a giant video screen. A man wearing a frown and carrying a clipboard approached me.

"Who are you?" he asked.

"I'm the star of the show," was my reply.

"Talent," he muttered as he walked away. He approached the stage and yelled, "Brian! Your talent is here."

A man with long black hair and a full beard that had been dyed gold came from backstage, jumped down, and approached me.

"You are?" he asked.

"I'm the talent. The star of the show."

"Sounds more like you're a smart ass. Your dressing room is the trailer right back there in the corner. The door with the star on it. You can tell it's yours because your name is on it. Stow your stuff and then let's talk."

I looked down at my empty hands and shrugged. I walked over to the trailer in the corner and opened the door. Inside was a dressing table with mirror, a couch, a bed, and a bathroom in the back. Yep, looks like a trailer. I closed the door and walked back to the man with the golden beard.

"Is Harvey Howard here?" I asked.

"Who?"

"The producer."

"Oh yea, right. No. He sold the idea to the studio, took his money and ran. I'm the producer now. And director. My name is Brian Goldstein."

"Oh." I guess that explains the choice of beard color.

"What do you think?" Brian asked, gesturing around the sound stage. "Nice setup, huh?"

"This stage you built. It needs to be bigger."

"What?"

"A bigger stage. I need more room for my throws. This stage isn't big enough. I need a throwing area that is at least half the size of this room. It must be at least 80 feet long and 50 feet wide."

"You know this is only a six-episode run. There isn't money in the budget to build a stage that size."

"Okay. Forget the stage. I'll do it on the floor."

After staring at me like I had lost my mind, Brian said, "I guess that will work. Do you have a name for the show?"

"A name?"

"Yes, a name. What do you call what you do?"

"A throw. I throw a star."

"*The Throwing Star Show*. No. We can't call it that. Too boring. The name needs to be exciting and give the TV audience some idea of what the show is about."

"I don't know what else to call it."

Brian waved it off. "Well, don't worry about it. That's what we have a creative staff for. Those writers can come up with anything."

"Writers? Why would this show need writers?"

"Let me ask you something."

"Okay."

I looked down at my dirty sneakers. I would need new shoes for this show.

"This throw of yours. How long does it take?"

"The actual throw? Probably around 30 seconds. Add in some prep time. Getting everyone in place. Final staging. Maybe fifteen minutes."

"This is a one-hour show. That means 40 minutes 30 seconds of airtime. Thirty seconds for your throw. That leaves 40 minutes to fill. How exciting is watching you getting set up?"

"Not very. Pretty boring really."

I still wore jeans with holes in them. Maybe I would get new jeans as well.

"Right. So we fill 5 minutes with you at various times walking around setting up. Those are the teasers. Those little tidbits before the commercial breaks. We fill 5 minutes with a video package about the person about to kill themselves. Show them doing things around their hometown. That's flavor. That is at the beginning. Then 30 minutes of the person telling their story while being interviewed by Phil. Now, do you know of any person who is about to commit suicide who can talk coherently and intelligently for 30 minutes?"

"No."

I didn't know anyone, about to commit suicide or not, who could talk coherently and intelligently for 30 minutes.

"And that, my friend, is why we need writers," he proclaimed with a hand flourish as he walked away.

After reminiscing, I walk over to makeup. They fuss with my hair, but since it is so short there isn't a lot they can do with it except put in a couple blonde streaks for excitement. They put paste on my face, mascara, and false eyelashes. I never used makeup before, not even blush. I feel like a two-bit whore.

When I return to my trailer, I want to scrub my face clean, but they say I need it for the cameras. I guess. Getting into my costume takes fifteen minutes and I definitely need an assist. With my left hand in as bad of shape as it is, I never would be able to fit into my skintight one-piece black leather outfit. The network says this outfit is going to make me look sexy. Sexy? I don't want to look sexy. I just want to do my throws. Instead, I feel like a bad Cat woman caricature. So far, I am not feeling good about any of this.

They want me to wear these shoes with three-inch stiletto heels, but I can't do it. Physically, I cannot walk in them. I try walking around in my trailer with them on and fall three times. I can't throw in these things.

My assistant calls Brian who comes over and asks me what I am going to do about the shoes. I reply with a smart ass comment about going barefoot. He says that can be sexy too.

As I walk from my trailer back to the studio in my bare feet, I notice they have let the fans in, and the bleachers are starting to fill up. I spy my sister parked in one of the handicapped spaces, and hiding my left hand behind my back, I give a little wave with my right hand. Of course, she can't wave back. I feel calmer seeing her. She is the reason I am here. I am doing this crazy show for her.

I owe her at least that much.

Brian checks in with me via my earbud, and I tell him I'm fine, ignoring the rumblings of my stomach. I am surprised he can't hear them, they're so loud. I quickly duck into shadows as the *Capping S'ers* theme music starts up.

"Welcome, California, to a new weekly show that will delight. It will thrill you and, yes, even shock you. Welcome to *Capping S'ers!*"

I follow the spotlights as the audience politely applauds. The lights are swinging back and forth. One of the spotlights stops and zeros in on a random audience member, an older gentleman scratching his bald head.

"For the next sixty minutes, we are going to meet Dawn Adams. We are going to visit her in her hometown of Bakersfield. We are going to do a live interview of her here in our studio, and then LIVE we will watch the Capp and see if Dawn commits suicide or not. Stick around. We will be back after the commercial break."

That's my cue. On the stage floor, three men are standing in an arc spaced about 20 feet apart from each other. Between the first and the second man is a post with an arm from which a length of rope hangs down about halfway to the floor. The rope post is repeated between the second and third man. After the third man, an unadorned square post stands alone. The men are dressed in black form fitting leather shorts. They are bare chested and are also barefoot.

Funny, they had shoes on before. They are all standing stiff and erect, with a decorated silver or gold metal collar around their necks.

The men are all built well. Six packs. Developed chests. Bulky arms. And they all seem to be wearing oversized cups.

I walk over and grab hold of the first man in the arc and move him two inches to the left. Looking at the first man's new position, I gaze at the other two men, and move the first man back one inch to the right.

I look over at the audience to check on my sister. She is still there, but I notice that seated above her is the same older gentleman who was scratching his head. He is now adjusting himself. That guy just can't get comfortable.

Commercial.

During the commercial break I walk over to the coffee and donut table. While I am tempted, I think if I were to have even a bite, I might burst out of my costume. I rub my left hand again. It aches bad.

The doc is at the table as well. Chowing down on goodies. Maybe I should ask him about my hand. And my right hand itches where the scar is. I guess I can't get comfortable either.

I look over at the giant screen against the back wall where the next part of the show is to be displayed. As the *Capping S'ers* theme music plays, the camera fades in on a pretty, young girl standing on a curb next to a bright yellow sign that says BAKERSFIELD spanning the road. She is smiling as she says, "Welcome to Bakersfield, my hometown."

Next shot is the same girl standing outside a building with a tall spire that says FOX. "This is the Majestic Fox Theater. It is one of the last of its kind built in the Gilded Age. It opened Christmas Day, 1930, and was actively showing movies and hosting concerts until the borders closed. My name is Dawn Adams, and I am ready to commit suicide."

The scene shifts and now Dawn is standing outside a church. She says, "This is the First Baptist Church, which survived the 1952 earthquake, and was used commercially until it closed."

The final scene shows Dawn walking into a plain stucco home. She says, "This is my parent's home, but I live here, too. Let me show you my room."

The camera follows Dawn down a hallway and into a room. It pans to show the small room filled with a bed, desk and chair, and a window. Nothing adorns the walls. No posters, pictures or decorations of any kind. The view out the window is of a neighboring house. The girl sits on the bed. She says, "I spend most of my time here in this room. I hide in here. This is where I go to cry. I just want to kill myself."

With the camera zooming in on Dawn's face, the announcer says, "We will get up close and personal with Dawn right after these commercial messages."

My cue again. This time I walk over to the first

pole that is holding a rope. I move it a couple inches one way, then move it part way back.

Commercial.

Once I receive the 'all clear' message that I am off camera, I put the pole back where it started. Just part of the show. I look for my sister again and observe the older gentleman above her vigorously scratching his arm and looking around. Does he have fleas? I hope he doesn't give them to my sister.

During the two-minute break, Brian tells me my interview is next. So once the theme music has played and Phil, who is also the announcer, is done saying "We're back," I walk up the five steps onto the stage and sit down in one of the chairs.

"Welcome Ricky," Phil starts, "Thanks for agreeing to be interviewed."

"I didn't realize I have a choice."

"Ha, ha," Phil laughs, "Such a kidder. Seriously, I am sure everyone here and at home would like to know more about you."

"Not much to tell. Pretty boring, actually."

"Well, why don't you start with how you prepared for the show today?"

"Okay, well, I really didn't have anything to do today. Just makeup and getting dressed. All the prep work was completed over the past three months."

"So all you did today was makeup and get dressed?"

"Yeah, pretty much."

"So all the prep work was done over the past three months?"

"Correct."

"While you were naked."

"Excuse me?"

"You said today was the first time you got dressed. So all the prior three months, while doing prep work, you were naked."

"Are you some kind of pervert?"

"Not really. Just curious. Tell me about this prep work. What did you do this past week?"

"I spent this week working with lighting and cameras. I did my thing while they ran around like crazy figuring out what they needed to do, best angles, close-ups, where and when."

"And prior to that?"

"Oh, there was a ton of stuff to do. Finding the people to stand in the line. Practicing throws. Picking contestants to be S'ers, although Brian did most of that."

"So, do you think you are ready?"

"I feel great. Yes, I'm ready."

"What is the purpose of the ropes hanging from the poles?"

"The ropes are there to prove the star really can cut and isn't fake."

"Okay, enough for today. I hope you interview better next week."

I am too stunned to say a word, so I just stare at Phil until we are off the air and all the way through the commercial.

Commercial.

The next part of the show is the interview with the S'er. I don't want to watch this part. I don't want to know anything about someone who may soon be dead because of my actions. I don't want to know their problems or why they are on the show. I don't want to see them until the Capp, but as I am about to descend the stage stairs, Dawn is at the bottom. We both do an awkward, "You first. No, you go.", before I go down and head out to my trailer. Damn. Didn't want that.

Even though I can't see Dawn and Phil, I can still hear them. The speakers for the audience are loud. I want to turn on some music or something to drown them out, but there is no radio in my trailer. Just a TV that only gets the one official state channel that is broadcasting this show, and I turn that off.

"Hello, everyone. I am Phil Ebenezer. I have a PhD in clinical psychology. Now Dawn, tell me why you want to end your life."

"I made a mistake. Now I'm afraid everyone will find out my secret. I would rather die than have that happen."

"I see. Now, this secret. That you would rather die than have revealed. Can you tell us what it is?"

"No."

"Would this secret perhaps be sexual in nature?"

"What? No."

"Could it be that your boyfriend Keven got too worked up one night at the end of your date?"

I hear crying.

"No. Don't say that."

"Could it be you were kissing him too much, got him too excited, then maybe he went too far, or did you want him to do it?"

"No,"

I hear the trembling of her voice amidst her sobs.

"And now you're pregnant with his child? Could that be the secret you don't want anyone to know?"

"I just want to die."

"Stay tuned. We'll be right back so Dawn can get her wish."

Commercial.

"Welcome back, folks. It seems that there are twenty minutes to kill before we can go to the Capp. Dawn, tell us a little about yourself."

"What do you want to know?"

"Oh, I don't know. What is the most embarrassing thing to ever happen to you?"

"That was just now. Five minutes ago. On this show. By you."

"Oh. I guess so. Well, what is the thing you are most proud of?"

"I taught my dog to do tricks."

"Wait a minute," Phil says as he consults a 3 X 5 card on the table next to him. "I know you are young, but training a dog is the greatest accomplishment of your life?"

"It wasn't easy. It was hard."

"But still, you can't come up with something better than that."

"Not really."

"How about school? Did you get good grades in school?"

"No."

"Did you go on to college?"

"No."

"Okay, I'm getting the signal it is time for another break. We'll go to commercials while Dawn tries to come up with a better accomplishment."

Commercial.

"Well Dawn, did you come up with anything better?"

"No."

"All right. Let's try something else. What do you do for fun?"

"I used to go to the Fox Theater until it closed. They had movies and concerts."

"What kind of movies do you like?"

"Oh, I love romance movies. I always cry at those. Or anything with dogs in it."

"So, I gather you like dogs."

"Oh, yes."

"What kind of dog do you own?"

"A collie. Female. Three years old."

"And who is going to take care of the dog after you are gone?"

Dawn starts crying again as she mutters, "My parents."

"I guess you cry at more than just movies. Okay folks, I just got the little voice in my ear saying it's time to do the Capp. Before that though, here are some commercials for you that you are sure to enjoy. Don't forget to stay tuned after the show for your XCAL 1 evening news, the only official state newscast. Remember folks, if you didn't see it on XCAL 1, it didn't happen."

I rush out of my trailer. I was so busy not listening that I missed my cue! Does my earbud not work in my trailer? I have no idea what the television camera is showing, maybe me running to the set looking all confused. Too late now to pretend to adjust something, so I look up at my sister. She seems fine but the gentleman above her is panting like a dog.

I grab a couple of stagehands and do what I was supposed to be doing before this commercial break, which is carrying off-stage the pole with a rope that is between the second and third man in line. This is where the S'er will be standing for the Capp.

Commercial.

The playing of the *Capping S'ers* theme music means we are back from a five-minute commercial break.

"Ladies and gentlemen, welcome back to the LIVE part of the show. Let me introduce you to Ricky Fordham, our Capper."

As the spotlights center on me, hiding my left arm, I wave to the crowd with my right. Holy crap, this is happening.

"Ricky has, through years and years of practice, perfected a technique of throwing a star that will allow Dawn, by simply standing still, to end her life. So, without further ado, we'll proceed to the LIVE Capp where anything can happen."

I am standing where the second pole was, the star held loosely in my right hand, both arms behind my back. Brian escorts Dawn from the stage over to me. I see the doctor and paramedics are still standing by the snack table. I study Dawn's neck. It will be a left sided strike. I feel the camera man right behind me. Dawn's jugular vein is throbbing nicely. This won't require a very deep cut. I pull away until I see Dawn's whole face. I don't want to look. I don't want to know, but despite trying not to, I look into her eyes. They are hazel, they are wide open, and they look terrified.

I move to Dawn's left side. I bend down and have her move her feet. I push on Dawn's back to get her to stand straight. I tell Dawn to breathe calmly. No big breaths.

I check Dawn's position in relation to the rest of the line, first looking up the line, then down. I look again at Dawn's neck and walk to my throwing spot.

I am standing 20 feet in front of the first of the barechested men. I stare down at the line assembled before me. I am holding the shiny star with the five white sharpened points up by my chest. I take a deep breath. I am doing this for my sister, I remind myself. While I normally hide my left hand, I must extend my arm out full-length to get the balance I need for the throw. I cock my right arm into its throwing position. I am doing this for my sister. I look down the line as I prepare to throw. Everything looks good except Dawn, who is shaking too much. A voice in my ear says, "Sixty seconds." Damn earbud works fine now.

I lower my arms and walk over to Dawn. Without any prior shows to watch, this must all seem so strange and overwhelming to her. I wonder what they even told her about how she was going to die.

I am taking too long to do the Capp, but I am confident the station will keep this show on the air for as long as it takes. Isn't this what everyone wants to see? If Dawn dies or not? The eleven o'clock news will have to wait. I lean in close to Dawn and whisper in her ear, "You don't have to do this. If you change your mind, step away. The star won't hurt you if you step away." Dawn stares straight ahead without a change in her expression. I am not sure she even heard me. Or understood what I said.

"Fifteen seconds."

I walk back to my starting position and cock my arm. My left hand aches, and the scar on my right itches, but I ignore them both. I am doing this for my sister. I throw the star. It flies straight at the first man. With a *clang* and a spark, the star bounces off the collar around his neck and continues at a slightly different angle.

The star cuts the rope hanging from the first post as it passes by on the way to the second man. The cut portion of the rope falls to the ground as the star bounces off the second man the same way it did the first. It flies on toward Dawn, grazes by her, cutting her neck in the process. Dawn's body shudders, falls to the ground, blood streaming. I stare at the ever-increasing pool of blood as another *clang* is heard, then a *thud*.

The *Capping S'ers* theme music starts up as the doctor rushes over to watch Dawn bleed out. The studio audience is so quiet I can hear her gasping for air. I did it for my sister. The in-line men all turn to watch. The camera is hovering two feet away from Dawn's face. I can see it clearly on the big screen.

Phil and Brian are standing on the stage, looking on. The doctor leans down to check her pulse and is finally satisfied. He gives Brian the thumbs up that she is dead. The audience erupts in cheers. Dawn is lying on the ground, her eyes still wide open. The star is stuck in the last post.

I walk over and look down at Dawn's body with her terrified eyes. I still have bare feet, so I avoid stepping in her blood. Why did she have to die? Why was being pregnant such a mistake? She not only killed herself, she also killed her baby. Why do I care? I don't. I only care about my twin.

Commercial.

We are off the air. I walk over to the square final post and pull out the embedded star. I walk back to my trailer with my head down, ignoring the cheering and shouts of congratulations. I don't talk with anyone until I am just outside my trailer.

"Hi, Steven."

"Hello, Ms. Fordham."

"Thanks for bringing my sister backstage." I bend down and gently kiss my sister's cheek. I can see from the light in her eyes how excited she is.

"I did this for you," I whisper.

"Thanks for bringing her to the show and taking care of her, Steven. I'm going inside now and get out of this monkey suit."

"Of course, Ms. Fordham. Great show tonight."

"Thanks." I wait as he wheels my sister away and then enter my trailer. My assistant peels me out of my costume, and I sit down naked in front of the mirror. I don't like my breasts. Across the top of them is what looks like freckles. I touch one of the spots. They are burn splatter marks. My breasts either need to be bigger, so I look like a girl or not there at all. Presently, they are just a bother.

There is a knock at the door.

My assistant answers it. "Oh, hello, Mr. Goldstein. Ricky isn't dressed yet."

"Don't worry," he replies as he forces himself in. "She hasn't got anything I haven't seen before."

He walks over and puts his hand on my shoulder. "Great start to a great show tonight. I think this is going to be huge!"

"Brian, my eyes are up here."

"Ah, yea. Right."

"And get your hand off my shoulder or I swear I will punch you in the balls."

"Oh, right. Well, I really must be going. We're off to a great start here."

I continue to sit and stare into the mirror. My assistant asks if I want some fruit or champagne, but I decline. I don't get it. I just watched someone die from my throw and then I am fighting off Brian's advances and refusing complementary gifts. Are we mourning or celebrating? Why didn't she step away? I dress slowly, not knowing what I am supposed to be feeling.

The door pops open and Phil sticks his head in.

"Oh, you're already dressed." He disappears and the door closes.

I go out and the limo drives me to my studio provided condo.

Season One, Episode Two

CAPPING S'ERS
XCAL - 1
10-11 pm
New "Ivory Beck"
S1/EP02, (2017), The second episode of the hit new TV show that highlights one individual who desires to commit suicide. With an assist from thrower Ricky Fordham, the individual may die or not.

I arrive at the studio too early again. Is this my routine now? As before, there are only a few people wandering around, so I go to my trailer to rest up before the show. Rest up. I have been getting too much time to rest lately. Too much time to think. I pull the star out of my backpack. It looks the same as always once I washed off Dawn's blood.

Dawn. Did she want to die? She acted more like a scared rabbit than someone who wanted to end their life. Or is that how all people getting ready to kill themselves act? Scared? Afraid? Did I kill someone who wanted to live? Plus her unborn baby? Was that a double death? No. I'm not responsible for her and her baby being dead. I told her she could step away. She didn't. The doctor didn't save her either. Didn't save them.

Their deaths are on her, not me. She could have gotten an abortion if she didn't want the baby. Besides, this show is not something I want to do. This is something I must do — for my sister.

Dawn isn't the first person to die from my throwing the star. She is the third. The second one was an accident. Not my fault. The first one was ruled justifiable homicide, so I am not guilty of that one either. As for here on the show, I have a letter signed by the Governor of California stating that I cannot be held liable, either criminally or civilly, for any actions taken while on the air.

Holding one of the points of the star, I remember a day during our first month of setting up the show. After lunch at the studio cafeteria, I was invited into a room with the writers. Brian was there along with a couple of other people I was not introduced to. They announced that the name of the show was "Capping S'ers." I asked if that name was exciting and gave the TV audience some idea of what the show was about. They explained that the name was exotic and mysterious, and that made it exciting. They also explained that once everyone knew what Capping and S'ers meant, then people would know what the show was about. They also thought the name would be hard for people to forget. I didn't know what Capping and S'ers meant, so they explained that Capping was the throw. That's from gangster talk, like you are going to go cap (kill) someone. S'er stood for a suicider (someone about to commit suicide). This was my first lesson in Hollywood spin.

"So what do you call the first in-line, the second in-line and so on?" I asked.

"You mean the ones who just stand there and don't do anything?"

"Yeah, those people."

"Well, we don't call them anything. They just stand there and don't do anything. They are barely part of the show. They are just props."

So went my second lesson. Neck gear or neck-wear became the name for the neck armor. Armor was too strong of a word, not vulnerable sounding enough. Too safe sounding. My third lesson.

Thinking back over the past week since the show's premier, I had been trying to keep busy. With no change to the setup of the show, not much practice was required. I visited my sister every day. I had Brian move her to a home closer to my condo, so I didn't have to travel so far. I would talk to her and brush her long hair. Of course, I told her everything that happened since my last visit, but I couldn't tell if she understood any of it.

Brian had me do a bunch of publicity photo shoots. Me in my cat suit and makeup, all the in-lines with their bare chests and beefy bodies. My favorite one was where the in-lines stood in a row. All five of them. Three for the show and two backups. They held their forearms straight out, elbows tucked in, and I laid across them as if I was lounging on a couch. Man, those guys are strong. Too bad that during the Capp they just stand there and don't move. Still, I do love that photo.

I went jogging one day to try to tire myself out, so I could sleep, but I was almost mugged, so I had Brian put a treadmill in the condo instead. But it didn't make a difference. Regardless of how tired I got, I lie in bed trying to sleep, staring up at the ceiling, and all I see is Dawn's face and her wide-open eyes. Looking at me with that surprised expression that says, "Hey, wait a minute. This isn't what I signed up for."

I feel the same way.

Holding one of the star's points, my mind flies back to how I first found the star.

Even though I was raised to be a man, I loved to dress up in all the old clothes I would find in my grandmother's attic. It was there that I found the box. It was a flat brown box, just over twelve inches square, and one-half inch deep and it was addressed to my grandfather from an address in New York, New York. It was postmarked May 13, 1955. Inside was a white metallic disc with five points, so it looked sort of like a star. Much too big to be a Christmas tree ornament. I picked it up and examined it. There was no hook or anything else to hang it with. There was nothing else in the box. No instructions or papers. Not seeing any use for it but intrigued, I decided to downstairs and ask Grandma about it.

As I was descending the stairs, I heard my mother shout, "Call 911!"

"What's going on?" I asked.

"Your grandma is having a heart attack," my dad replied. "So stay out of the way."

I watched, still clutching the box with the star inside, as 911 was dialed, paramedics arrived, and grandma was loaded into an ambulance. My heart was beating fast. I prayed that grandma would be okay. She was the last grandparent I had. She was always nice to me. She would have fresh baked cookies and was never mean to me. I spent many hours in her attic playing make believe. When we were younger, my twin would join me, and we would play act and stuff. I would dress up in man clothes and her in woman clothes, and we had pretend weddings, pretend marriages, and pretend fights. Now, since she is confined to her wheelchair, she has to stay downstairs, and I must play both parts as I pretend alone.

"I'm going with her," mom said. "Take the girls home," she instructed my father.

My father grumbled and packed my sister and me into the car and drove us home. I had stuffed the box into my backpack when he wasn't looking. "Stay here and watch your sister," he said. "I'm going to the hospital."

I wheeled my sister in front of the TV, set the parking brake, and made sure she was comfortable. I had carried the box home but now I had to figure out what to do with it. I took the star out and looked at it again. I still didn't know what it was for, but I did know dad would never let me keep it. I wasn't allowed to have anything unless he approved it first. I grabbed my dog's leash, turned on the National Geographic channel so my sister could watch the animals, and walked out the back door with the star. Fluffy was jumping up and down, so excited to see me. After she covered my face in kisses, I gave a few tummy rubs, hooked her up, and together we tromped off through the woods down at the end of the block.

Beyond the woods was a neglected field with an old broken-down barn. No one ever came there. The roof sagged, and several boards were missing from its sides. It smelled old and musty. There was a dirt floor and a loft with a single hay bale sitting in it. I used to climb up the rickety ladder with missing rungs and hide behind the hay bale and pretend I was shooting bad guys. There was also a small door up there that gave a great view of the field behind the barn. I went inside the barn and sat in the middle of the floor. I examined the star. The points around its circular body were dull and unimpressive. Not sure what to do with it, I buried it and walked home.

While waiting for word about grandma, I changed the channel to something I wanted to watch and brushed and braided my sister's hair. She liked it when I did things like that for her. I could tell it pleased her because her eyes lit up and became animated. It was the least I could do for her.

When my parents got home, Dad said, "Your grandma died." Mom said, "I'll miss her. She was a good mother." Oh no, now it was just Mom and Dad, my twin sister, and me.

My dad walked into the kitchen and came out a minute later with the box. "Ricky, what's this?"

Oh shit. I had forgotten to dispose of the empty box. "I don't know. A box?"

"Don't get smart with me. Isn't this the box you found in grandma's attic? How did it get here?"

"I brought it home in my backpack."

"Okay. Why were you hiding it? What was in the box?"

"Nothing. It was empty."

"Then why did you take it?"

"Because it was old."

"What are you going to do with it?"

"I don't know. Just keep it." I was stalling. Trying to think of a reason to have taken it. "It used to belong to grandpa, and I don't have anything of his. I barely remember him."

"Okay. Keep it in your room then. But there had better not have been anything in that box. If I find you with something you are not supposed to have, I will beat you to within an inch of your life."

I believed him, so I took the box up to my room and put it on my dresser. Then I laid on my bed and cried myself to sleep. Why did grandma die and leave my sister and me alone with these two monsters?

When it was time, I went to makeup and then back to my trailer for dressing. I walked onto the studio floor just as the show was starting.

"Welcome, California, to the new hit show that

will delight. Last week's premier set new records for the number of viewers to watch any show ever. If you thought that was something, we will really show you how it is done tonight. Welcome to *Capping S'ers!*"

I look in the audience for my sister and give a little wave. I notice that behind her is a young couple kissing. Ah, young love. Good for them.

"For the next sixty minutes, we are going to meet Ivory Beck. She lives right here in Hollywood. We are going to do a live interview with her here in our studio, and then LIVE we will watch the Capp and see if Ivory goes through with it or not. Stick around. We will be back after this commercial break."

I walk over in my bare feet to the first in-line and adjust his position. I look for my sister again and notice that the young couple is kissing passionately. Young love or young lust?

Commercial.

On the big screen, while the *Capping S'ers* theme music plays, the camera fades in on a thirty-five-year-old woman with the famous Hollywood sign visible over her right shoulder. Her lips are pressed tightly together.

Then the same woman is standing outside the Grauman's Chinese Theatre. "This world-famous theater opened on May 18, 1927, but is no longer in use today. My name is Ivory Beck, and I am ready to commit suicide."

A change in scene and Ivory is kneeling on the Hollywood Walk of Fame, pointing to a star. She says, "This is the star for Natalie Wood, my favorite actress."

The final shot is of Ivory walking into an older apartment building. She says, "This is my apartment. A one bedroom, one bath unit."

The camera follows Ivory up three flights of stairs and through a doorway. It pans to show a small kitchen, no dining room, and a living room filled with a recliner, a portable TV, and a bookcase made from bricks and boards. The lone window shows a view of the building next door. Ivory stands by the window. She says, "If I stand right here, I can get a partial view of the street and the people walking by. Otherwise, I get to look into the windows of my neighbors. Most keep their blinds closed all the time, but there are a few who don't. There is the pervert flasher, the wife beater, and an older man who just sits and cries all day. Very depressing."

"We will get up close and personal with Ivory right after these commercial messages."

I adjust the position of the first pole holding the rope. Behind my sister, the man is cupping one of the woman's breasts. Hers are a good size. Nice.

Commercial.

My turn to be interviewed again. I am beginning to hate this part. Phil starts it off by asking, "How did you feel after killing Dawn?"

Talk about hitting below the belt. And with the very first question. We are going to have to start rehearsing these interviews.

"I didn't kill her. She committed suicide."

"I guess that's one way of looking at it. Who else have you killed with that star thing?"

"This interview is over." I storm off the stage, looking for Brian.

"Well folks, it looks like we have some time to kill. Earlier this week, we did a follow-up segment where we interviewed Dawn's parents to see how they reacted to her death. We weren't going to air it because, quite frankly, it is boring. All that crying and stuff. But, since there is time, we're going to show it anyway. Enjoy, and then we'll go to commercial."

I find Brian at the snack table. "You have got to

do something about him!" I begin.

"Him who?"

"Phil. That man is out of control. And an asshole."

"Why? What did he do?"

"Did you not hear my interview just now?"

"I heard it."

"And you are okay with it? You think those questions he asked are acceptable?"

"Look. I know Phil can be a little upsetting at times, but he is good for ratings. And don't you think you're being a little over sensitive?"

"Over sensitive? No!"

"Then why didn't you answer the question? Look, I know all about your past. And so does Phil. We did a complete investigation on you before we ever agreed to taking on this show."

I can't think of a thing to say. Those records were supposed to be sealed.

"Look, if you don't want to do the interviews anymore, that's okay. We won't do them. Just do the Capp and be happy. Okay?"

"Okay."

"You must do me a favor though."

"What?"

"Last week you were in your trailer during Dawn's interview and you missed your cue. I need you to stay here in the studio. No visiting your trailer during the show, unless it is an emergency."

I look over to the stage where Phil and Ivory sit slightly facing each other. We are about to go live.

"Okay," I agree reluctantly.

"Hello, everyone. I am Phil Ebenezer. I have a PhD in clinical psychology. Now Ivory, tell me why you want to end your life."

"I am just so tired of it all. I just want to stop living."

"I see. And why is that?"

"I just find the endless searching so exhausting. I'm never going to be able to find love. Not real love. Not the kind of love where someone cares for me so much they would rather die than be without me."

"Why do you think you can never find that kind of love? You are not unattractive."

"No, I guess not. But all the men I meet are attracted to girls younger than me. Prettier than me. Do you know how many beautiful young women are in Hollywood? With more flooding in each day?"

"Well no, I don't. Maybe you are looking for love in the wrong places? Instead of bars, try libraries."

"You don't understand."

"I don't understand what?"

"I met a guy at the library. He seemed like a wonderful man. Smart, caring, thoughtful," her voice trembles and tears are flowing freely now.

"And what happened with this guy?"

"We went out a couple times. At first, he was so considerate. Holding the door for me. Sending me flowers."

"Go on."

"At the end of the third date, I invited him up for a drink. We hadn't even kissed at that point. I didn't intend to go to bed with him, but we had that drink, then another. We were sitting on the sofa and started making out."

"I'm listening."

"It just felt so good. I thought maybe he was the one. And it had been so long since I had been with someone."

"Then what happened?"

"We moved to the bedroom. He made love to me. Glorious sweet love."

"Sounds great so far. And after that?"

"After that. He got up and started putting his clothes back on. Then he pulls out his cell phone. I was wondering who he was going to call. He then snaps a picture of me, naked, there on the bed. Said he had to have proof."

"Have proof of what?"

"That he got me to sleep with him. He said he had a bet with his buddies. And that he had just won 500 California dollars."

"Did he offer to share some of his winnings with you?"

"No. I'm not a prostitute. Just a fool."

"So now you want to end your life?"

"I do."

"Because you were taking advantage of by one jerk of a man?"

"You don't understand."

"You said that before."

"I am the victim here."

"Only if you allow yourself to be. Otherwise, you are just going to be a statistic.

Don't forget folks to stay tuned after the show for your XCAL 1 evening news, the only official state newscast. Remember folks, if you didn't see it on XCAL 1, it didn't happen."

I do my pre-commercial routine, then check on my sister. She seems okay. I wonder where Steven, her caretaker, is. I don't see him anywhere near her. I do see, however, that behind her, the man has his hand under the girl's sweater. He must be getting an under bra feel. Or maybe she isn't wearing one? Better and better.

Commercial.

"Ladies and gentlemen, welcome back to the LIVE part of the show. Let us welcome Ricky Fordham, our Capper."

While the crowd applauds, I step into camera range and wave.

"Ricky has, through years and years of practice, perfected a technique of throwing a star that will allow Ivory, by simply standing still, to end her life. So, without further ado, we'll proceed to the LIVE Capp where anything can happen."

I am standing where the second pole was. Brian escorts Ivory to me. She has a very determined look on her face. I study Ivory's neck. The camera zooms in. I pull back slowly until I can see Ivory's face with her quiet eyes squeezed shut. I saw them before she closed them. They are pale green, like my sister's. Don't think about it. I check Ivory's position by looking up the line, then down the line.

I fuss with Ivory's positioning, then put my mouth next to her ear. The microphone boom closes in tight, so everyone can hear me say, "You don't have to do this. Just step away, and the star won't hurt you." Ivory gives no sign of acknowledgment, her eyes still tightly closed.

I look over to make sure the doctor and the paramedics are ready, then turn and walk over to my starting spot. My left hand aches as I extend that arm out. I am doing this for my sister. My right hand itches. I cock my arm back and throw the star. It flies straight at the first in-line. With a *clang* and a spark, the star bounces off the first man's neck armor and continues on.

The star cuts the rope as it passes by on the way to the second in-line. The cut portion of the rope falls to the ground as the star bounces off the second in-line. It flies on toward Ivory, grazes by her, cutting her neck in the process. Her eyes fly open wide as her body shudders. She falls to the ground, blood streaming from her body. I can't pull my eyes away from the ever-increasing pool of blood as another *clang* is heard, then a *thud*.

The crowd is silent as the doctor walks over and bends over Ivory. She is struggling. Trying to get up? She falls back down again and is still. The doctor gives the thumbs up to the crowd which erupts in cheers. The *Capping S'ers* theme music starts up. I am still standing on my spot. Ivory is lying dead on the ground. Her dead pale green eyes open. The star is stuck in the last post. The crowd is going crazy.

I look down at Ivory. She shouldn't let one man ruin her life. She would find true love, maybe. Eventually. She never will now, that is for sure. And who needs a man anyway? I certainly don't.

I look up at my sister. "I did this for you," I whisper. Behind her the young man has his hand between the girl's knees. Hey, get a room.

Commercial.

I go back to my trailer, after visiting briefly with my sister. Steven says he was in the bathroom when he wasn't by my sister's side. I have no backstage visitors this week. Is it ironic that Ivory died because she couldn't find love while a couple in the audience didn't even notice because of their young love? I guess there are different kinds of love.

There is the young passionate kind of love that is more like lust. There is the mature partnership kind of love where two people can depend and rely on each other's trust and faith. There is the love between siblings. There is the deeper sibling love that twins feel. There is the love of a parent for their child; that I never felt. There is the love that a child has for its parents. Something else I never had. There is the love for a pet, or a toy or doll.

Ivory never found, and felt that she would never find, the type of love that she was looking for. I would hope that I find the type of love I am looking for, someday.

If I was looking for love.

Season One, Episode Three

CAPPING S'ERS
XCAL - 1
10-11 pm
New "Rob Bennett"
S1/EP03, (2017), The third episode of the hit new TV show that highlights one individual who desires to commit suicide. With an assist from thrower Ricky Fordham, the individual may die or not.

I like arriving at the studio early. It gives me time to review my week and reflect on how I got to this point in my life. The only eventful thing that happened this past week was when Brian showed up at my condo one night, drunk. I know the studio owns the condo and lets me use it for free, but that still doesn't give him the right to barge in. I didn't even know he had a key. Quite frankly, I think he dropped in thinking he could take advantage of me. Or catch me naked again. I never gave him a chance. I lectured him and hustled him out the door so fast he didn't know what hit him. Neither one of us have spoken about it since. He may not even remember. The next day I went out and had my hair cut even shorter.

Holding one point of the star, I remember back to when I first started throwing.

The day after grandma died, I went back to the barn. I dug up the star and took it behind the barn. Ahead of me was a field filled with waist-high grass turned to seed. The field looked to be about fifty yards long before the woods started again. With my left hand being useless, I gripped the star in my right hand, cocked my arm back and flung it away from me. It took off, banked sharply to the right, and buried itself in the ground. I tried again. Same thing. I changed my stance. Better, but still nothing to brag about. After several hours, I got it to fly about fifty feet before it plowed into the ground. I couldn't keep it aloft.

I climbed up into the hay loft and went to the edge of the door there. I had to kneel to make the throw. There was a faint whistle as it moved through the air, and it became nearly invisible and silent as it got further away. I lost sight of it after it hit a tree, but I heard it hit two more.

I ran out looking for the star but couldn't find it that day or the next. Great. All the hiding, all the wondering, all the risk taking, and I only got a few throws out of it. I finally found it stuck in a tree. I had been looking on the ground for it, and I found it by almost walking into it. I had better be careful. One of those points could put an eye out.

I pulled the star out of the tree, walked back to one corner of the barn, and hid it by piling some leaves on top of it. This was the first time I had done something like this. The first time I had hid something from my dad, and I didn't want to risk losing it if he got mad. He was always getting mad, so you never knew what would set him off. The next day, I took a spray can of red paint out of the garage and covered the star. Maybe now it would be easier to find.

I also remember one time when my dad had been out driving his big rig. When he came home, he was complaining that the feds were screwing everything up. My dad drove truck long haul across the country and back, so I guess he saw a lot and obviously seemed very concerned about national issues.

It seemed the federal government was in its usual financial crises, and the politicians refused to do anything about it. My dad said it was all the Republicans' fault. They weren't willing to work with our Democratic president to address the hard problems. It started, my dad said, with Congress refusing to raise the debt ceiling. They said the national debt was too high and needed to be reduced. They said there needed to be a balanced budget. Not that anyone wants an unbalanced budget, but no one could agree on how that debt reduction or balanced budget was going to happen. No one wanted to cut any spending in their area, and tax revenue was stalled due to the lack of increases in wages. At least, that was what my dad said the newspapers said.

All I knew was that my dad and I went out for cheeseburgers, fries, and chocolate shakes because I had gotten a C on my report card. And then he beat my mom before he left to go back to work because he said she was stupid.

While sitting in the makeup chair, I reflect on the three months I spent preparing for this show. The only props needed were the poles they built and hung ropes from. They didn't think the ropes needed weighs.

We had to find people for in-lines. Getting the in-lines to stand still and trust that I wasn't going to hurt them was the hardest part. I figured out every-one's spots where they had to stand.

At the same time, they were also interviewing candidates for S'ers. I was glad I wasn't part of that portion of the show. I didn't want to know who was going to die at my hand. I didn't want to know their name. I didn't want to know their problems. I didn't want to know anything about them.

The three people that I had been using as my in-lines prior were unsuitable, said the studio. "Why, if this show is successful, those people will be famous! We must have the right kind of person in that role. Someone we would be proud to call Californian." Quite a big deal for persons the creative staff initially thought were just props.

I had a lineup of new people to choose from. All young and movie star beautiful. Part time actors. Body builders. It isn't easy being an in-line person. That sharp cutting edge of the star flying towards your neck at high speed tends to make people nervous. I probably went through fifty people to find one who could hold still for thirty seconds.

Also, Brian wanted to plant the poles permanent-ly in the ground. It took me two days of explaining as to why that wasn't possible. I had to be able to move them. Even if I moved them a tiny amount, that would make the difference between a successful Capp and one that failed, I explained.

I didn't want to participate, but they started including me in the pre-production meetings. They said it was part of my contract. I was really going to have to read that thing someday. There were always more S'er applicants than what we had openings for, so the pre-production meetings were basically about picking who was going to be on the show.

"What about this one? He's gay and got jilted by his boyfriend."

"I don't know. I think the female sex maniac

will pull in more points in ratings. Sex always sells."

"What about the fat guy?"

"No. Everyone is fat. That's not a good reason to kill yourself."

"How about her? She says she can't cope."

"Can't cope with what? Next!"

"Rape victim?"

"We already scheduled one of those. Find me something different."

"This one says he wants to be an S'er because he can't wait to ascend to heaven."

"Nut case. Audience won't relate. You know we don't do religion here."

"How about this guy? In the space of a month, he lost his business, his wife, and son."

"Now that's a good one. We need more like that."

I don't enjoy being more involved. I never express an opinion. I don't enjoy any part of the show. Except throwing the star. All I wanted to do was my throws. Not Capps. Throws. I didn't want people dying because of my talent. I just wanted to do bigger and longer and more complicated throws. I wanted to test my talent to see how far it would go.

It's funny, but growing up, whenever I was asked what I wanted to be later in life, I had no answer. No aspirations of being an astronaut, cowboy, or doctor. My dad wanted me to be a man, but I didn't know if that was what I wanted, or even what it meant. I guess I was too busy trying to survive. I did my throws for therapy. Because it got me out of the house and there was nothing else to do. I never thought I was making a career with it. It just happened. And when I talked with Brian about how I wanted to do different Capps, he turned it around to where all they wanted was to put in two S'ers instead of one. The audience would love it, of course. I would not.

I walk into the studio just as Phil is starting his welcome speech.

"Welcome, California, to the new hit show that will delight. Last week's show busted through the record books again. It makes us very happy here at XCAL 1 as more and more of you are really enjoying the show. The show is so successful that after only two airings, it has already been renewed for next year. While this first year is just a short six shows, next season is a full ten show slate. Now, isn't that exciting? Thanks to all of you who are making *Capping S'ers* part of your late Sunday night. But if you thought last week was something, we will really show you how it is done tonight. Welcome to *Capping S'ers!*"

Yes, the show is a huge hit. We have been signed for ten more weeks. It sounds like an eternity. We are the biggest show on TV. We even topped the *Running of the Bulls in San Francisco* special that was on at the same time as last week's show.

I look for my sister. The bleachers are full. She is there and behind her is a young boy holding a sign that reads "When I grow up I want to be an S'er." No Steven in sight. Where does he go?

"For the next sixty minutes, we are going to meet Rob Bennett. He is a resident of San Diego. We are going to interview him live here in our studio, and then LIVE we will watch the Capp and see if Rob goes through with it or not. Stick around. We will be back right after this commercial break."

I walk out of the shadows and give a hearty wave to the audience. Behind my sister, the boy with the sign waves back. Does the boy realize what his sign says?

Commercial.

On the big screen, while the *Capping S'ers* theme music plays, the camera fades in on a fifty-year-old man standing by the lion's cage at the San Diego Zoo in Balboa Park. He has a slight smile on his face.

The music dies as the same man is standing on a pier with the ghostly *USS Midway* aircraft carrier evident over his right shoulder. "This is the third ship to bear the Midway name. She was commissioned on September 10, 1945, and has served her country well in various actions. She was abandoned here when the federal government collapsed. My name is Rob Bennett, and I am ready to commit suicide."

Then Rob is standing on a road where a street sign that says 'Normal Heights' is visible over his left shoulder. He says, "This is the neighborhood where I live, just two blocks up from Antique Row."

Next is Rob walking into a worn-down single-story home. He says, "This is my home. Let me show you the inside."

The camera follows Rob as he tours the house, pointing out all its features. The home appears to have been built in the 1930s, but it is neat and clean. He comments, "I live alone now. My wife died two years ago. We had been married for thirty-two years. Childhood sweethearts."

"We will get up close and personal with Rob right after these commercial messages."

I do my usual pretend to adjust the in-lines routine. My sister looks cold. Behind her the boy with the sign is tugging on his dad's sleeve and pointing at the in-lines. I wonder who helped him with that sign. Do they realize what it says? Steven should be giving my sister a blanket.

Commercial.

Since I am not doing interviews with Phil anymore, and since they decided not to do follow-ups with S'ers' relatives, I see that Phil is ready to go with his interview with Rob. I guess they will just make this segment longer to fill the time. More work for the writers.

"Hello, everyone. I am Phil Ebenezer. I have a PhD in clinical psychology. Now Rob, tell me why you want to end your life."

"Well, I lost everything. And I am too old to start over."

"I see. And what is it that you lost, exactly?"

"Well, I lost my wife. Like I said in the video piece. That house I showed off was foreclosed on last week. I lost my son in the riots. He was my only child. I lost all my money when the stock market crashed. I lost my business when the state took it over. I lost everything. I have nothing left."

Phil picks up a 3 X 5 card that is on a table next to him, stares at it for a full ten seconds before he asks, "What do you attribute these losses to?"

"It's all because of the collapse of the federal government. That's when the states closed their borders. That's when the rioting started, and California started taking over all the businesses. Martial law and…"

While the camera shows Rob talking, there is no sound.

"Whoa. Easy there, Rob. I'm glad this segment of the show has a five-second delay before it is broadcast."

Rob's eyes squeeze shut tight as Phil asks, "So now you are ready to end your life?"

Camera zooms in for a tight shot as Rob opens his eyes before replying, "I am."

"Stay tuned folks. We'll be right back."

Commercial.

"Hey folks, we're back. Still twenty minutes left on the clock until we can do the Capp. So Rob, what else do you want to talk about?"

"I don't care."

"Okay. In your video you mentioned that your son was killed in the riots. You didn't mention how your wife died."

"Yeah. It was a home invasion. I was away on business; my son was sleeping over at a friend's when someone broke into our house. Apparently, from what the police could figure out, the robber had hold of a pearl necklace that I had given my wife for our twentieth anniversary. She fought him for it, and he killed her. Pearls were scattered all over the floor from when the necklace broke."

"That's sad. All that work, and they didn't even get the necklace."

"What?"

"In one of your video shots you were standing by the *USS Midway*. Were you in the Navy?"

"Yes. For six years."

"What did you do there?"

"I was an electronics technician."

"I see. And what kind of business did you run?"

"An electronics business."

"You weren't using military secrets in your private business, were you?"

"No, of course not."

"Had to ask. In one video shot, you were standing by the lion's cage at the zoo. Do you like lions?"

"Yes."

"Wow. That generated a lot of response. Let's go to another commercial."

Commercial.

"Okay, we're back again. Still here with Rob. Trying to find something interesting. Do you have anything interesting that you want to talk about?"

"No."

"Okay, well I'm done. I'm bored. We will just fill the empty time with more commercials."

Commercial.

"Don't forget to stay tuned after the show for your XCAL 1 evening news, the only official state newscast. Remember folks, if you didn't see it on XCAL 1, it didn't happen."

Commercial.

I get a couple stagehands to move the second pole off the floor. I look up at my sister. She has a blanket on her, so I guess Steven is up there taking care of her. Next to her is two men swearing so loud that I can hear them from here. The young boy is still holding the sign while his dad is covering the boy's ears. So the boy can hold up a sign that says when he grows up he wants to commit suicide, but he can't hear a little swearing. Talk about a double standard.

Commercial.

"Ladies and gentlemen, welcome back to the LIVE part of the show. There is no five second delay on *this* portion of the show. Let us welcome Ricky Fordham, our Capper."

I wave to the audience. Phil explains how I have years and years of practice. Blah, blah, blah.

I am standing where the second pole was. Brian escorts Rob over to me. Rob is dressed like a businessman with a suit and tie. I check out his neck. Even with the suit coat and tie on, there is still enough exposed. Rob's pale blue eyes appear calm and resigned. I look up the line, then down the line.

I adjust Rob's position, then say, "You don't have to do this. Just step away, and the star won't hurt you."

I turn and walk over to my starting spot. My left hand aches. I'm doing this for my sister. I look over at the snack table. The paramedics are there. Where is the doctor? I see him a little further away talking with a cute redhead. God, he can't even be bothered to get ready.

I continue to stand there and stare. Brian glances around to see what the holdup is. He sees that the doctor is not paying attention, so he runs over to him and slaps him on the arm. The doctor looks apologetic as he takes his place by the table.

I cock my arm back and throw the star. It flies straight at the first in-line. With a *clang* and a spark, the star bounces off the first man's neck armor and continues without losing altitude.

The star cuts the rope as it passes by on the way to the second in-line. The cut portion of the rope falls to the ground. The star bounces off the second in-line the same way it did the first. It flies on toward Rob, grazes by him, cutting his neck in the process. His body shudders. He falls to the ground, blood streaming. I stare at the increasing pool of blood soaking into his suit and power red tie as another *clang* is heard, then a *thud*.

There is silence as the doctor casually walks over to Rob. He watches the blood flow as it slows and then stops. The doctor looks frustrated. Brian comes over and says, "Can't you do something?" Brian looks like he wants to say more until the notices the camera in his face and the microphone boom over his head.

Rob is lying there, his pale blue eyes looking up into the overhead lights until the doctor finally calls the paramedics over, and they put Rob on a gurney and hustle him out the door. On the big screen, the gurney is loaded into an ambulance. With lights flashing and siren screaming, the ambulance leaves. The crowd starts booing and throwing objects. The in-lines and I all scatter. I pull the star out of the last post and run to my trailer.

Okay Rob. You lost everything, except maybe your

life. I hope you get another chance because from what I can tell, your death will not change anything.

I wonder about the boy with the sign. He obviously didn't make up that sign himself. It looks too professional. So, are his parents encouraging him to have the ambition in life to die on a TV show? Is that what kind of influence this show is having on children?

If so, I am not happy with what is going on. I don't want to know about the S'ers. I tried hiding in my trailer but was told I couldn't. I try not watching the interviews, but I am standing right off-stage and can't avoid it. I didn't want to go to the pre-production meetings, but now I must. They are forcing me to do this show in a way that I hate. Must someone die for me to do a throw? And now little kids are making it their life's ambition to die on this show? I don't like the direction that all this is going in.

Season One, Episode Four

CAPPING S'ERS
XCAL - 1
10-11 pm
New "David Miller"
S1/EP04, (2017), The fourth episode of the first season that highlights one individual who desires to commit suicide. With an assist from thrower Ricky Fordham, the individual may die or not.

I am sitting in my dressing room, ready for the fourth show of *Capping S'ers*. Four weeks. One month. I spent most of this past week pestering Brian to live up to what had been promised me. First, he denied that there was any such promise. And while I don't have it in writing, Harvey Howard certainly did say it, or I wouldn't be here. I kept bugging Brian. Then he said that the studio didn't have to abide by any promise that Harvey had made. I threatened to quit the show then and there. Brian finally agreed to check into it. We'll see.

He also lectured me on not making my cuts deep enough. He said it is taking too long for the S'er to bleed out and that Rob's closed altogether. I didn't know how to respond to that. The cut can't be too deep, or I will hit bone. And different people bleed at different rates. That is not my fault. Anyway, I promised to do better with the Capp.

Holding the star by its points, I remember back to a Sunday shortly after I found the star. My mom, my sister, and I all went to church. We had to walk there because dad had our only car at work. He worked in the city which was an hour's drive away. He was usually gone ten days at a time, then home for three, although he rarely stayed at home that long. I was pushing my sister in her wheelchair. We didn't go to the church closest to us; we went to a special church that was about three miles away. It was hot that day. I was all sweaty before we were even halfway there. I noticed my sister was sweating as well. She had a blanket covering her legs and mom wouldn't let me take it off her.

"If I can take it, she can take it," is what she said.

"But mom, you're sweating too."

"Don't sass me, girl, man, whatever."

So we continued our walk in the heat. Mom walked slowly and swore at anyone who looked our way.

If it was a man who looked, she would say, "What are you looking at? Bet you wish you had a piece of this, don't you? Well, keep wishing buddy."

If it was a woman who looked, she would say, "What are you looking at? Bet you wish you looked this good, don't you? Well, keep wishing sister."

If it was a kid who looked our way, she would say, "What are you looking at? Crybaby."

Was it any wonder that I had no friends?

It was just another typical Sunday. I hated that church. During a certain part of the service, I would be standing in the pew while my mother would be rolling in the aisle and speaking gibberish. She wouldn't be

the only one doing it, but it was still embarrassing as hell. For a long time, that was my vision of
hell. Fire, brimstone, rolling in aisles, speaking in
strange tongues, and embarrassment. Later in life, I
would add lawyers and tax accountants.

This particular Sunday, after we got home from
church, my mom took a nap. I parked my sister in front
of the television, so she could spend her day watching
cartoons and sermon shows. I quickly finished all my
chores, took my dog, and snuck off through the woods
to the barn. I dug up the star and threw it again and
again. Not throwing from the loft in the barn, it never
made it into the woods. It always flew straight into the
ground after fifty feet. After about the tenth throw,
I stopped for a moment. My dog was looking up at me,
her tongue hanging out and her tail wagging, anxiously
waiting for another run down the field. I could hear the
birds chirping but otherwise it was silent. No one was
yelling at me or hitting me. While the sky was cloudy,
my mind was clear. Even if throwing the star was a flop,
I was, I don't know, happy.

The next time I saw my dad, my single outstand-
ing C grade had fallen back to its normal F, so he
whipped my behind with his belt. He also slapped my mom
because he said she wasn't being responsible enough.

With the debt ceiling maxed out, no new treasury
bonds or bills could be sold. The federal government
simply ran out of money. The feds stopped sending out
social security checks and started denying Medicare
payments. Things fell apart from there.

I walk out onto the studio floor just in time.
"Welcome, California, to the fourth edition of
Capping S'ers! We have a really big show planned for

you tonight. Before we get started, I have some great news for you. Rob Bennett, who was hustled out of here on our show last week, died in the ambulance before it could get to the hospital. So, Rob got his wish and ended his life. Way to go, Rob! Stay tuned."

Rob died in the ambulance? How did that happen? Didn't Brian say that Rob's cut closed?

I look for my sister and find her in her usual spot. Her being here is such a comfort to me. Behind her I notice a beautiful blonde woman wearing neckwear. Steven is sitting beside my sister, staring at the blonde. Since when did neckwear become a fashion accessory?

Commercial.

"For the next sixty minutes, we are going to meet David Miller. He is a resident of San Francisco. We are going to interview him live here in our studio, and then LIVE we will watch the Capp and see if David goes through with it or not. Stick around. We will be back right after this commercial break."

I walk out to the center of the floor and wave. The crowd cheers. I wave to my sister and notice that the beautiful blonde woman wearing neckwear is powdering her cheeks. The neckwear on our in-lines looks very attractive. The silver and gold show up well in the lights. I guess that is why other people are starting to wear them. It looks gorgeous on her.

Commercial.

I walk over to the donut and coffee table. This time there is also some fresh fruit. Tempting, but I better not. I ask the doctor about Rob. He says that the wound opened again while they were moving him, and he bled out before they knew it. Do I believe him? Do I still need to do deeper cuts?

According to what I had been told, my troubles started before I was even born. They began when my parents were in the doctor's office. My mother was pregnant for the first time and was getting an ultrasound. The ultrasound technician, after fussing around for a bit, exclaimed, "You're having twins!"

"What? Are you sure?" asked mom.

"Oh yes, two babies in there all right. Not identical twins it doesn't look like, because I am seeing one as a girl and the other looks like a boy."

"A boy!" was my father's comment. "Yes, my prayers have been answered."

"Well, it's a little crowded in there but … right here," the technician pointed at the screen, "a penis."

My dad squinted. "I see it. Great. Good news." He thanked the technician as if she had been the one to determine the baby's sex instead of him. They left the doctor's office in a euphoric mood.

Like most parents, my mom and dad had already picked out the babies' names before they were born. They were in the hospital and Mom was ready to deliver. One baby came out.

"It's a girl," said the doctor.

"Her name is Roberta," was Mom's quick response.

Then I came out.

"It's another girl," said the doctor.

"What?" was my father's response, "What happened to the boy? Is there another baby in there?"

"No, no more babies. You are the proud father of two beautiful perfect baby girls."

"I wanted a boy."

"Yeah, I saw on the chart that you were expecting twins. One was indicated as a girl and one as a boy. Guess there was a mix-up with the ultrasound.

Happens all the time."

"Not to me it doesn't. I still want that boy."

"Well, then you are just going to have to try again."

"What are we naming her?" Mom asked.

"Her name is still Ricky. I want my boy."

"But she needs a girl's name."

"No, she doesn't. I'm going to get my boy one way or another. If we can't have another one, then she will have to be it."

Even though they did try again, there were no more babies. My dad was left with just me. Me and my boy name.

My parents came to an agreement. Mom would raise Roberta and do all the girlie things with her. Mom was ecstatic. She had a hope chest full of little girl things she had been saving ever since she was a girl. My dad would raise me. He had been looking forward to having a son to play ball and wrestle with, so I had to be it.

On screen, while playing the *Capping S'ers* theme music, the camera fades in on a thirty-six-year-old black man standing by a cable car starting to descend a hill. A broad smile lights up his face.

Then he is standing with the Golden Gate Bridge visible over his right shoulder. "Construction started on this bridge January 5, 1933. Taking four years and four months to complete, its cost of $35,000,000 was $1,300,000 under budget. My name is David Miller, and I am ready to commit suicide."

David is standing by a prison cell, and as the camera pulls rapidly away, it becomes obvious David is on Alcatraz Island. He says, "I have always been fascinated by history and crime. You can find both right here."

The camera watches David walking into a modest two-story home. He says, "This is my home. I live here with my parents. Let me show you my room."

We watch as David walks through the house. Mom and Dad Miller wave weakly as the camera hurries by. David's room is small, and his walls are adorned with posters of female singing stars. He comments, "This is where I spend all my time. Especially now that I dropped out of college."

"We will get up close and personal with David right after these commercial messages."

I adjust the first in-line. Stewart is his name. My sister is still in her wheelchair. Like where else would she be? The beautiful blonde woman wearing neckwear is applying lipstick. Red to match her outfit. Hmm. I lick my lips.

Commercial.

I would love to go to my trailer now, but I have been forbidden to do so, so I hang out by the exit and watch as Phil and David, both dressed in suits are seated in chairs facing each other.

"Hello, everyone. I am Phil Ebenezer. I have a PhD in clinical psychology. Now David, tell me why you want to end your life."

"All my life I have been depressed. Growing up, I never felt joy and happiness like other kids. They would be out jumping and laughing, and I would be watching out from the window inside the house. I never liked being outside. Trees scare me. Noises scare me. Life has always been a struggle, and now it is too much to bear. My parents try to help, but they don't know what to do. Nothing they do helps. Doctors don't know what to do. Nothing they do helps. They give me drugs, but then I am living in a haze. Everyone would be better off without me. I can't hold down a job. I make no money. I'm a burden on my parents. I can see

it in their eyes. I sit in my room all day. I don't
have any friends. No one comes over to visit with me.
My aunts and uncles don't want to be around me. I am
ready to end it all."

Phil refers to his 3 X 5 card and tears it into
tiny pieces, "I see. So now you are ready to end your
life?"

"I am."

"Stay tuned. We'll be right back."

Commercial.

"Hi folks. We are back with David. Another
boring guest who leaves us with too much time to fill.
So David, what's going on?"

"Nothing."

"In your video piece, you showed us all the
tourist hangouts around San Francisco. Why?"

"Because everyone always seems so happy there."

"Okay. You say you are fascinated by history
and crime. How does this fascination manifest itself?"

"Well, I like visiting historical places where
there was a big battle, or where there was a famous
crime."

"How about Alcatraz?"

"Yes. Alcatraz also."

"Where else have you been?"

"Oh, all the big battlefields back East. Gettys-
burg and such. The Alamo. Little Big Horn. Places like
that."

"Wow. That is quite a variety. Civil War. Texas
Revolution. The Great Sioux War. Fascinating. Don't
forget to stay tuned after the show for your XCAL 1
evening news, the only official state newscast. Remember folks, if you didn't see it on XCAL 1, it didn't
happen. Let's go to another commercial."

Commercial.

"Okay. We are back with David. Still with another ten minutes to fill. Tell me David. These are trying times, are they not?"

"They are."

"How does a man of color cope these days? Is it easier or harder now? I mean, there is plenty of rioting going on. You should be used to that, right?"

"Wrong," David says, getting angry, "Just because I'm black doesn't mean I like to riot. I hate riots. Being black is hard enough as it is. But these days, people are so ready to be angry, to get upset and to start shooting over nothing."

"Angry? Like you are getting now? I think I made my point. Anything else you want to talk about?"

"No. Look, I'm really depressed. Can't you help me?"

"Help you? We are not here to help you. What do you think we are? The national suicide hotline? Call them if you need help. My job on this show is to make sure you are ready to kill yourself. That is what I have been trained for. And in my opinion, you are ready. Are you?"

After a moment of silence, spoken softly, "Yes."

"Okay then. We'll be back with the LIVE Capp right after this."

That seemed to end abruptly, so I hustle over to in-line number two and pretend to adjust him. His name is Martin, I think. I look for my sister. Yep, still there. The beautiful blonde woman wearing neckwear is applying mascara. Don't you normally do all that at home beforehand?

Commercial.

"Ladies and gentlemen, welcome back to the LIVE part of the show. Let us welcome Ricky Fordham, our Capper."

The crowd applause is strong as I step into

camera range and wave to the crowd. I notice that the beautiful blonde woman wearing neckwear is checking herself out in the mirror. She looks good to me.

After Phil's normal spiel, I am standing on the S'er's spot. The star at my side. Brian escorts David to where I am standing. David is staring at the star. I study David's neck. Nice good vein. My normal cut should be fine. I look at David's face. His dark brown eyes are nearly hidden by lazy eyelids weighed down with heavy black lashes. I must prod David twice to get him to stand straight.

I check David's position by looking up the line, then down the line. I fuss a bit, then say, "You don't have to do this. Just step away, and the star won't hurt you." David gives no response.

I then turn and walk over to my starting spot. This time the doctor is Johnny on the spot. The paramedics also look ready.

I cock my arm back and throw the star. David faints and falls to the ground. The star flies straight at the first in-line. With a *clang* and a spark, the star bounces off the first man's neck armor and continues. I start moving toward David. Brian jumps off the stage and starts running toward David. The doctor also rushes to him.

The star cuts the rope as it passes by on the way to the second in-line. The star bounces off him and flies on toward where David stood. David is lying on the ground, unhurt as another *clang* is heard, then a *thud*. I arrive and kneel beside David as Brian shouts and gestures, the doctor watching.

I hear the *Capping S'ers* theme music play as Phil says, "The late-night news broadcast is being delayed, so we can show you the conclusion of this live Capp. This is one of the adventures of live television, my friends. Sit back and enjoy."

The conclusion? Isn't this Capp over?

Brian and the doctor lift David up. Brian

tells me to get the star and throw it again, so after retrieving the star from the final post and getting the in-lines on their spots again, I return to my starting spot. Brian is standing next to David, his arm around his waist. The doctor is standing nearby.

After staring at Brian for a full minute, he gives an impatient nod of his head, so I cock my arm back and throw the star. The star flies and bounces off the first in-line. It passes by the rope without disturbing it. It bounces off the second in-line. It flies on toward David, still being held by Brian, grazes by him, cutting his neck in the process. His body shudders. Brian releases him. David falls to the ground, blood streaming from his body. Another *clang* is heard, then a *thud*.

The doctor watches the blood flow. His hand twitches, but he waits until he is satisfied that David is dead before giving the thumbs up.

The *Capping S'ers* theme music starts up. I am still standing where I began, watching the big screen. The in-lines are still at attention on their marks, as if we were going to do a third throw. David is lying dead on the ground. His dark brown eyes are closed. The star is stuck in the last post. Brian is walking away, back to the stage where he came from. The crowd is going crazy with shouts and cheers.

David, why didn't you just get out more? You could have talked with strangers until they became friends. All that you got for sitting in your room all day, replaying all the reasons for being sad; is dead.

I look at my sister who, of course, doesn't give any response. I notice that the beautiful blonde woman wearing neckwear is looking around as if to see if anyone else is looking at her. She sees me looking and smiles. I blush and look away.

Commercial.

After retrieving the star, again, I walk to my trailer and greet my sister. I kiss her on the cheek and watch as Steven pushes her away. He has a goofy looking grin on his face, and as he walks away, he glances back. Does he like me? Sorry buddy, you are barking up the wrong tree.

Sitting at my dressing table, I wonder if I should have warned David a second time to step away. Maybe he changed his mind after his fainting spell. Maybe Brian shouldn't have held him up like that. Then, at least, he wouldn't have gotten David's blood splashed on him. Oh well, too late now. Thru the trailer walls, I hear the crowd chanting, "Ricky! Ricky! Ricky!"

My assistant tells me that there is a blond woman waiting to see me. I tell her to let the woman in and I let my assistant go home early. Something tells me that I won't be needing her help to get out of my suit tonight.

Season One, Episode Five

CAPPING S'ERS
XCAL - 1
10-11 pm
New "Janet Forbes"
S1/EP05, (2017), The latest episode of the first season that highlights one individual who desires to commit suicide. With an assist from thrower Ricky Fordham, the individual may or may not die.

      I am back in the studio for show number five. Brian says they decided they would honor Harvey's promise. He says that in a couple of weeks, they will have the best specialists in California study the problem and then begin procedures after that. I thank him.

      Since I am early again this week, I go to my trailer to reflect on how I got here. I hold a point of the star as my mind fills with the thoughts and feelings of the day after we went to church.

      It was a Monday, and after school and chores,

I went back out to the barn again. It had rained the night before, and I noticed the Star's points had a dull white look where some red paint had been rubbed off from hitting the ground. I ran back home, stole a file from my dad's garage and hurried back to the barn. I filed all the rest of the red paint off those points. I kept filing. I filed one edge of the points until they were super sharp. I thought about adding more colors to the body of the star. Maybe to highlight the design that was there. Underneath each point there was a dot and a line. All five lines ran into the center of the star. But all I did was color those dots and lines in black.

I cocked my arm back for the first throw of the day, then propelled it forwards as I always did and, "Ouch!" The thing bit me. I didn't have my hand in the right spot on the star's body to prevent one of those now super sharp points from cutting me as I released it. I got blood all over the star. I quickly buried it and went home bleeding.

So mom and I, leaving my sister at home in front of the TV, walked to the hospital where the doctor put in ten stitches to sew up the cut in the web part of my right hand between the hand and thumb. "It's still better than your left hand," the doctor said. I told my Mom I had slipped while climbing over a barbed wire fence. She called me an idiot and a clumsy lazy ass but didn't question me any further. I went to bed with my hand sore and later itching like crazy.

My dad came home the next day, took one look at my hand and laughed.

"You idiot," he said.

He gave me a gift to make me feel better, though. A model airplane. Then he hit my mom twice for letting me cut myself. I tried putting the plane together while listening to my mom crying as my dad slammed the front door on his way out, but the instructions were too difficult to understand. I couldn't concentrate and they were blurry.

It would only take four months from the time the federal government stopped paying their bills to its total collapse. After two months, Congress realized its mistake and raised the debt ceiling, but it was already too late. While the Treasury did go back to issuing bonds, no one was buying them. There was nothing backing the U.S. government's debt but faith in the U.S. government. And that had been lost.

After the bleeding incident, my throws got a lot better. The star would fly without crashing. It would fly straight where I wanted it to. It would fly level without any loss of altitude. I never tried to find out how far it could fly. I didn't want to risk losing it, so I kept bouncing it off trees. Later, I could even predict where it was going to hit on each tree and where it was going to end up. If I threw it a certain way and aimed for the side of this one tree, then I knew which tree it was going to hit after that, and then the next one too. Not bad for such little practice. Maybe I was not such a big loser after all. Maybe there was something, however insignificant, that I was good at. Maybe even the best in the world at.

I walk onto the studio floor just as Phil is announcing.

"Welcome, California, to the latest edition of *Capping S'ers*! We have a really big show for you tonight. Stay tuned."

I look for my sister and give her a little wave. I notice that behind her, a middle-aged man suddenly stands up, pulls off his t-shirt, and waves it over his head. These fans are getting crazy.

Commercial.

"For the next sixty minutes, we are going to meet Janet Forbes. She is a resident of Los Angeles. We are going to interview her here live in our studio, and then LIVE we will watch the Capp and see if Janet has the guts to go through with it or not. Stick around. We will be back right after this commercial break."

On cue, I walk out to center stage and give the crowd a big wave. It seems a little chilly tonight. I hope my sister is warm enough. The middle-aged man behind her is jumping up and down, making his fat stomach jiggle. Crazier and crazier.

Commercial.

On the big screen, while playing the theme music, the camera fades in on a very young looking woman standing on a beach with waves crashing nearby. She has a tight smile on her face.

I know the age to be on the show is twenty-one, but this girl looks at least four years younger. Why would someone want to end their life before it has even begun?

The scene shifts to the same person reading a map while standing with a 'Welcome to Beverly Hills' sign over her right shoulder. "Beverly Hills is home to many movie stars. I have a map to all of them right here. My name is Janet Forbes, and I am ready to commit suicide."

Then Janet is standing by a gate, and as the camera pulls away, it becomes obvious she is outside of the La Brea Tar Pits. She says, "I have always been fascinated by how fossils are preserved and what they tell us about the past."

Finally, Janet is walking into an older two-story home that has been carved up and turned into a fourplex. She says, "This is my apartment. I have one-fourth of this beautiful 1920s home. Let me show you my place."

Janet walks through her front door. Her apartment is spotless. She comments, "I love it here. I have only been here for six months, but I feel like I made it my own."

"We will get up close and personal with Janet right after these commercial messages."

I am on cue again as I adjust the position of the first in-line. I think Stuart is married. Or has a significant other. I know he is on the phone a lot, calling someone sweetheart. My sister still doesn't have a blanket. The middle-aged man is putting his shirt back on. Well, at least he calmed down.

Commercial.

Phil and Janet are seated in chairs slightly facing each other.

"Hello, everyone. I am Phil Ebenezer. I have a PhD in clinical psychology. Now, Janet, tell me why you want to end your life."

Janet cries throughout the interview, pulling tissues out of a box next to her chair in almost a continuous stream. "I was happy in life. I had a good job. A loving boyfriend. We were going to announce our engagement in the fall and get married next year in the spring. I have caring parents who always loved me and given me everything. I never wanted for anything. That is, until the accident."

Phil picks up the 3 X 5 card that is on the table next to him. He folds it in half and slips it into his shirt pocket before he says, "Tell me about the accident."

Janet's crying increases as she explains haltingly, "I was driving my car. It was late at night. I had been out with friends, but I hadn't been drinking. Only one beer."

"Go on."

"I was tired. I had been working a lot of overtime that week. I shouldn't have gone out. I should have stayed home and gone to bed. But one of my girlfriends had gotten a new job that had a cute guy working there, and she wanted to tell me all about it."

"Then what happened?"

"After we left the bar, I was driving down the road. It was late. It was dark. The road was straight and dry."

"And then?"

"I guess I fell asleep. My eyes were closed for only a second, I swear. The car drifted across the yellow line. It hit an oncoming car. We were both doing sixty."

"And what happened to the people in the other car?"

Janet was wailing now. "Their car went off the road. It hit a tree and split in two. They all died. A mother and two children. One of them a two-month-old. I killed them! I killed a little baby!"

Janet says in a whisper, "Now I just want to die."

Janet's shakes her head from side to side while Phil asks, "So you are ready to end your life?"

"I am."

"Stay tuned. We'll be right back."

Commercial.

"Welcome back, folks. I thought that was a great way to end the interview, but Brian tells me I still have fifteen minutes to fill. So Janet, what would you like to talk about?"

"Nothing."

"Well, I don't think Brian is going to be very happy if we just sit here and stare at each other, so, let's see. What can we talk about?" After a pause as

Phil scratches his chin, "What did you do to prepare for the show today?"

"I put my affairs in order. I said goodbye to everyone I wanted to say goodbye to. Most of them tried to talk me out of it. I donated all my furniture or gave it away to friends. I gave my landlord his keys back. My car was totaled, so I didn't have to worry about that. I just got ready to die today."

"I see. Very organized. I like that. So you aren't going to change your mind and step away?"

"No."

"What about your boyfriend and loving parents? How do they feel about you being on the show?"

"They don't know I'm here. I had to deceive them."

"Good. Very good. In your video you were at the beach. Do you like the beach?"

"Oh, very much so. I go there every chance I get. That's where I spent the night last night."

"You slept on the beach last night?"

"I didn't sleep. I walked in the surf or sat and watched the waves all night long."

"Huh. That makes me feel funny. Like you were trying to pack a lifetime of beach going into one night. That makes me feel a little sad. Oh well, time to die. We will be back with the LIVE Capp right after these commercials."

Commercial.

I adjust the third in-line. It looks like Steven finally gave my sister a blanket. The middle-aged man is sitting down. I guess he spent all his energy early.

Hearing Janet talk about her accident reminded me of the day everything changed for my sister and me.

Of course, it was all my fault. I don't remember where we were going, but my sister and I were in the back seat of the car with mom and dad up front. Dad was driving. And I was tormenting my twin, like always.

We were ten, and she still liked to play with dolls. She had her favorite Barbie with her until I snatched it away from her. She screamed and started hitting me. I held the doll out my window and acted like I was going to drop it onto the street. My dad started yelling at us to behave. My mom turned around, glaring. My sister unbuckled her seat belt and was trying to climb over me to retrieve her doll. A dump truck ran the red light and hit us broadside.

The truck hit right at my sister's door. Our car spun and flipped, over and over. My left hand was smashed between the road and the car. My sister was thrown from side to side, seat to ceiling. It sounded like a lone shoe during a dryer cycle. *Thunk*, *thunk* as she hit each hard surface. The roof, the floor, the door. She ended up in my lap, looking peaceful and asleep. I thought she was dead. The doll had disappeared. I didn't realize my hand had been hurt. I didn't feel any pain. I was in shock, I guess. I reached down to touch my twin's face and wondered where the blood was coming from. Then I saw my hand and realized the blood was mine. That's when I started screaming.

I heard later that the dump truck driver was drunk and already had a DUI on his license. He shouldn't have been driving, but the company was short-handed that day. I shouldn't have taken my sister's doll. It was all my fault.

The crowd applauds after my introduction while I, in my skintight black leather outfit and bare feet, step into camera range and wave. The scar on my right hand is itching like crazy. My left hand feels like someone is holding it over a flame.

I stand in the empty space where the second pole with the rope was. The in-lines are standing at attention on their marks. Brian escorts Janet to where I am standing. I study Janet's neck. Should be no problem. I pull back to see Janet's face. It is swollen and puffy. Her amber eyes are filled with tears. I check Janet's position by looking up the line, then down the line.

I say, "You don't have to do this. Just step away, and the star won't hurt you."

"But I want to die."

I turn and walk to my starting spot. The doctor and medics are ready. I hold out my left arm with its mangled hand and cock my right arm back and throw the star. It flies straight at the first in-line. With a *clang* and a spark, the star bounces off the first man's neck armor and continues.

The star cuts the rope, then bounces off the second in-line. It flies on toward Janet, grazes by her, cutting her neck in the process. Her body shudders. She falls to the ground, blood streaming. Another *clang* is heard, then a *thud*.

The doctor comes over to watch. Janet is holding her hand pressed against her neck. The doctor acts confused.

"She doesn't want to die!" I scream.

The doctor motions the paramedics over and holds a compress against her neck as she is lifted onto the gurney and hustled out the door.

The music starts up. I am still standing where I began. The in-lines are still at attention. On the big screen, the ambulance hasn't moved. The star is stuck in the last post. The crowd is growing restless. Security guards are moving in as on the big screen, the ambulance slowly leaves the parking lot.

I look at my sister but can't read any expression. Soon sis. Soon. The middle-aged man behind her is fast asleep. Wow, guess this isn't exciting enough for him.

Commercial.

In my trailer, after retrieving the star, greeting my sister, and ignoring Steven, I think about Janet and her reaction to her automobile accident. She sincerely wanted to die because of it. I never felt that way after our crash. Was it because my sister lived? All I felt afterward was a deep desire to make it up to my sister. To make up to her that she must spend the rest of her life in a wheelchair.

After all, I am the cause of her injuries.

Season One, Episode Six

CAPPING S'ERS
XCAL - 1
10-11 pm
New "Sally Henderson"
S1/EP06, (2017), The final episode of the first season that highlights one individual who desires to commit suicide. With an assist from thrower Ricky Fordham, the individual may or may not die.

It's been a quiet week. The only interesting thing that happened is my assistant who helps me into my costume had been eyeing me a little too much. I don't know if she saw me naked too often or what. I'm not ready for a relationship, so I may have to ask Brian for a new assistant.

Remembering events after the car wreck, everything changed. My sister was confined to a wheelchair for the rest of her life. No use ever of her legs. She had limited use of her arms. They could move some, but she couldn't push herself in her wheelchair or use them for anything meaningful. She couldn't speak anymore. Just grunts and groans. She still had her long beautiful wavy hair. Her soft skin. Her eyes were the same. A spellbinding pale green. Only now, everything she wanted to say, every emotion she felt, every thought she had, had to come out through those eyes.

My mom, of course, became bitter and depressed. I had stolen her companion, the child she was raising in her image. She wanted nothing to do with what that child had turned into. And she hated me for causing it.

My dad. My pal. The one who raised me to be a man. He turned his back on me. He started hitting me, beating me, berating me. Even more than he used to. Calling me stupid, clumsy, and worthless.

And I deserved it all.

I was the cause of so much misery and anger. I felt so ashamed of what I had done. I was the curse, the black sheep of the family.

After I had been successfully throwing the star for about a month, I came home from school one day and heard groaning coming from my room. I had seen our car in the driveway, so I knew dad was home. Both he and my mom were standing in my room. My sister was there too. She was the one groaning, and her pale green eyes were as big as saucers. I noticed my baseball bat was lying on my bed. I keep it in the corner behind the door.

"What happened?" I asked.

Mom just stood there while dad replied, "Your sister fell off the porch and hurt herself."

My eyes returned to the bat. "Are we going to take her to the hospital?"

"Why? She never could use her arms. Nobody ever died from a broken arm."

I couldn't see any bones sticking out but both arms were completely covered in deep red and purple bruises. Looking at the terror in my sister's eyes, I could tell what happened. I'm not stupid. But what could I do? I felt angry and compassionate at the same time. Anger at my parents. Compassion for my twin. Both feelings mixed together seemed to cancel each other out, leaving only confusion. I felt dull, and my stomach hurt.

My parents left my room, leaving my sister there. I went to my twin, knelt down beside her wheelchair, and said, "I'm sorry. I'm sorry," repeatedly. I didn't know what else to do. I closed the door to my room and laid on my bed. I finally fell asleep while staring at my sister's battered arms and listening to my dog whining outside my window.

The next morning my dad was gone again. Sis was still in my room. She had soiled her diaper and it stank. I went out and Mom was sitting at the table, smoking a cigarette. A cup of coffee was on the table in front of her. There was toast burning in the toaster, but my mom continued sitting there without moving. Her eyes followed me, but she didn't move as I fished the burnt toast out with a fork and threw it away.

"Are you going to clean up Roberta?" I asked.

"Not my problem anymore. You caused her to be like that. You take care of her."

I went back to my room. Even though it was a school-day, I couldn't leave her like that.

I wheeled Roberta into the bathroom, lifted her out of the chair and sat her on the toilet. I then started removing her dirty clothes. She stared at me with her pale green eyes. I could tell she had been crying.

I cleaned her up as best I could, wiping her everywhere. I then carried her to her room and laid her on the bed. It was hard. She was as big as me and weighed only slightly less.

I combed the tangles out of her hair and then brushed it for an hour. I was just going to have to miss school today. I could see the 'thank you' in my twin's eyes.

I left my sister on the bed and since it didn't look like my mom was going to stop me, I went to the field behind the woods, buried the baseball bat and threw the star as hard as I could. I wasn't doing any bouncing off trees. I was just throwing hard straight at the trees, as if I wanted to make them hurt too.

It was nearly dark by the time I returned home. Mom was still sitting at the table.

"What's for dinner?" I asked.

Mom streaked out of her chair and knocked me to the floor. "Fix your own goddamn dinner!" She kicked me in the ribs and then in the face. "I'm not your slave!" She kicked me in the back and stomach. I curled up into a ball. "I'm tired of being responsible! And getting the shit beat out of me every time something doesn't go right around here!" She picked me up, punched me in the stomach, face and knocked me down again. "It's about time you got your ass kicked!" She kicked me one last time. In the ass.

It hurt to breathe but there was no trip to the doctor. She wrote a note for school that said I had the flu and would be out two weeks and gave the note to the bus driver.

I still had bruises after the two weeks was up but since I had no student or teacher friends, no one asked what happened.

Spring led into summer, which led into fall, which led into winter. I practiced with the star every moment I could. My sister seemed to recover from her injuries. Her arms hung crooked, and they didn't move at all anymore except for an occasional uncontrollable jerk.

On school days, I would wake up an hour early, so I could take care of my sister. I would escort her to the bathroom, so she could take care of business. I would manually stimulate her to get her bowels moving. If she was having a difficult time with it, I would hum her a tune. Either a current one from the radio or one I would make up. That always seemed to help.

I would get her dressed and park her in front of the television. Mom was always there but never did or said anything. Just sat at the table smoking a cigarette and drinking coffee.

After school, I would fix dinner for my sister and me. I would change and wash the bed sheets once a week, or earlier if they needed it. When her clothes wore out, or just for variety, I would go into my closet and give her mine.

Fixing my sister and myself a meal was always a scary time, especially if I was making something hot. Mom would suddenly leap up from the table and knock me down. I stopped counting the burn marks once I got past thirty. If my dad saw this while he was home, he would laugh and give my mom a high five.

Wasn't it funny that these were the only times I saw them together and happy? It wouldn't be long, however, before he would hit my mom and knock her to the floor over something, and then leave for weeks at a time.

It was fortunate that he would give me the grocery money at the beginning of his visits rather than at the end. That was how I could buy food for my sister and myself. I never bought any for my mom. I always wondered where she got the money for her cigarettes and coffee.

I got tired of just hitting trees with the star, so I hung a heavy piece of wood from a rope tied to one of the tree branches that ranged out over the field. I then threw the star to see if it would cut the rope. It did. Apparently, the star was spinning fast enough, and the points were sharp enough and extended out far enough that it worked. I did that a few times. Then I moved the rope so that the star would hit a tree, bounce off and then cut the rope. Once I perfected that,

I moved it again so that the star would hit two trees and then cut the rope. That was okay, but the star was getting a little too far back in the crowded woods, so I was going to have to think of something else.

As my dad's visits home became more frequent, his anger grew. His world was shrinking, and he didn't like it. He said it started with the senior citizens not having any money to spend when social security was cut off. Then the people they would have bought from didn't have any money and so on and so on. People were laid off. Stores had to close. There wasn't any inter-state freight to haul anymore. Banks were closing. Homes had become worthless. Air travel just stopped. Barter was the norm.

After making sure my sister was taken care of, I would go to school.

School.

I wasn't sure why I was even there. They weren't teaching me anything that I needed to know.

They weren't teaching me how to take care of my sister.

They weren't teaching me how to avoid getting beaten by my parents.

They weren't teaching me how to fight back.

They weren't teaching me the best way to run away from home.

They weren't preparing me for life after school.

They weren't showing me how to survive.

Survive.

The only reason I got up in the mornings was to take care of my sister. If it wasn't for her, I wouldn't bother. I would just lie in bed and rot to death. Everything I did, I did for her.

Walking around school, I felt like I was living in a bubble. All the girls giggling and laughing. Talking about dating, football games and penis sizes.

All the boys standing around looking all macho. Puffing out their chests and eyeing the girls as they walked by.

I didn't feel connected to either group. I felt alone. Alienated. I stared out the window and wondered what I would be doing five years from now. Ten years from now. Twenty.

Sometimes I saw someone else across the room, standing alone, watching, and not participating. I thought about talking to them, but doubted if they would understand.

I closed myself off. Built walls. I told myself none of it mattered and I didn't care.

I couldn't care. If I cared, I would cry. And I couldn't do that because I was a man, and men don't cry.

I missed my twin when I was off at school. When I was around her, I had a purpose. I had no purpose at school. I was just wasting time there.

I missed my sister at night. I missed her sleeping next to me, putting the day's torments behind us and just enjoying being with each other. Now, most nights, after I put her to bed, I would lie there next to her. I didn't speak. I would just listen to her breathing. Listen to how it slowed and became softer as she fell asleep. This provided some comfort to me, and maybe her too. But it was not like it used to be before the accident.

There was no life without my twin.

I remember one fight my dad had with my mom was about green eyes.

"Where did they come from?" he shouted. "Those green eyes! No one in my family has green eyes. No one in your family has green eyes. So, where did they come from?"

Every time he said green, I could hear a slap. I was looking at my sister and every time there was a slap, her pale green eyes got bigger and rounder. I wheeled my sister into my room and kept her there all night with the door locked.

"Welcome, California, to the final episode of *Capping S'ers'* first season! We have a really big show planned for you tonight! Also, let's give some applause for our special guest here at the studio. Governor Johnson, the chief executive officer of this fine state. Isn't he grand? Stay tuned."

If it is possible, the audience applause is louder than usual while the spotlights fly back and forth at an overheated frenzied pace. Extra seating was added between the two big sets of bleachers. In it is the Governor and his entourage. He stands up and waves.

The Governor arrived to visit a few hours before show time. I had been told about it the day before, but I figured he was just out for a photo op. He was running for an unprecedented fifth term. He came early, during rehearsal. He met with Brian and the creative staff, and then came out onto the studio floor. He was introduced to me, and then he went to talk with the in-lines.

I was surprised when he came back to me. He really did seem interested. He asked me some questions about the star and how I learned to throw it with only one good hand. I was sure he already knew all the answers. He probably had a file on me a mile thick. He asked if he could hold the star.

While I was fanatical about no one else touching the star, he was the Governor. How could I refuse? Especially with all these people standing around staring at us. No one since Irene had touched it, and that was years ago. And my mom, of course. Wait, somebody had packed it into my box at the foster home, but I don't know who that was.

I couldn't think of a reason to say no, so I handed it to him. He shuddered.

"Wow," he said. "This really is light. And cold. Can I throw it?"

"Sorry, sir, but no."

He ran his thumb along one of the points. It cut, and he bled a few drops. "Sharp too," he added before he sucked on his thumb to stop the bleeding. His aides wanted to spray disinfectant and bandage the cut, but he waved them off.

Then he said, "Let's get a picture. Ricky and I can stand here in front, holding the star. The in-lines and Brian gather around behind us."

When the photographers indicated they were ready, and everyone was standing facing forward, I reached out and grasped one of the points of the star that the Governor was still holding by a different point.

I was instantly flooded with all the knowledge, thoughts and feelings of the Governor. At that moment, I probably knew him better than he knew himself. I knew how he felt when he sucked on his mother's breast. I knew what he was thinking when he first ordered a person to be executed. I knew how he really felt about his wife and her affairs and what he was planning to do about it.

While the light bulbs were flashing, and everyone was smiling, I explored every bit of this man. There were no areas hidden from me. I wondered if he was doing the same with me.

The photographers indicated they were done. The Governor let go of the star, and the connection was broken. Still smiling, he leaned toward me and said, "Sorry about your mom. Such rage you had. So intense. So beautiful."

How did that happen? Why did that happen? Irene and I had spent hours both holding the star all those years ago, and nothing like that had ever happened.

"For the next sixty minutes, we are going to meet Sally Henderson. She is a resident of Chino. We are going to interview her here live in our studio, and then LIVE we will watch the Capp and see if Sally becomes an S'er or not. Stick around. We will be back right after this commercial break."

I walk into the studio and wave to the audience. My sister is there. The Governor is in his special section talking with an aide.

Commercial.

On screen, music plays as the camera fades in on a very good-looking twenty-five-year-old woman standing in front of a field where hundreds of cows are segregated into separate pens. She is holding her nose while smiling.

Next up is the same person standing with a Chaffey Community College sign over her right shoulder. Sally addresses us in sign language as she says, "This is where I went to school. I got my Associates Degree in Sign Language Studies. My name is Sally Henderson, and I am ready to commit suicide."

Then there is Sally standing by a booth, and as the camera pulls back, it becomes obvious she is amid a well-attended farmers market. She signs and says, "This is where I come once a week to buy fresh produce and flowers."

Lastly, is Sally walking up the driveway of an older single-story home. She signs and says, "I rent the room over the garage. They made it into a cute little apartment. Let me show you."

We see Sally as she walks up the stairs to her front door. Her apartment is furnished with a futon and an end table. It has a mini kitchen and a closed door that presumably leads to the bathroom. There is a clear glass door that leads out to a one-person balcony. She comments, "I just moved in a month ago. If I die on your show, do you think they will let me out of the lease?"

"We will get up close and personal with Sally right after these commercial messages."

I adjust the position of the first in-line. I think his wife's name is Martha. I give a wave to my twin who can't wave back. The Governor is smoking a cigar.

Commercial.

Phil and Sally are seated.

"Hello, everyone. I am Phil Ebenezer. I have a PhD in clinical psychology. Now Sally, tell me why you want to end your life."

"I just want to start by saying that this is not about my father."

"Okay."

"It is just that I don't want to live anymore. I think about killing myself all the time. So, it is now time to do it."

"But this isn't about your father?"

"Correct. I don't care what it says on your little card over there. He didn't do anything wrong."

Phil picks up his 3 X 5 card and flings it into Sally's lap. "Well, according to this, he molested you."

"He didn't do anything wrong."

"So what he did was right? Did you do something wrong? Did you lead him on, somehow?"

Sally looks startled. "No. I didn't do anything

wrong either."

"Well, if no one did anything wrong, why are you here?"

"To kill myself. Isn't that what happens on this show?"

Sally's eyes narrow as she shakes her head from side to side. Phil asks, "So you are ready to end your life?"

"I am."

"Don't forget to stay tuned after the show for your XCAL 1 evening news, the only official state newscast. Remember folks, if you didn't see it on XCAL 1, it didn't happen. We'll be right back."

Commercial.

"Welcome back, folks. Sally, you haven't been very forthcoming about why you want to die. We have twenty minutes left in this interview. Do you want to try explaining why again?"

"No."

"Anything else you want to talk about?"

"No."

"I seem to be getting that a lot. In your video piece, you said that you graduated from Chaffey College with an AA in sign language. Why did you want training in that?"

"My dad is deaf. Has been his whole life. My mom would sign to communicate with him. So, I pretty much grew up around it and knew it well. I studied sign in college, so I could do it better."

"This is the same dad who is not at fault here?"

"That's right."

"Did you do anything with your training after you got your degree?"

"I went to work for the California School for the Deaf in Riverside."

"And what did you do there?"

"I taught in their elementary school."

"Did you like it?"

"Oh, yes. I loved it."

"Won't the children there miss you?"

"Yeah, probably. They made a six-foot tall heart, and everyone signed it on my last day there." Sally's eyes fill with tears. "It was beautiful."

"Are you ready yet to tell us what your dad did?"

"My father didn't do anything. This isn't about him."

"Then what is it about?"

"Nothing. It is about nothing. Can I die now, please?"

"Sure. We'll be back with the LIVE Capp right after this."

I adjust the third in-line. My sister seems to be staring into space. The Governor is leaning forward in his seat.

Commercial.

The crowd applauds after my intro, while I, dressed in the outfit my assistant helped me into, step into camera range and wave to the crowd.

I am standing in the S'er spot while Brian escorts Sally to me. I study Sally's neck. It looks like a normal cut is all that is needed. I pull back slowly to see Sally's face. It looks youthful. Her hazel eyes appear clear and bright. I check Sally's position by looking up the line, then down the line.

I then say, "You don't have to do this. Just step away, and the star won't hurt you."

I turn and walk to my starting spot. The medical team is in position. I see we have a new doctor.

I hold out my left arm. I ignore the itching of my hand as I cock my right arm back and throw the star. It flies straight at the first in-line. With a *clang* and a spark, the star bounces off the first man's neck armor and continues.

The star cuts the rope, then bounces off the second man. It flies on toward Sally who steps back. I stare at the slightly smiling Sally as another *clang* is heard, then a *thud*.

The *Capping S'ers* theme music starts up. I am still standing where I began. The in-lines are still at attention. Sally is beginning to walk away. The star is stuck in the last post. Brian is running toward her. The crowd is silent and stunned. The Governor is looking angry.

Commercial.

After assisting me out of my outfit, I dismiss my assistant and sit for hours staring into the mirror. What just happened? The Governor showed up for my performance. Why? Just curious? What does that mean? Then, when we both held the star, I entered his mind, his soul. I accessed every feeling and thought he ever had. How did that happen? What is this star thing? Then Sally stepped away. That hadn't happened before either. I guess she didn't want to die. She never said why she was on the show. Something about her dad it sounded like. Maybe it was too horrible to talk about? Boy, I have a lot to process.

Season Two, Episode One

CAPPING S'ERS
XCAL - 1
10-11 pm
New "Sally Henderson, Part 2"
S2/EP01, (2018), The premier episode of the second season that highlights one individual who desires to commit suicide. With an assist from thrower Ricky Fordham, the individual may or may not die.

First show of season two. Time for a fresh start. Got a new assistant. I had Brian fire the old one after one torrid night of sex. Didn't see how I could work with her every day after that. They are going to have Sally on again since, so far, she is the only S'er to step away. That was probably not the original plan, but a lot of fans were upset they didn't get to see her blood, so we are trying again.

We didn't have much of a season break, and I didn't do a lot with it. Growing up, I used to wonder if I was a boy or a girl. I mean, I know I have girl parts. But did I feel like I was a boy or a girl inside, in my soul? I knew about transgender people. My eighth-grade class had one. One day I asked him why he was always wearing girl clothes. He said even though he had boy parts, he knew he was really a girl. Deep down inside. Just knew it. I couldn't say if I felt anything that strongly deep down inside.

Boys were supposed to be tough. I was even tougher. Just ask any of the many boys that thought they could pick on me. That was one thing my dad taught me. How to fight like a man.

Boys were dirty and smelly. Girls were clean and cover themselves in fragrances. I was always clean, but I didn't drench myself in perfumes. Just a dab in case I had body odor that day.

Boys liked to play sports. My dad made me watch and play sports. I enjoyed it and was good at it but never seemed to be as good as the boys were.

Boys seemed to be unaware of other's feelings. Girls often used other's feelings to inflict hurt and pain. Girls may not fight with fists. Instead, they fought with words. I felt more like a boy in that aspect.

Girls were more prone to obey rules. Boys were more likely to break them. Check one for the Boy column.

Not very conclusive, but I guess I was more like a boy than a girl. I thought about that for a long time. Tried acting and thinking like I thought a boy might. Nope, not feeling it. So, I want to be a girl. I thought about that for a long time. Tried acting and thinking like a girl might. Not feeling that one either. In truth, I just felt like me. Whoever or whatever that was.

Sitting in my trailer, touching a tip of the star, I went back in time to a day when my dad was gone as he usually was. My mom was drinking coffee and smoking cigarettes at the kitchen table when she said,

"Your sister and I are going for a ride. I need you to meet me at the bus station later."

"Ride? What ride? Dad has the car."

"Don't worry about the ride part. Just meet me at the bus station. It's a long walk so you better start now. And take a snack. And some water."

I went into the kitchen, grabbed a package of peanut butter crackers, a bottled water and left the house. I was curious about what was going on, so I hid behind the neighbor's bushes and waited.

About ten minutes later, an EMS vehicle and a fire truck came screeching around the corner, lights flashing and sirens wailing. They stopped in front of our house, and men in uniforms jumped out just as an ambulance pulled up. A man and a woman got out of the ambulance and rushed into the house.

After about five minutes, the two ambulance workers went to the back of the vehicle, pulled out a stretcher bed and carted that into the house. "What is happening?" I wondered.

I was just about to climb out from behind the bushes to find out when the stretcher was wheeled out of the house, and as my mom walked alongside it, says, "I don't know what happened. She just stopped breathing. She's never done that before." I could see my sister on the stretcher as it was loaded into the ambulance, but she wasn't moving, so I couldn't tell if she was dead or alive. My mom climbed in and the ambulance drove off.

The EMS guys came out of the house, closed the front door, and then left along with the fire truck. The street was quiet again, as if nothing had happened. I climbed out of the bushes and went back into the house. Nothing looked different, but it felt emptier.

Not knowing what else to do, I started walking to the bus station.

When I got there, my mom was already inside.

"Where have you been?" she asked. "You made us almost miss our bus."

"Where's sis?"

"Don't worry about her. She's fine. I left her with our neighbor."

I knew that was a lie. I had seen her taken away in the ambulance. I also tried to recall the last time I had seen my mom talking with a neighbor. I drew a blank.

"Where are we going?"

"To Las Vegas."

"Why?"

"To teach your dad a lesson. That's why."

I don't know where she had gotten money for the bus. Same place she got her coffee and cigarette money, I guess. First thing after arriving in Las Vegas, we went into the nearest bar. Then after an hour and forty-five minutes of making out with a stranger, she took off with the guy and left me sitting there. When it got to be closing time, the bartender, not knowing what else to do, took me home with him. I didn't like the bartender. He smelled like cigarettes and alcohol.

"What are you going to do to me, mister?" I asked.

"I don't know. Wait for someone to come looking for you, I guess. Although your mom was pretty wasted. She probably doesn't even remember what bar she left you in."

So, I waited.

I guess it could have been worse. The bartender didn't try to kill me or rape me or anything else like that. He fed me; let me sleep on the couch and pretty much left me alone. He would take me to the bar when he worked. I guess in case my mom was to show up, which she never did.

When the bartender wasn't at work, I would stare out the picture window of his house and wait. I would start to get excited every time a car I hadn't seen before approached the house, but each time it either turned off or sped by.

I remembered when I first entered his house, I was wondering why there were so many Christmas cards on the walls. I knew it was December, and a lot of people hung up all the cards they receive, but these seemed to be placed at random. Several were yellowed like they were years old, some weren't signed, and others looked like they had never even been sent. Then one day he got into a yelling match with the woman who also lived in the house. His wife maybe? They were arguing about something she had bought. He was saying that they couldn't afford it, and she had to return it. She kept saying no. She needed it, and it wasn't ever going to be returned. He kept getting madder and madder until finally — *BAM*! He punched the wall so hard he put a hole in it, and up went another Christmas card.

So, I waited some more, and my dad finally showed up a week later. At the bar. He had gotten my mom out of jail already, so he took us all home. My dad had my sister with him, who, as far as I could tell, seemed the same as always. I cried when I saw her and gave her the biggest hug of her life. Her pale green eyes seemed so alive and joyful when she saw me. They were also leaking tears.

Dad said the police had come and visited him at work. Apparently, they wanted to arrest him for child abandonment. It seems that my mom just walked away from the hospital after my sister had been admitted because she stopped breathing. They couldn't find a medical reason why that happened. The hospital people were mostly mad because their facility had been treated like an animal shelter or a day care center. My dad managed to convince the police of his innocence and that he didn't know where his wife was. He promised to let them know when he found her. He did, and then he had to pay a whole big bunch of money too.

It was the phone call from the Las Vegas police who notified him of my mom sitting in their jail that let him know where she was. He had to pay even more money for that. My mom couldn't remember the bar, so they went around to all of them until they found me. My dad was mad by that point and threatened to kill my mom if she even pulled another stunt like that again. She told him that if he left her alone for more than five minutes, she would take off again. She may have said it, but I don't think she meant it, because it never happened again.

There were a few beatings that came out of all that as my dad stayed with us for the whole Christmas break. Meanwhile, life for everyone was getting worse. The grocery stores were mostly empty. People were rioting. Travel was restricted. Martial law was in effect, and after a time, California closed its borders.

I threw the star a lot. Threw it. Tromped down the field to retrieve it. Threw it again. My dog yapping the whole time like it was great fun. Holidays. Nothing like them.

"Welcome, California, to the premier episode of *Capping S'ers'* second season! We have a really big show planned for you tonight! Stay tuned."

I am standing next to the bleachers as the audience applauds, and the spotlights swing back and forth at a frenzied pace. I am standing by the side where my sister is always parked. I smile at her. Steven is standing next to her. Another season. I heard her procedures are supposed to be starting soon. I notice that in the seat above my sister, a teenage boy wearing a baseball style *Capping S'ers* cap is staring at the breasts of an older girl sitting next to him.

Commercial.

"We have a really special treat for you tonight. We have already met Sally Henderson. She was on the last show of the first season. She was the first, and so far, the only person ever to step away from the Capp. We are going to interview her again here in our studio, and then LIVE we will watch the Capp and see if Sally finally becomes an S'er or not. Stick around. We'll be back right after this commercial break."

I walk into the studio and wave to the audience. The teenage boy wearing a baseball style *Capping S'ers* cap is talking with the girl next to him. You go boy.

Commercial.

I stand by the snack table and watch Phil and Sally.

I remember one day when I was five, my sister was inside with our mom sewing dresses. My dad and I were playing football in the front yard. We weren't playing flag football. There was no sissy cloth hanging from a belt. So tackling was an option, even though just a shove or push would be enough. How much force does a grown man need to bring down a little girl?

I had the ball, and dad tackled me. I went down hard. Very hard. I started crying. My dad became outraged. The more I cried, the madder he got.

"Stop your crying! Be a man!"

"What?"

"You heard me. Stop crying. Be a man."

"I'm not a man," I said between sobs. "I'm a little girl."

My father moved and stood astraddle me, "You are not a little girl. I am going to make a man out of you, whether you want that or not."

I would never forget that day. My father's face

towering high above me, red with rage. Those words would echo in my head for the rest of my life.

"Stop crying! Be a man!"

"Be tough! Be a man!"

"Hit me! Hit me hard! Be a man!"

"Hello, everyone. I am Phil Ebenezer. I have a PhD in clinical psychology. Now Sally, tell us what happened the first time you were on this show."

"Well, I remember I was in line waiting to die but I kept hearing Ricky's voice saying over and over, 'Just step away,' so I did."

"So, you didn't want to kill yourself."

"No, I did. I mean, I do. You see, we are really poor."

Phil consults his 3 X 5 card. "And you are afraid of your parents losing their home?"

"Correct."

"So, are you going to go through with it this time?"

"Yes. Absolutely."

"Okay then. I must ask. Sally, are you ready to end your life?"

"I am."

"Don't forget to stay tuned after the show for your XCAL 1 evening news, the only official state newscast. Remember folks, if you didn't see it on XCAL 1, it didn't happen."

Commercial.

"Okay Sally. I think we established why you were on the show in the first place, and why you stepped away. What I don't understand is why you are back."

"Because I really want to die."

"I don't believe you. I am a clinical psychologist, and I don't believe you."

"But I do."

"No, you don't."

"You are right; I don't. Not really."

"I knew it. All those years of college finally paid off. So why are you here?"

"Can I whisper it in your ear?"

Phil appears startled. "Sure, I guess so."

Sally leans over and whispers something into Phil's ear. The boom man is trying to pick it up, but he is too slow.

"Now that I believe. You don't want to share it with the audience?"

"No."

"Why not? I am sure that on one of these episodes I will be interviewing someone who is being bullied. Oops. I said it. Do you want to talk about it now?"

"I might as well as long as you already blurted it out."

"Go ahead then."

"Well, after I stepped away on your last show, I started getting threats and nasty phone calls and emails. People called me coward and said I was chicken and weak. They said they were cheated out of what the show promised, and they would get their blood one way or the other. Someone found out my address and posted it and told people to trash my parent's house."

"I see. Well, you don't need to worry about those bullies. If you decide to step away again the show will protect you. So, do you still want to die?"

"I think so. I'll try not to step away."

"Not good enough, Sally. You must commit to die. You must say it. You must say that you are ready to die. That's the rules."

With hesitation, Sally whispers, "I'm ready to die."

"All right then. We have the LIVE Capp right after this."

I adjust the first in-line. If I remember correctly, he has three children. I glance at my sister and notice that the teenage boy wearing a baseball style *Capping S'ers* cap is having his face slapped by the girl who is seated next to him. She knocks the cap off his head. Struck out. Too bad. I wonder what he said to her to get that reaction.

Commercial.

"Ladies and gentlemen, welcome to the LIVE part of the show. Let us welcome Ricky Fordham, our Capper."

The crowd applauds while I step into camera range and wave. I am dressed in the normal skintight suit that my new assistant helped me into. She is very cute, but I am keeping my hands off. Good assistants are hard to find.

After Phil talks about my years of practice, I am ready in the usual S'er spot. Brian escorts Sally over. I fuss with Sally's positioning. I have her stand straight. I examine her neck. I pull back to see her entire face. I feel like I almost have a relationship with Sally. Seeing her for the second time like this. I know that Brian and the fans wanted her back, but I'm curious as to the real reason why she wanted to come back, so I ask, "Why are you here again? You stepped away."

"I had to come back."

"Why?"

"Like I said in the interview, everyone was calling me chicken. Because I didn't go through with it before."

"So what? You are still alive."

"They also said I would have to give the money back."

"Money? What money?"

"The money they give you for being on the show. They pay 100,000 California dollars to the families.

And we need that money."

"Sixty seconds," says the voice in my ear.

"What are you doing?" asks Brian after he rushes over in a panic. "This is not the time to be having a conversation. This is live TV."

"You're paying people to be on this show?" my anger now directed at Brian. "You're paying people to kill themselves!"

"Look. We'll talk about this later, okay?"

"Thirty seconds."

"Like hell we will." I start walking away.

Brian tries to grab my sleeve, but the black leather is too slick. "We have a Capp to do!"

I jerk my arm away as he tries to grab me again. "Not tonight we don't," I say as I walk out of the building with the star.

As I walk past the stands, I look up at my sister. She shows no reaction. I notice that the teenage boy has his cap back on his head and is staring at the breasts of the girl on the other side of him. I hope he uses a better pick up line than last time.

Commercial.

"Ladies and gentlemen, it appears that there will be no Capp tonight. Tune in next week for what I promise will be a REALLY big show. Good night."

Commercial.

Brian pounds on my trailer door for about an hour before giving up. I won't let him in. I am mad and not ready to talk about it.

They pay people to be on this show! So, this isn't about saving lives, or wanting to die, or hoping someone watching the show decides their life isn't so bad and stops contemplating suicide. It is all about the money. And ratings.

Season Two, Episode Two

CAPPING S'ERS
XCAL - 1
10-11 pm
New "Season One Recap"
S2/EP02, (2018), A recap of season one highlights.

There are six of them pounding on my door at 6:00 a.m. the next morning. Brian, of course. He does most of the talking. Says stuff about contracts, breaches and severance options. There are three others talking on their cell phones, relaying the action to people not identified. There is also an old gentleman with white hair and beard who sits quietly in the corner, staring at me with one of the best poker faces I have ever seen. The last person to enter must be Brian's personal aide because he flutters around Brian like a moth around a flame.

Brian is furious, "What do you think you are doing? Walking out on the show like that."

"You pay people to be on the show?"

"Yeah, so what? We don't actually pay them; we provide some relief to their families after they are gone. As a humanitarian thing. That's all."

"That girl last night. Sally. She didn't want to kill herself. She just wanted the money."

"Some people are like that. We screen them out, but she had special appeal because she had already been on the show before. So far, she is the only one to chicken out. But you! You can't walk out like that."

"Sir," interrupts one of the persons on the phone, "We just got the results. The show has gone hyper viral. A survey done this morning says more people than ever want to watch the show now, sir."

"So" I interject, "I guess I can walk out."

"Once. Just once," Brian warns, his teeth and fist clench tight, his face a lovely shade of red. "Now get your ass to the studio on time today, so we can get started on next week's show."

They leave, all six of them, without waiting for my reply.

I go back to the studio, but I tell Brian I am still too upset to do a Capp this week. He rants on about ratings, losing momentum, and delaying my sister's procedures. I promise him I will feel better later, but I convince him of my distress by missing the ropes a couple of times during practice. Out of all the bad things that Brian is predicting, he decides the worst would be if an S'er who wants to die doesn't because I miss. So, he gives me the rest of the week off, and they show a recap of season one instead.

Sitting on my studio paid couch, in my studio paid condo, I watch the show on my studio paid television. It is the first time I have seen the show on TV.

The camera fades in on Phil Ebenezer.

"Hello, California. We have a really special show for you tonight. Ricky is feeling a little under the weather, so tonight, we are going to recap *Capping S'ers'* first season. God, I hope she isn't pregnant.

That girl does get around, you know.

   We are going to spend about ten minutes on each of the six shows that made up season one. I am going to provide special insight into each S'er and into what makes this show so great. But before we start off with season one, episode one, I apologize for the technical difficulties we experienced with our sound system on our last show. We lost the sound feed for our cameras right there at the end of the show, but don't worry. You didn't miss anything. Just some yelling. Stick around. We will be back right after this commercial break."

   Holding a point of the star, my mind drifts back to that spring when I tore down part of the barn and used some of the rounded poles. With my dad's tools, I cut them to eight-foot lengths, so they stood six feet tall after I planted them in the ground. It was hard, but I manhandled them okay. I built some with an arm on top, so I could hang the weighted rope. I then used the poles instead of trees for my throws. Hit the first pole, cut the first rope, hit the second pole, cut the second rope, hit the third pole and then watch the star go flying off into the woods. I would set everything up; practice till I had it down pat, then change the starting spot, dig up the poles and set them up again in different places. Just eyeing it the whole time. Practice that until I had it perfect, then change the whole setup again. Digging up eight-foot poles. Dragging them around and burying them again. Man's work. Wasn't that what my dad raised me for?

   While playing the theme music, the camera fades in on the stage where Phil is sitting alone.

   "Hello, everyone. I am Phil Ebenezer. I have

a PhD in clinical psychology. Now, on our very first show, we had a young girl by the name of Dawn Adams. I should point out that, while some of our contestants look quite young, they all must be at least twenty-one years of age. They are all volunteers. And as you will see, they can step away, and bear no consequences. Now, Dawn allowed her boyfriend to go a little too far, in the heat of the moment, shall we say? She ended up pregnant and was afraid everyone would find out. Which, of course, everyone did find out when she came onto the show. But she doesn't have to worry about that now. Here is the replay of how her Capp went down."

The TV replays Dawn's Capp.

My dad was now home for good. He had been laid off. On the news they said that California, which had always had an economy larger than most nations, pretty much could continue as before. The state did take over the banks and insurance companies, but those had always been highly regulated anyway. It started printing its own money to replace those worthless federal dollars. California dollars. My dad didn't know how that worked with imports or exports with other states or nations or even if there were any of that kind of thing anymore, but then, that wasn't something he was involved in. The state also took over the media (radio, television, and internet). Migration between states was prohibited.

The state could produce enough food for everyone if it could get the water. California's water comes from two sources: snowpack and the Colorado River. Both were threatened, so he didn't know how the state did it, but there was always water out of the tap. Watering the lawn and washing the car was prohibited, however. Overall, California seemed to be able to do well on its own. The only problem that it couldn't get a handle on was the violence. Year after year there were more shootings, stabbings, riots, robberies, and domestic abuse than the year before. Oh well. No place can be called paradise, I guess.

While the theme music plays, the camera fades in on the same stage where Phil is sitting alone.

"Hello, again, everyone. I should point out that the man with the golden beard who you saw bring Dawn out is our own producer and director, Brian Goldstein. Now, on our second show, we had a young girl by the name of Ivory Beck. Like our first show, Ivory was also a victim of love. A man, trying to win a bet with his friends, toyed with Ivory's affections. He treated her nice, pretended he cared, and acted like he loved her. Ivory, apparently, did fall in love with him. Or at least, what he represented. So, she was easily fooled and can't tell real love from pretend love. She won't make that mistake again. By the way, we got even with that gentleman later. Too bad *that* wasn't live on the show. That would have been justice. Here is the replay of how Ivory's Capp went down."

The TV shows Ivory's Capp.

I remember one night when I was young, I was in a deep sleep, dreaming that I was drowning and couldn't breathe. I woke up startled. My mother was standing there, looking down at me with a strange expression on her face. She was breathing heavily and smelled of alcohol. Why was she just standing there? I wondered. I could hear my dog barking furiously outside. There must be a raccoon or something out there for my dog to be so wound up. Eventually, my mom left the room, and I went back to sleep.

I remember sitting through school the next day.

I rubbed the scar on my hand that the star made when it cut me, and I had needed stitches. I stared out the window and wished I were throwing it. The teacher was talking. I could hear words but didn't recognize any of them. I don't know why I remember that day so clearly. It was just one out of so many. I know that I did feel uneasy about going home that day.

When I got home from school, my mom told me that Fluffy had broken her chain and had run away. I had that dog for as long as I could remember. It had never once run away. It was a puppy when I was a baby. We grew up together. We were inseparable. She followed me around like a, well, like a dog. And now she was gone? Broke her chain? She wasn't strong enough to break her chain. Ran away? Every other time she got loose; she would be waiting for me on our back step. Ready for a treat or to play. What did my mom do with my dog? And why? I wanted another one, but mom said, "You ain't bringing no mongrel bitch into this house." I begged and begged, but the answer was always no.

I put up flyers. I asked all the neighborhood kids. No one knew a thing, and I was sure she was gone forever. I don't know what Mom did with Fluffy, but she destroyed a piece of my heart that day.

"Hello, again, everyone. Now, on our third show, we had a real loser by the name of Rob Bennett. Rob was a loser who tried to blame all his problems on bad government. While what he said about the federal government and the consequences of its collapse are true, there is assuredly no basis for blaming the great State of California for any of his problems. This state is in tip-top shape. It is a great place to work and play. Rob was such a loser that he deserved to die. Here is the replay of how Rob's Capp went down."

The television replays Rob's Capp but I take a bathroom break instead of watching.

Brian calls to see if I am watching the show. I tell him I am. I don't tell him that I am not enjoying it. He says the studio is pissed. Online real time ratings this recap week are down, so they are going to cut my pay by 10%. I tell him I don't care. I really don't. With the studio paying for everything but groceries and clothes, I don't need much money.

"Hello, again, everyone. Now, on our fourth show, we had a young man by the name of David Miller. David suffered from depression all his life. No one could help him. Not his parents, doctors, priest, no one. Sounds to me like he is better off dead. I mean, who would want to live like that. David does have one distinction, however. He is the only one to faint on this show. So far. Here is David's Capp."

During David's Capp I go into the kitchen and make a sandwich.

So, I was throwing the star in the field behind the barn, hating my life, when I got a creepy feeling I was being watched. I spun around but didn't see anyone. I did a slow 360-degree turn and saw grass, trees, posts, and the barn, but I still didn't see anything else. I went back to throwing again, but that feeling never left me. Not that day or the next, but on the third day, after picking up the star, my eyes happened to catch someone standing very still in front of a tree. It was a girl. She had pale green eyes.

I walked back to my starting spot and looked over at her again. She hadn't moved. She wasn't in the way, so I threw the star again. As I was walking over to retrieve it, she said, "Watcha doing?"

"Throwing the star."

"Why?"

"Why not?"

She didn't have an answer to that, so I did another throw.

"I've been watching you," she said. "From up there," pointing and indicating the loft in the barn.

"Why?"

"Why not?"

I did another throw.

"Can I try?"

"No."

"Why not?"

"Because."

"Because why?"

"Because it's mine, and I don't want you to. Because I don't want you to touch it. Because it is too dangerous for a girl."

"But you're a girl."

"Yeah, but not a girly girl. I'm a manly girl."

Another throw.

"I'm not a girly girl either."

I looked over at her. She was wearing jeans, a shirt and tennis shoes. Just like me. "Well, you still can't."

Another throw.

"I can get one too, you know."

"Bet you can't."

"Why not?"

"Because I don't think they make them anymore."

"Why do you think that?"

"Because I found this one in my grandma's attic. In a box. Mailed a long time ago. And I have never seen or heard of anything like this."

"What is it for? What is it supposed to do?"

"You sure ask a lot of questions."

"Well, I wouldn't be asking so many questions if you were telling me more answers."

I got ready to throw. "I don't even understand what you just said. Go away. You're bothering me."

Silence. I did my throw and looked over. She was gone, but I still had the feeling of being watched. Dumb girl.

"Hello, again, everyone. Now, on our fifth show, we had a beautiful young woman by the name of Janet Forbes. Certainly, no love life problems with that beauty, hey? Janet had it all. She had a great life, loved her new apartment, and loved God as well, I'm sure. But then she blew it. Fell asleep at the wheel for one second and killed three people. A mom, a five-year-old, and a two-month-old baby. Oh well, it was a good life while it lasted. Right Janet? Here is the replay of how Janet's Capp went down. At the end you will notice she is taken away in an ambulance. I never did get an update on her status. I think she died."

I mute the sound for Janet's Capp.

I remember when my sister and I were twelve. I had full use of my body. Well, all except for my mangled hand. And my sister, my twin, had no use of hers. I spent every spare moment trying to make it up to her. I would get a chair from the kitchen and set it next to her wheelchair so we could watch television together. The chair was hard and would get uncomfortable after a while, but that was okay.

I didn't deserve comfort.

I would spend hours brushing and braiding her hair. Then take out the braid and do it again. I had my hair cut shorter than most boys, too short for even a ponytail.

I would rub lotion into her skin. Her soft silky

skin.

I would get the dolls out of her room and set them up in and around her wheelchair. I sometimes even played with them, a little. But never when our dad was around.

I used to whisper in her ear, all the time. I would repeat over and over. "Don't worry. I will take care of you. I promise. I'm sorry I caused you all of this. I will make it up to you. I will take care of you. Forever and ever."

"Hello, again, everyone. And now we come to the highlight of our show. The last show of season one, and what a controversy it caused. Of course, I am talking about the Capp that didn't happen. Sally Henderson was the S'er, but she backed away. She is the only one so far to come on our show and survive. Sally never did tell why exactly she wanted to die. Just that it wasn't about her father. As if we believe that one. We think thou protest too much, Sally. And then, of course, there is the issue of what happened on last week's show when Sally showed up again, and Ricky got upset about something, argued with Brian, our awesome producer and director, and then walked off the set. More on that later, but first, let's look at what happened during Sally's Capp."

I ignore the ringing of the phone as I watch Sally's Capp.

The dumb green-eyed girl was back the next day. She stood and watched me throw for over an hour before she asked, "What's your name?"

"Ricky. What's yours?"

"Irene."

"Why are you watching me?"

"I don't know. I just like to, I guess."

She continued to watch me, all that day and the next and the next. When she wasn't there the following day, my throws seemed a little, I don't know, empty, sort of. I guess I liked having an audience.

She wasn't there the next day, either. She had told me where she lived, so I went off through the woods until I came upon her house. I stayed in the woods and watched it for a while. It was dark. Empty. I hoped she hadn't moved away. I wanted her to come out and watch me again. I looked down at my empty right hand and smashed left one. The scar on my right hand was itching. My left hand felt like it was on fire. The star was still buried in the field by the barn. I hadn't gotten it out that day. I felt kind of sad. No one else to share with now that my dog was gone. I wanted to see her green eyes again. They were so like my sister's, so expressive. After a while, I went home and didn't throw that day at all.

While playing the *Capping S'ers* theme music, the camera fades in on the stage where Phil is standing.

"Thanks everyone for tuning in on our special recap show tonight. Brian, our great producer and director, assured me that we will be back to LIVE Capps next week. Apparently, Ricky ate a bad donut on our set last week and had indigestion. Thank goodness she isn't pregnant. See you all next week."

Playing no sound other than the theme music, the TV replays the scene starting with Ricky advancing toward Sally and ending with Ricky leaving the building.

About a week later, Irene was back. I felt but-terflies in my stomach.

"You're back," I said.

"We went away on vacation. To Disneyland."

"Wow. Was it nice?"

"It was okay. Crowded. I would rather be here and watch you."

My face got hot suddenly. I threw the star again and again without looking at her or speaking to her. Finally, when I had finished for the day, she came over and kissed me on the cheek. My face turned red and I felt flushed.

With my heart racing, I ran all the way home.

Season Two, Episode Three

CAPPING S'ERS
XCAL - 1
10-11 pm
New "Lucy Doyle"
S2/EP03, (2018), The third installment of this weekly show that highlights an individual who desires to commit suicide. With an assist from thrower Ricky Fordham, the individual may or may not die.

It's funny how neckwear evolved as a fashion statement. At first, women (and later men) wore it because it was pretty. Silver or gold, intricate carvings, bright paints. Later, it became a statement. "I am wearing this because I am not an S'er. I am not ready to die. I want to live."

But that slowly changed, because on the show, neckwear was worn by the in-lines who never ever move. Wearing neckwear came to mean that you were inflexible, rigid, and cold. What happened next was neckwear kept getting narrower and narrower until it was only one inch tall. That seemed to satisfy most people as it carried a meaning that said "I am not an S'er. I am also not an in-line. I am a person who likes pretty jewelry, and I'm a fan of the show."

Brian found it strange that I had never put on neck gear. He bugged me about it often enough. Said it would enhance the show. I received lots of offers to be photographed and promote the various makers of neck gear. But I never did it. I equate it to the prostitute who will let you do whatever you like with her body, but you can't kiss her on the lips. They keep that one little part for themselves. That way, they are not fully engaged in an activity they were forced into but don't agree with. I think I was doing the same thing with my neck, even though I never wear any kind of jewelry anyway.

Holding two of the tips of the star, I relive how Irene started showing up at the field nearly every day. My dad got a new job. Driving trucks locally, so he was gone during the day but home every night. It was now the start of summer, and I spent ninety percent of the hours he was gone in that field behind the barn. Sometimes Irene would be there before me, but mostly she came after. I would set up all my poles and ropes how I wanted them and practice that setup until I could do a perfect throw ten times straight. Then I would change the setup and do it again.

One day Irene was there before I was, and she was holding the star. I ran over to her, "Give me that!" and I jerked it from her hand. It was lucky that neither of us got cut.

"I wasn't hurting it. I was only holding it. It felt cold when I first touched it, but its fine now."

"How did you find it?"

"You always bury it in the same place, dummy."

"Well, I won't now. I will bury it in a different place every night. And you will turn your back, so you can't see where."

"I don't want to see. And I don't want to watch

you throw. I'm leaving."

Before she exited the field, she turned and said, "That star is very light. It hardly weighs anything. Also, it spins way too fast for as slow as it is going. I don't know how you can make it spin that fast."

Irene was back the next day.

"Why are you here?" I asked, "I thought you were never coming back."

"I'm only here because my mom wanted me out of the house. She's vacuuming. I'm not here for you."

"Fine." I had set up an extra complicated throw for that day. It took me almost a week to master it.

"Welcome, California, to the newest edition of *Capping S'ers*!"

I am standing next to the stands. My sister is parked almost near enough to touch. Above her, I notice a young dad bouncing a baby on his knees.

"The newest member we are welcoming to the *Capping S'ers* family is Lucy Doyle. We are going to visit her in her hometown of San Diego. We are going to interview her here live in our studio, and then LIVE we will watch the Capp and see if Lucy does commit suicide or not. Stick around. We will be back after the commercial break."

I walk to the center of the studio floor and wave to the crowd. I find my sister in their midst. Behind her, the young dad is handing the baby off to its mother.

Commercial.

On the big screen, while playing the theme music, the camera fades in on a drab middle-aged woman standing next to a road where a sign says El Camino

Real. "This translates as 'The King's Highway.' It was the major thoroughfare connecting California's twenty-one missions." She has a broad smile.

Then the same woman is standing outside a building that is the Old Point Loma Lighthouse. "This lighthouse was built in 1855, and when it was built, it had the highest elevation of any lighthouse in the United States. My name is Lucy Doyle, and I am ready to commit suicide."

Lucy is standing next to an orange and white building. As the camera pans out, it is revealed she is on Balboa Island. She says, "On what were originally mudflats, dredging started in 1906 to create three artificial islands. Waterfront lots were then offered for $750. I try to come here every Sunday. It is so beautiful here."

Lucy enters a plain white stucco house. She says, "This is my home. Let me show you around."

Lucy walks slowly around the small house that appears as if it needs a good cleaning. And a dumpster for all the trash. She says, "I know the house needs more storage space. I filled up two storage units down the street, and I still don't have enough room."

"We will get up close and personal with Lucy right after these commercial messages."

I adjust the position of the first pole holding the rope. I look over, and the young dad is standing up and shouting.

Commercial.

I take a bite of a donut and look to the stage where Phil in a suit and Lucy in an old house dress sit facing each other. I know I'm running a risk of bursting out of my outfit, but I am starved.

One day, when I was very young, I was lying in the grass playing with a neon blue toy pony. I'd had the toy for a while but only took it out of hiding and played with it when my dad was out of town. I was humming to myself as I imagined the pony jumping over giant fences represented by twigs. Gallop, gallop, jump. Gallop, gallop, jump. Suddenly a hand reached down and jerked the pony away.

"I didn't know you were home," I said.

My dad shouted, "Is this what you do when I'm away? Play with a fake pony?"

"No. I just found it, and I was putting it away."

"Don't lie to me. Where are the toy soldiers I bought you?"

"In the house."

"Well, get them and play with them instead. I'm putting this in the trash."

"Hello, everyone. I am Phil Ebenezer. I have a PhD in clinical psychology. Now Lucy, tell me why you want to end your life."

"Well, my husband and I separated."

"I see."

"Ah, he didn't pay any attention to me."

Phil leans over to peek at his 3 X 5 card, then asks, "And what would be the reason for that?"

"What? Ah, I don't know."

"Could it be that your husband beats you?"

"Yes. Yes, he does. He beats me."

"So, he doesn't completely ignore you?"

"Well, he does. Except when he beats me."

"Tell me about the voices in your head."

"They talk to me. They tell me to do things."

"What kind of things?"

"You know, things. Beautiful things. Hurtful things."

"Don't you take medication for these voices?"

"Yes. But I can't take it."

"Why not?"

"It gives me gas."

"Did the voices tell you to come onto this show?"

"Yes."

"Did the voices tell you to kill yourself?"

"Yes."

"Anything else the audience should know about you?"

"I'm tired all the time."

"Good to know. Lucy, are you ready for the Capp?"

Lucy squeezes her eyes shut as she says, "Yes. Shut up in there!"

"Don't forget to stay tuned after the show for your XCAL 1 evening news, the only official state newscast. Remember folks, if you didn't see it on XCAL 1, it didn't happen. We'll be right back."

Commercial.

"Welcome back, folks. Brian tells me there is still twelve minutes to eat up. So Lucy, let's talk about something else."

"Okay."

"You said in your video that you go to Balboa Island every Sunday. Today is Sunday. Did you go there today?"

"I did. I had a lovely time."

"You did? What did you do?"

"I walked around some. Looked at all the boats. They are so pretty and colorful. And of course, I went window shopping down Marine Avenue."

"Did you buy anything?"

"I got a coffee. And a frozen banana."

"What else did you do today?"

"Came here."

"Of course. I have a question for you. All that stuff in your house. And your storage units. What is happening with all of that?"

"Well, I talked with Goodwill, but they didn't want it. So, I guess I'll just leave it. Hey, maybe my storage units will be on TV someday. One of those *Storage Wars* TV shows. Where someone is going to pay 200 California dollars for the contents of my unit sight unseen. Then they open it and see all my stuff! Wouldn't that be exciting?"

"I can hardly contain myself in anticipation. Are you ready to be an S'er?"

"Yep, the voices say full steam ahead."

"All righty then. We will be back with the LIVE Capp right after these commercial messages."

I direct two stagehands to pick up and carry off camera the pole holding the rope that was between the second and third in-lines. I look over, and the young dad is sitting back down.

Commercial.

I step into camera range and wave to the crowd. I am standing where the second pole with the rope was, and all the in-lines are at attention. Brian escorts Lucy over. I study Lucy's neck. Looks good. I pull back to see Lucy's face and her distant, tired looking dark brown eyes. No makeup adorns her face. I check Lucy's position by looking up the line, then down the line.

I move to Lucy's left side. I bend down and move Lucy's feet. I push on her back to have her stand more erect. I tell her to breathe. I say, "You don't have to do this. Step away, and the star won't hurt you."

I walk to my starting position, check that the medical team is in place, cock my arm back, and throw the star. It flies straight at the first in-line. With a *clang* and a spark, the star bounces off the neck armor and continues.

The star cuts the rope, bounces off the second in-line, and flies on toward Lucy, grazes by her, cutting her neck in the process. Her body shudders. She falls to the ground, blood streaming from her body.

The doctor rushes over and bends over Lucy. The blood flow slows until the doc reaches over and touches the wound. The blood flows faster until the inner light fades out of her eyes. I stare at the pool of blood as I realize I didn't hear the other *clang* and *thud*. I look over at the final post and the star is there, so I guess the rest of the Capp went okay.

The *Capping S'ers* theme music starts up but is barely heard above the crowd noise. I am still standing where I began, staring at Brian. He seems pleased. The in-lines are starting to leave. Lucy is lying dead on the ground. The crowd is still going crazy with shouts and cheers.

The Capp is back.

My sister is being wheeled away while behind her the young dad is bouncing the baby on his knees.

Commercial.

We are off the air. Lucy is the first person to die on the show since the Governor was here. I walk over to the final post and pull the star out. I walk over to Lucy's body. I wait a minute while the doctor pronounces her dead and walks away. I take the star and place one of its tips in her hand while I hold onto a different tip.

Nothing happens.

I dip the star into the pool of Lucy's blood until one of the tips is covered. I again hold her fingers onto one of the tips while I hold the other.

Still nothing.

I guess it doesn't work on dead people. Or maybe it only works with certain people. I straighten up and

notice that most of the crew is staring at me strangely. I go back to my trailer.

I thought of asking someone alive to cut themselves and then hold the star with me, but I don't
dare. Besides the fear of sounding like an idiot, I
didn't want to let anyone else into my mind like that.
Much too intimate.

I am not happy the show is back. I thought it
stood for something, but if it doesn't, then what am
I doing here? Oh yeah, that's right. I'm doing it for
my sister.

Season Two, Episode Four

CAPPING S'ERS
XCAL - 1
10-11 pm
New "Herb Jones"
S2/EP04, (2018), The latest installment of the weekly show that highlights an individual who desires to commit suicide. With an assist from thrower Ricky Fordham, the individual may or may not die.

This week I skipped two rehearsals. I told Brian I was sick. I don't think he believed me. I was visiting my sister in the hospital.

While holding the star, I remember back to a day filled with panic. It was about mid-summer, a bright sunny day when I walked onto the field and the barn was gone. Where it had stood was torn up dirt and there were tractors and excavators parked around the field. There were no workers there. All the machines were idle.

"The star!" I shouted. "What did they do with

the star?"

I tried to remember where I had buried it, but my mind was all in a haze. Irene wasn't there yet, so I couldn't ask her. I know she had been peeking the last few times I had buried it. Also, with the barn gone and all the ground chewed up, I had no point of reference.

I looked around. Most of the field was still intact. I started digging wildly. I didn't have a shovel, so I used my hands. Irene arrived after I had dug about ten holes, and she started digging as well. I was in a real panic. I could hardly breathe, and my chest hurt. I heard what sounded like a diesel engine approaching when Irene shouted, "Found it." I ran over to her, grabbed her hand, and pulled her into the trees just as a truck pulled in and parked.

I was panting heavily, both from running and from relief that I had the star back. I realized that I was still holding Irene's hand, so I quickly dropped it. She handed me the star, "Here."

"Thanks," I said. Tears wanted to form in my eyes, so I quickly looked away from Irene. I couldn't cry. I had to be a man. I looked back onto the field and watched two men get out of the truck. They started talking, pointing into space, kicking the dirt, and walking around. Irene and I watched for about a half hour, but they weren't leaving, so I buried the star amongst the trees, and we went back to our homes.

"Welcome, California, to the latest episode of *Capping S'ers!* Exclusively on XCAL -1."

I am standing by the bleachers. My sister is not there. Above where she would have been is a toddler standing in the aisle waving a *Capping S'ers* flag. The logo, which is the star with white tips—one with some red on it—and the black inside design, is popping up everywhere.

There are *Capping S'ers* hats, flags, t-shirts, polo shirts, coasters, soap dishes, plates and bowls. I hear they also have action figures of me and the in-lines, even one of Brian. My action figure is advertised as complete with my mangled left hand. I wonder if it also has the scar on my right hand. There is a *Capping S'ers* app where you get a more in-depth interview with the S'ers and behind the scene coverage. Coverage of what, I don't know. There are always cameras running around all over the place. I also hear there is a *Capping S'ers* video game. There is a little Ricky in the game that runs around throwing a disc and cutting everyone's heads off. Neat. Sort of like those movies my dad made me watch.

"Tonight, we have an S'er who I am sure you are all going to love. His name is Herb Jones. We are going to visit him in his hometown of San Jose. We are going to interview him here live in our studio, and then LIVE we will watch the Capp and see what Herb does. Will he, or won't he? Only Herb knows for sure. Stick around, folks. We will be back after the commercial break."

I walk onto the studio floor and wave. The toddler is hitting the person seated next to him with his *Capping S'ers* flag.

Commercial.

On the big screen, as the music starts up, the camera fades in on an older gentleman standing next to a building where a sign says Winchester Mystery House. He wears a comforting smile while pointing out, "This used to be a popular tourist attraction until it closed."

Next, he is standing on the sidewalk outside of the Odd Fellows building. "The Odd Fellows are a fraternity that dates to 1730 in London, England. My name is Herb Jones, and I am ready to commit suicide."

Herb is standing next to a wall. As the camera

pans out, it reveals a sign that says International Business Machines. He says, "This is where I work. I am a systems analyst. Which means I work on whatever I am assigned that day."

Herb enters a Cape Cod style house. He says, "This is my home. Let me show you around."

Herb walks throughout the two-story home that is well cared for and filled with movie posters. He says, "My wife and I love to go out to the movies. We have a poster of every movie we've seen. The best ones are on display. The rest are down in the basement."

"We will get up close and personal with Herb right after these commercial messages."

I adjust the position of the first pole holding the rope. The toddler is crying, and the mom is now holding the *Capping S'ers* flag.

Commercial.

I stand by the snack table. No donut this week. It took an extra five minutes to get my costume on today. I am going to have to start watching my weight.

When I was young, my dad would select which movies we were going to watch. My mom and sister didn't have to watch, and they usually didn't. The movie was usually a war movie, or a horror film, or a documentary. Never a romantic comedy. Whatever it was, it was sure to have lots of blood and guts on the screen. Not only did I have to watch, I wasn't even allowed to turn away. When I did, my dad would force my head back around. He would even pull and hold open my eyelids. Eventually, I could watch without his assistance.

Phil and Herb are both in suits and ties.

"Hello, everyone. I am Phil Ebenezer. I have a PhD in clinical psychology. Now Herb, tell me why you want to end your life."

"Well, I have terminal lung cancer. The doctors have given me six months to live."

"I see."

"Death from cancer is not pleasant. I would like to die on my own terms."

Phil consults his 3 X 5 card before he asks, "Well, nothing wrong with that, right?"

"No, there isn't."

"Good. So Herb, are you ready for the Capp?"

Herb calmly answers with eyes open, "Yes."

"Stay tuned, folks. We'll be right back."

Commercial.

"Welcome back, folks. Well, that interview was so boring we still have over twenty minutes to fill. Herb, let's talk about your job. Can you explain in more detail what a systems analyst at IBM actually does?"

"Well, system analysis is the study of an activity, really any activity, by mathematical means in order to define its purpose and to discover operations and procedures for accomplishing them more efficiently."

"Okay. Nice definition, but what do you do?"

"I use analysis and design techniques to solve business problems using information technology."

"Right. But what do you do?"

"I write computer code."

"Why didn't you say that in the first place? Let's go to commercial."

Commercial.

"All right. We are back. So, you and your wife

are big movie goers?"

"Oh yes. We go to every movie as soon as it comes out. And then we get the poster. Our local theater gives them to us for free."

"I'll bet. You must be their best patrons."

"That's what they say."

"What is your favorite movie?"

"Wow. That is a tough one. I have several, of course. I guess my all-time favorite is *Logan's Run*."

"Why is that one your favorite?"

"Well, it has everything. It's sci-fi. It's a possible future. It shows how a common belief built up over time can be so wrong. It shows how parts of the past can be ignored and forgotten. It shows how an idle life can degenerate into a hedonistic lifestyle. It shows how a closed society devolves over time. There is a robot in it. A brief nude scene. A long chase scene. It may seem a bit clunky by modern movie methods, but the underlying themes are as current as ever. And in the end, all those young people want to be near an old person. What other movie has that?"

"Well. That was very thought out."

"I have thought about it. A lot. I spend hours thinking about the movies I've seen. Movies that should have been made. And how I would make them. Anything but this damn cancer."

"Just curious. What is your wife's favorite movie?"

"Oh, that's easy. *Beauty and the Beast*."

"Well, looking at you, I can see why. Okay. On that note, let's take one more commercial break, and then we will get down to business."

I direct two stagehands to pick up and carry off one of the poles. The mom, still holding the *Capping S'ers* flag, is now bent down face to face with the toddler, and they are engaged in a serious discussion.

Commercial.

I stand on the S'er's spot as Brian escorts Herb out. I study Herb's stubby neck. It looks like Herb missed a shave or two. Not that it matters now. The jugular vein can be plainly seen. I pull back slowly to see Herb's face and his accepting copper eyes. I check Herb's position by looking up and down the line.

I fuss for a bit, then say, "You don't have to do this. Just step away, and the star won't hurt you."

I walk back to my starting position, check that the medical staff is ready, cock my arm back and throw the star. It flies straight at the first in-line, then cuts the rope, and then bounces off the second in-line.

It flies on toward Herb, grazes by him, cutting his neck in the process. His body shudders. He falls to the ground, blood streaming.

The doctor runs over but the blood is pouring out so fast that Herb is already gone. The doc gives his thumbs up and the crowd reacts.

The *Capping S'ers* theme music starts up. Herb is lying dead on the ground, his eyes open. The crowd is going crazy with shouts and cheers.

The toddler is again standing in the aisle waving his *Capping S'ers* flag.

Commercial.

This show is getting out of control. They are selling merchandise now, beyond just the neckwear. There is talk of spin-offs. They already have a bloopers show, although what is on it, I don't know. There is a talk show on Thursday nights dissecting the Capp, the S'er and speculating about what the next show will bring. We are already the most viewed show in California history. How am I ever going to get out from under all this? It is getting too big. They are never going to let me go.

Season Two, Episode Five

CAPPING S'ERS
XCAL - 1
10-11 pm
New "Amanda Hart"
S2/EP05, (2018), The latest installment of the weekly show that highlights an individual who desires to commit suicide. With an assist from thrower Ricky Fordham, the individual may or may not die.

My assistant tells me that Brian is looking to replace me. Apparently, he doesn't like the rehearsals I've been missing. Even though I didn't miss any rehearsals this week after I convinced Brian to mix up the throw. Anyway, that is what she heard. I believe her, but I think there is more to it than that. I think they don't—or can't—live up to the promise that was made to me, and that is why they want me out.

My mind flies back fifteen summers. As the rest of that distant summer progressed, a house rose on the site where the old barn was. It was a big house. A majestic house. While part of the field was still there, my poles and ropes had been hauled away. I could have used the trees again for my throws like I use to, but I had progressed too far beyond that. Mostly, Irene and I sat up in a tree near the edge of the field and watched the workers build the house. I don't think the workers ever knew we were there. Or else, they didn't care. We never did anything but watch. I wasn't throwing at all then, but I still felt relatively calm.

Irene didn't show up every day like I did. My mom didn't care if I was around or not. My dad was working again, so after taking care of my sister, I was free to come and go as I wished.

Irene sometimes had to go shopping or do other stuff with her mom. She would usually tell me what she had been doing, but sometimes she didn't. On those days when she wasn't there, I would go to the woods by her house, climb up a tree there and stare at her empty house. The days she came home early, I would watch her through the windows as she moved about the house. On other days, she would be off to our tree by the field. I would silently follow, sneak up behind her, and surprise her. She would laugh and say she knew that I was following her. But if that was the case, why did she jump so much when I tapped her on the shoulder?

It was nice sitting in the tree, doing nothing. There were no more kisses on the cheek, but I did like holding her hand. After a bit, I got used to it, so my hand wasn't sweating as much. Her hand always felt dry, smooth, and soft. Like my sister's. The days she didn't show seemed lonely, but the rest of the time seemed sort of…peaceful. I let Irene hold the star all the time now. Or on some days, I left it buried in the woods. Life wasn't so bad then, even with my dad being home every night.

"I want a big house like that," Irene mused.

"A house like that would take a lot of money."

"You could build it for me someday. After you become rich and famous from throwing your star."

I laughed and after a moment, I asked, "Why do you ignore me at school?"

It took her a few minutes to reply, "People talk about you. Not just the kids. Even parents. Even my parents. They say you're bad. And that your mom has the evil eye. They talk about your mom a lot. And your dad, too. My parents have forbidden me to hang around with you."

"Then why do you? Don't you think I'm bad?"

"No. I think you're good. Other people don't know you like I do. At first, I came around to see what you were up to. This girl who was so bad. I found this field by accident and hung around to see if you were, like, killing small animals or doing something evil. But you weren't. You were just throwing your star. So that's when I let you see me. Because, by then, I already knew that you weren't bad."

"I really am bad, though. Sometimes I'm very bad."

"But you're not. I know you're not. Do you think I would be here now, with you, if you were bad?"

So, I told her about my twin. It's funny, we had been talking for months now, and I had not once mentioned my sister. I explained what happened to her and how it was all my fault. Irene said it wasn't. I said it was.

After being silent for a while, I looked into her pale green eyes and asked, "So are you going to hang out with me when school starts?"

She stared back at me a moment before replying, "Sure. My friends are going to like you, too. And if they don't, I'll hang out with just you instead."

I kept my voice calm as my heart swelled, "Good. That will be nice. Thank you."

"Welcome, California, to the latest episode of *Capping S'ers!*"

I am standing by the bleachers and smell hot dogs. There. Right above me. A very fat man eats half of a hot dog in one bite.

"Tonight, we have an S'er who I am sure you are all going to love. Her name is Amanda Hart. We are going to visit her in her hometown of Los Angeles. We are going to interview her live here in our studio, and then LIVE we will watch the Capp and see if Amanda goes through with it. Stick around, folks. We will be back after the commercial break."

I go out on the floor and wave. The usual in-line setup has changed. There is more distance between the in-lines, stretching the whole thing out. The line now goes almost from wall to wall in the studio. Also, the curve to the thrower's left that the line normally makes now breaks to the right, away from the audience. Another set of bleachers was added. I notice that most of the audience wears neck gear now. The very fat man in the audience is stuffing his face with a handful of nachos. He isn't wearing neck gear. Maybe he is afraid it would interfere with his eating. Or else he can't find one in his size.

Commercial.

On the big screen, while playing the *Capping S'ers* theme music, the camera fades in on a thirty-five-year-old woman standing next to an entrance into Dodger Stadium. She smiles as she says, "We come here to the ballpark every chance we have. Well, we used to. There are no baseball games anymore."

Next, she is standing on the sidewalk outside of the Los Angeles Memorial Coliseum. "This is where the University of Southern California football team used to play. There are no football games anymore, either. My name is Amanda Hart, and I am ready to commit suicide."

Then the big screen shows Amanda standing on a bridge. As the camera pans out, it reveals a concrete basin with sloping concrete sides. She says, "This is the Los Angeles River. There is no water in it right now. There seldom is."

Amanda is shown entering a two-story pink stucco house. She says, "This is where I live with my husband. Let me show you around."

Her husband is sitting in a recliner in front of the TV. He is dressed in shorts and a T-shirt. He holds out a can of beer in a salute. She says, "Dan and I just love sports. As you can see, he's watching a replay of a Dodgers game from 1983."

"We will get up close and personal with Amanda right after these commercial messages."

I walk out and adjust the position of the first-in-line. I think his three kids are all under the age of six. He has been a very busy man.

The very fat man is consuming half a burger in one bite.

One Christmas before the accident, Roberta had gotten a paint by the numbers set. The next day, she did one picture in the set (there were three), and then put it aside. I asked if I could do one of the pictures. With some hesitation, Roberta agreed.

I sat on the floor and put the paint set on the coffee table. My back was to the front door. I got water and napkins and proceeded to work. I was concentrating so hard I didn't hear my dad come home early.

Sensing his presence, I quickly glanced at my mom to see if she was also surprised. She had a smirk on her face. I looked over at Roberta, but she had her head down with her hair hiding her face. My dad didn't say anything. He picked up the paint set, walked into the kitchen, placed the set on the stove and lit the burner. With the paint set burning on the stove, dad walked over to mom and slapped her across the face. Mom's head snapped back as dad asked, "How could you have let this happen?" Then he walked out of the house.

I sat as still as I could as I heard the car start and roar away. I was afraid to move a muscle. Roberta had her head down, hair still covering her face, not moving either. Mom rose slowly off the couch and walked over to the stove. Some cardboard had fallen to the floor, slowly burning itself out. Plastic had clogged up most of the vents of the burner and the flames were barely sputtering out. Mom watched it burn and melt before she turned it off and sniffed the air. It smelled like burnt plastic.

Mom walked slowly over to me. "This is your fault."

She grabbed me by my left wrist and pulled me upright. She pulled me over to the stove and turned the burner back on, at its highest setting. The flames grew larger as some melted plastic fell away. She forced my hand to the burner. I could feel the intense heat.

Just as my hand was about to touch the flames, I used my other hand and pushed my mom away. She fell against the sink, glaring at me. I ran out the door but as I reached the street, I heard my sister scream.

I ran back into the house and saw my mother dragging my sister into the kitchen. I grabbed a knife off the counter and held it out in front of me.

"Come back to take your punishment, have you?"

My mom let my sister go. Sis ran to our room. I heard the door slam.

My mom knocked the knife out of my hand and proceeded to beat me and beat me and beat me. I let her. My sister was safe in our bedroom. Even though I tormented my twin constantly, she didn't deserve anything like this. She was safe, for now. That was all that mattered.

On stage, Phil and Amanda are ready. Amanda wears a necklace with a cross hanging from it.

"Hello, everyone. I am Phil Ebenezer. I have a PhD in clinical psychology. Now Amanda, tell me why you want to end your life."

"I want to join God."

"I see."

"I feel that he is calling me, and it is time to go."

Phil searches for his 3 X 5 card but it is not on the table next to him. He sees it on the floor, picks it up and lays it on the table without looking at it, then asks. "Aren't you afraid of what God will think of your alcohol and drug addiction?"

"All is forgiven through Jesus, who died for our sins."

"You know that was over 2,000 years ago, right?"

"Time doesn't matter to God. He is immortal."

"I understand that. But, do you think that at the time Jesus died, was he just forgiving everyone who had sinned so far? Don't you find it a little far-fetched that he would be forgiving every sin yet to come? By everyone? Forever?"

"No. I don't find that to be far-fetched at all."

"Okay. The power of faith. Amanda, are you ready to move to the LIVE portion of our show?"

"I am."

"All right then. Let's get to it. Don't forget to stay tuned after the show for your XCAL 1 evening news, the only official state newscast. Remember folks, if you didn't see it on XCAL 1, it didn't happen."

Commercial.

"Welcome back, folks. Brian tells me there is exactly twenty minutes left to fill. I will keep my eye on that clock over there while we find out if Amanda has anything interesting to say. Amanda, you're a sports fan?"

"I am. I love all sports. Baseball, football, soccer, tennis. It's too bad there aren't any sports being played anymore."

"Well I think we still have Dodge the Bullet."

"What?"

"Never mind. So, what do you do for fun?"

"We watch all the old games on XCAL 1, of course. I used to jog but can't do that anymore."

"Why not?"

"It isn't safe to be outside."

"I can agree with that. What else?"

"Sometimes there is dancing at the local bar. But my husband doesn't like to do that."

"Party pooper. What else?"

"I don't know. That's all, I guess. Just watch TV."

"So, you like the Dodgers?"

"Oh yes. They have always been my team."

"Do you know where the name comes from?"

"What name?"

"The Dodgers. Do you know where the name 'Dodgers' comes from?"

"No."

"Would you like to know?"

"I guess."

"Back when they were in Brooklyn, they were the best at dodging trolley cars. Dodging — Dodgers. Get it?"

"Sure."

"Okay. Well, that was stimulating. We'll be back after this."

Commercial.

"So, Amanda, you are a USC fan?"

"Not really."

"But you mentioned them in your video."

"Oh, that was just for that. I do like football though."

"Yeah. Which team was your favorite?"

"I don't know. They keep moving into the city, and then moving out, and then moving back in. It is so hard to get invested in any one team. The Angels maybe?"

"That's baseball."

"Oh, yeah. That's right. Well, did you know that when the Dodgers signed Jackie Robinson in 1947, that he was the first black player to be in the big leagues?"

"Of course. Everyone knows that."

"Oh."

"Well. That is about all the excitement I can take for one day. Ready to do the Capp?"

"Yeah. Hey, throwing that star thing could be a sport."

"Right. We'll see if we can't get a league started. We'll be back with the LIVE Capp right after this."

The pole is carted off as the very fat man in the audience is gorging himself with a fistful of fries.

Commercial.

Brian escorts Amanda out. I study the opposite side of Amanda's neck. It still won't require a very deep cut. I pull back to see Amanda's face and her faith-filled gray eyes. I check Amanda's position, fuss for a bit, then say, "You don't have to do this. Just step away, and the star won't hurt you."

I walk back to my starting position, check with the staff, cock my arm back, and throw the star. Even though the star is hitting the opposite side of the in-lines necks, the star's path requires only a minor adjustment to my stance. It flies straight at the first in-line. Instead of hitting the left side of the in-line's neck gear like always before, it hits the right side. With a *clang* and a spark, the star bounces off the neck armor and continues further on to the right.

The star cuts the rope as it passes by on the way to the second in-line, then bounces off, flies on toward Amanda, grazes by her, cutting her neck in the process. Her body shudders. She falls to the ground, blood streaming. I stare at the blood as my nostrils fill up with the smell of it.

The doctor rushes over as another *clang* is heard, then a *thud*. He stoops down and doesn't move for a good five minutes while the pool of Amanda's blood slowly increases. Finally, he gives the thumbs up.

The *Capping S'ers* theme music starts up. Amanda is lying dead on the ground, her empty gray eyes staring straight into the camera. The cross on her necklace is lying flat on the ground with blood flowing around it. The crowd is going crazy with shouts and cheers.

Now, I don't know much about God and religion, except for rolling in the aisles and speaking in strange tongues but isn't it God who decides when it is time for someone to go? Maybe he doesn't like it when people decide their time of death on their own.

The very fat man in the audience is draining half of his soda without a straw in one head-thrown-back gulp. Good. He is keeping plastic out of the ocean.

Commercial.

After the show, I try to go to a bar, but the crowd there won't leave me alone. They recognize me even without makeup and the cat suit. They keep telling me what a big star I am, what a great show *Capping S'ers* is, and how they like the excitement and suspense. They want my autograph on their cocktail napkins, they

want to give me a hug, and they want smiling selfies.
I get three marriage proposals before I can't stand
it anymore, so I go home, lock the door and heat up a
frozen pizza to go with my beer.

Season Two, Episode Six

CAPPING S'ERS
XCAL - 1
10-11 pm
New "Mathew Morgan"
S2/EP06, (2018), The latest installment of the weekly show that highlights an individual who desires to commit suicide. With an assist from thrower Ricky Fordham, the individual may or may not die.

Brian came up to me this week in rehearsal and asks if I would be willing to let someone else practice with the star.

"No way," was my response.

"Why not? What if something happens to you? What if you get run over by a bus?"

"Then the show is over."

"That is not acceptable. There is too much invested in this show. The Governor doesn't want it to fail. This is the number one rated show in the state. The show must go on."

"Sorry. It's my star, and no one else gets to touch it."

"You are not being reasonable. Please, let someone else try a throw."

"Do you not believe this show's own hype? Haven't you heard the part about 'Ricky has, through years and years of practice, perfected a technique of throwing a star that will allow' blah, blah, blah?"

"Yeah, that is just hype."

"Seriously? You are doubting my talent now?"

"Oh, your throws are okay. But from what the audience and I see, anyone can do it."

With that, I stormed off. But I was back the next day.

And no one was touching my star.

In my dressing room, I replay the events immediately after Irene agreed to be my friend.

When I came back to the woods by the field the next day, I couldn't find the star where I buried it. Irene was the only one who knew where I kept it, but she wasn't there either. I waited a while, and when she still hadn't shown up, I walked to her house. It was dark and empty.

I went back to the trees by the field and searched for the star again. It was still not there. Did the builders take it? None of them were there to ask and I had never spoken with any of them before anyway. I didn't know what I would do without the star. It was pretty much the only thing I had ever played with, in like, forever. That and my dad's toy soldiers, which I hadn't touched in years. I walked home with my head down. Missing the star, my dog, Irene.

When I got home, Mom was in the kitchen. "Missing something?" she asked.

"What?"

"Are you missing something?"

I thought of all the things in my life that were missing. "No."

"Because I know what you been doing. I followed

you out into the woods by that field. Sitting up in that tree with your girlfriend all day. Holding that round thing. Or giving it to that girl to hold. Holding hands with her all day long. So are you a lesbo now? Well, you don't have to worry about your toy anymore, because I took that round thing with the points, and I destroyed it."

"What!"

"And I told that little whore of yours to get lost. You don't have to worry about her anymore either. She ain't coming back after what I told her."

I felt my face getting hot. My hands were shaking, and my voice got squeaky.

"Where is it? What did you do with it? Why did you talk to her?"

"So how do girls do it to each other anyway? You got one of those dildo things stashed away somewhere, too?"

"Where is the star?" I shouted.

"In the trash. I smashed it all up and threw it out in the trash."

I ran to the trash can, which I had wheeled out to the curb that morning. I prayed that the trash truck was running late. I hit the can at full speed, and everything spilled out into the street. I tore into the pile. The star was there. The top was dented and all but one of the points was bent back. I could hear her inside the house, laughing. I grabbed the star and ran back inside. She was standing there, one hand on her hip and the other holding a cigarette.

"What are you going to do now, you little shit?" she asked.

It was hard to see through my watery eyes; my heart was beating a mile a minute and my hands were shaking. What I did next was throw that battered star at her. It whistled and wobbled but the one point that was left was enough. She tried to scream, but with all the blood pouring out of her throat, she just gave off a faint gurgling sound as she was pinned to the wall. I watched the blood pour out of her until her mean dark brown eyes told me that she was dead.

I pulled the star out of the wall and watched her body fall to the floor. I knelt beside her, blood soaking my pants. I held the star with both hands as I walked into the living room where my sister was watching television. Her broken arms were shaking, her head was flopped to the side, but her eyes were quiet. I brought out a chair and sat next to her as *The People's Court* came on.

No matter how many times I replay that scene in my mind, I can't figure out what happened. How could it fly in the shape that it was in? I didn't think I was throwing the star straight at my mom. I thought I was throwing it a little off to the side. To scare her. Maybe nick her ear. But I don't know. I was so mad that maybe I had no control over the throw. I threw the star hard, and I usually don't. The only other time I threw the star that hard was after my sister's arms were broken. And then I wasn't trying to aim it. I was trying to put it through a tree.

Maybe throwing hard alters my angle of release or something. All I knew was, in every replay in my mind, my eyes were fixed on my mother, and when the star first enters my field of vision, it was already headed right for her. Maybe I meant to kill her. Maybe I didn't. I just don't know.

"Welcome, California, to the latest episode of *Capping S'ers!*"

I notice that everyone in the audience is in neckwear. The lights bouncing off the shiny silver and gold in the stands seem to add another layer of chaos to the proceedings.

"Tonight, we have a new S'er for your entertainment. His name is Mathew Morgan. We are going to visit him in his hometown of Fresno. We are going to interview him live here in our studio, and then LIVE we will watch the Capp and see if Mathew is a true S'er or not. Stick around, folks. We will be back after the commercial break."

I walk onto the stage floor and wave. The applause is deafening. The in-line setup from last week has changed again. There is still more distance between the in-lines, but the curve is back once again toward the audience. The extra set of bleachers is still there.

Commercial.

On screen, while playing the theme music, the camera fades in on an unhealthy looking twenty-one-year-old man in a wheelchair next to a drainage canal. He smiles as he says, "The Fresno Municipal Sanitary Landfill was the first modern landfill in the United States. It is still in use today; they dump a lot of riot victim bodies here."

The man is sitting next to a large planter that has a dying tree growing up and out of an open-air ceiling. "This is the Forestiere Underground Gardens. It is closed now. My name is Mathew Morgan, and I am ready to commit suicide."

Mathew is sitting next to a sign that says African Adventure. As the camera pans out, he says, "This is the Fresno Chafee Zoo. I like to come here to watch the animals."

The camera is behind Mathew as he enters a two-story Craftsman style house. He says, "This is where I live with my parents. Let me show you around."

Mathew wheels his chair throughout the first floor of the two-story home and into his room. He says, "This is my room. I have watched every episode of *Capping*

S'ers, and I am very thankful that they have selected me for their show."

"We will get up close and personal with Mathew right after these commercial messages."

I adjust the position of the second-in-line. I don't know his name.

I notice that a lot of the neckwear in the audience has bright red painted in intricate patterns on the portion covering the throat.

Growing up, not only did my sister and I share the same room, we shared the same bed. It was all our family could afford. There, late at night, we shared the bond that only exist between twins. We giggled and played, although very quietly when dad was home, or else he would barge in and beat us both. Mom didn't mind at first, but after a while, she also seemed to get upset if her two daughters were having any fun together.

Roberta usually fell asleep first, and after she did, I would reach out and caress her hair and wonder if mine would be as curly if I were allowed to let it grow out. I would also touch Roberta's silk nighties and revel in the feel compared to my own cotton t-shirt and shorts. I liked to rub Roberta's cheek and arm and always confirmed in my mind that my sister's skin felt better than anything I had ever touched. I would touch my own cheek and arm and thought them to be rough and abrasive.

Nighttime was our time, and it was never long enough.

As I stand next to the snack table, eyeing an apple, the music starts up. Phil and Mathew are sitting in chairs slightly facing each other. Mathew wears an orange necktie that extends down over his potbelly. Mathew's face is flushed, and his neck has dark fatty deposits. His arms and legs strike a queer note and appear to be too skinny and too hairy. He is sweating heavily.

"Hello, everyone. I am Phil Ebenezer. I have a PhD in clinical psychology. Now Mathew, tell me why you want to end your life."

"I have a disease."

"I see. What is it called?"

"Hypercortisolism."

Phil doesn't even look at his 3 X 5 card before he asks, "How does that make you feel?"

"Fatigued. Hungry. Weak. I can barely stand. I have constant headaches, and I bruise easily."

"But there is a cure for this disease, right?"

"They want to do surgery. I have tumors. They also want to do radiation on me. Radiation kills, you know."

"You don't want these treatments? You don't want to get better?"

"No. I don't think it will work. Besides, my life is over. I have nothing to live for."

"What about your parents? Won't they be sorry to see you go?"

"I have always just been a burden to them. My dad lost his job. My mom waits tables. We have no insurance. They would be better off without me. Can't we just end this, please?"

"Of course. Of course. So, Mathew, are you ready to move on to the LIVE portion of our show?"

"I am."

"All right then. Let's do it."

Commercial.

"Welcome back, folks. We still have fifteen

minutes to fill. Mathew, what should we talk about?"

"Anything."

"Anything, huh? Well, in your video piece, you said you liked animals."

"That's right. And trees. I am constantly amazed at the diversity of life that can be found here on this planet."

"Right. What is your favorite animal?"

"Oh, I don't have a favorite. I love them all. But if I did, it would be the red panda, or the kiwi, or the beluga whale, or the wombat, or the fennec fox, or the pygmy hippopotamus, or the cassowary, or the manatee, or the... No, wait. That's it."

"OK. I know we just had a commercial, but I feel a need for another one. Back after this."

Commercial.

"OK, we're back. Mathew, dare I ask what your favorite tree is?"

"Oh, that's easy. Japanese maple."

"That's it? Japanese maple. No others?"

"No. That's it."

"Well, I am curious about one thing. In your video package, you lead off with a landfill site. Not a usual first pick, or anyone's pick really. Why did you want to feature that?"

"Because the landfill, I feel, represents the state of the world as we know it right now. Just a giant heap of garbage that we are living in, looking for a nice area to settle, a bit of food that someone else didn't eat first, and maybe finding someone who can put up with it all."

"Well, on that happy note, I'm ready to end this interview. If Brian has more time to fill, he can do it with commercials. They are bound to be less depressing than you are."

Commercial.

The pole is carried away. I notice that, in the audience, all the shiny silver and gold neckwear also have little XXs painted on the striking portions on the sides.

Commercial.

"Ladies and gentlemen, welcome to the LIVE part of the show. Let me introduce you to Ricky Fordham, our Capper."

I step into camera range and wave to the crowd. I try to catch Brian's eye to make sure he is listening to the next part of Phil's commentary, but he is avoiding me.

"Ricky has, through years and years of practice, perfected a technique of throwing a star that will allow Mathew, by simply standing still, to end his life. So, without further ado, let's proceed to the LIVE Capp, where anything can happen."

I am standing on the S'er's spot. Brian escorts Mathew out. I study the side of Mathew's neck. The fatty deposits hide the jugular vein. I take more time than normal studying the neck. I pull back to see Mathew's face and his resigned hazel eyes. I check Mathew's position, fuss a bit more, then say, "You don't have to do this. Just step away, and the star won't hurt you."

I walk back to my starting position, check with the medical team, cock my arm back, and throw the star. It flies straight at the first in-line, then continues on to the rope and the second in-line. It reaches Mathew, digging in more than usual, but cutting his neck nonetheless. His body shudders. He falls to the ground, blood streaming. I stare at the blood as another *clang* is heard, then a *thud*.

The doctor walks over and examines Mathew. He

jumps back as Mathew rises up on one knee. Blood is continuing to pour down his side as he stands. The doctor is fascinated. Mathew tries to take a step but collapses. The doctor examines Mathew again, then gives the thumbs up.

The music starts up. Mathew is lying dead on the ground, hazel eyes seeming to look straight at me. The crowd is going crazy with shouts and cheers.

Knowing the lack of healthcare in California these days, the best thing he could have done was leave the state. I don't know the conditions of things in other states, but some state somewhere must have better healthcare than we have here.

Commercial.

My mother was the first person to die from my throwing the star. I examine my feelings and even after all this time I still feel no remorse. She was a horrible person. I don't know if it was all her fault or if my dad contributed. In either case, I can find no evidence that she fought it or expressed a desire to change. Would I hold back and not throw the star if I could go back in time and have a do-over; knowing now what comes after?

Probably not.

Season Two, Episode Seven

CAPPING S'ERS
XCAL - 1
10-11 pm
New "Cook Sisters"
S2/EP07, (2018), The latest installment of the show that this week highlights two individuals who desire to commit suicide. With an assist from thrower Ricky Fordham, they may or may not die.

Brian badgered me and badgered me and badgered me, so I finally let someone else throw the star. I didn't know what was going to happen. I was hoping for an epic fail. I would be devastated if someone else threw a perfect Capp, just like that, no practice or anything.

Brian wanted to use our regular in-lines, and I argued for using poles instead. Brian said no. Doing it my way, they wouldn't be able to tell if the bounce was accurate or not. I didn't have a counter argument to that, so on Thursday, during rehearsal, the full line was assembled, and someone else was standing in my starting spot holding the star. The medical team stood nearby.

I worried what would happen when I handed over

the star to him, but there was nothing. He shuddered, remarked how light it felt and that it seemed cold. He got ready, held out his left arm (no mangled hand), and cocked his right arm. He extended his right arm as he let the star fly. The star didn't cut him. It flew straight for about twenty feet and then tilted and dived. It hit the first in-line in the leg.

Yes! I was talented. While the doctor and paramedics ran around trying to save the in-line's life, Brian cursed, "Damn it! Now we must use one of the in-line backups."

I picked up the star where the doctor had tossed it aside, walked over to Brian and said, "Told you so."

Sitting in my trailer, waiting to go to makeup for the twelfth time, my thoughts go back to the time after my mother's death.

When my dad came home, he looked at my mom's body, then came into the kitchen where I was feeding Roberta burnt toast. He sat at the table and looked at the dried blood on my pants and shoes.

"Well, I guess you're finally a man now. At least I don't have to worry about that cheating bitch anymore."

I don't remember too much of what happened after that. It's all lost in a big blue haze. I know I was taken away at some point. I was locked up in what I think was a jail, then I came before a judge and was put on trial in an empty courtroom. It was ruled justifiable homicide based on years of abuse. I spent some time in a hospital. Under observation and counseling.

My dad said, "I don't want that good for nothing whore or her worthless twin sister either. You can have them. I only married their mom because she was knocked up."

I never saw him again. My sister and I were placed in foster homes. Different ones because she was special needs.

The home I went to was big with four bedrooms. One for the couple who ran the home and three for kids. Double bunkbeds per room. There always seemed to be a rotation of kids, in and out. I don't remember any who stayed there more than a couple months. Hard to make friends that way. I do remember opening my box of possessions on that first day in the home. On top sat the star, still battered and blood spattered. I don't know who put it there.

That box sat under my bed unopened for years while I was shuffled from one home to another. I didn't know where my sister was, and no one would tell me. Apparently, I was a troubled child. They thought I might try to hurt her. I know I used to get into trouble all the time, on purpose. I would break things. Windows. Doors. Furniture. I even punched holes in walls. Just because. They sent me to therapy for a while, but that didn't last long. It wasn't long before the foster parents decided to fake the doctor visits and pocket the money instead.

When the system decided I was old enough, I was told where my sister was staying. She hadn't changed much. Older, of course. Heavier. Still loving cartoons. Still had those calm, peaceful, pale green eyes. Sometimes I envied my sister. I didn't know if she couldn't comprehend what was happening to her or if she was just accepting of it all. I wished I could be like that. Either not knowing or just accepting. No thoughts or concerns other than eating, sleeping, and dirtying a diaper. Spending the whole day watching cartoons or staring out the window. Unfeeling. Untouched. No thoughts of destruction or death. Was that how she was? Or was she just pretending also?

I made sure to visit my sister at least once per

week. It was a two-hour bus ride with three transfers, one way. I would leave the home at 8:00 a.m., and I had to be back before 8:00 p.m. Minus the transit time, that gave me eight hours to visit with my twin.

If it wasn't raining, I would push her to the park and we would sit by the pond. I would spend the next two hours telling her about all the events that happened to me since our last visit. I would tell her everything. She was never judgmental or critical of the things I did. I would watch her eyes, and I could tell which things delighted her and which things disappointed her. My twin's body was broken, but I didn't think that her mind was.

At noon, I would push her up two blocks to the Dairy Queen. I would order us lunch. I would eat mine in five minutes and then take sixty minutes feeding her, one small bite at a time. I would give her a sip of her drink after every three bites. I would wipe off her drool as needed.

After we were done eating, I would take her into Dairy Queen's bathroom. They had a huge handicapped restroom. There I would lift her out of the chair onto the toilet and make her bowel movement happen. Sometimes it would take a while, but I always made sure she did before we left the room. If she seemed extra plugged up, I would softly sing her a song. Sometimes several songs. I knew I was not a very good singer, but my sister never complained.

After I cleaned her up and put on a fresh diaper, I would wheel her back to the park, and we would sit silently watching the squirrels, ducks, and birds. After a while, I would push her back to her home and into her room, and I would brush and braid her hair until suppertime when I would leave. If it was raining, we would stay in her room all day and eat lunch there at their communal dining area.

On the bus ride back, either it was already dark, or it was getting dark. On those rides, my mood always matched the growing darkness. The further from my twin I got, the more depressed I became. By the time I arrived at my foster home, I didn't care if I lived or died. The only thing that kept me going was the promise I had made to my sister. I had promised to take care of her, and I wouldn't be able to do that if I gave up. I wasn't doing enough for her now, but I was doing all I could. How could I do any less?

After a while, I took the star out of the box, cleaned it up, bent the points back and sharpened them. Got out the dents best I could. Had the body silver-plated to help cover up the hurt places. At last, it didn't look too bad. You could still tell, but you had to look closely. I had to see if it could still fly.

It performed like it had never been hurt.

Once I started throwing again, a peace came over me, and I settled down. I wasn't a troublemaker anymore, but I still got treated as if I was.

No matter in what home I was placed, I would find somewhere to throw. A field, a park, or an empty parking lot. I used trees, telephone poles, or light posts. I used rope, thin wire, or electrical cord. I used rocks, weights, or scrap metal in a bag. I would bounce that star off buildings, dumpsters, or walls. No matter what the environment, I managed. I managed to throw and throw and throw.

"Welcome, California, to the latest episode of *Capping S'ers!*"

The in-lines are in place. The replacement one is at the end, and everyone else moved up a spot. I talked with the paramedics. The injured first in-line (Stewart) will survive, although it was touch and go for a while. Since it had tasted his blood, I thought about touching the star with him to see what would happen, but I didn't want anyone else entering my mind. In the audience, I notice a teenage girl wearing gold neckwear with matching bracelets, nose ring, and earrings.

"Tonight, we are doing something we have never done before. We have identical twins on the show. Their names are Mandy and Candy Cook. We are going to visit them in their hometown of San Diego. We are going to interview them live here in our studio, and then LIVE we will watch the Capp and see if Ricky can handle two S'ers in one Capp. Stick around, folks. We will be right back after this commercial break."

I walk out onto the stage floor and wave. The crowd responds. The distance between the in-lines has been brought down to be the same as when the show first began, and the curve is also back to normal. The extra set of bleachers is still there. The end post, which used to be after the last set of bleachers, is now in the middle of the last set. The audience there can see the star heading straight for them when it hits the final post. Fun.

I am not happy that there are twins on the show tonight. A little too close to home, I guess. I am glad my sister is not here to see it. She is still in the hospital. She had her third surgery, and they are calling it a huge success even though she is still in intensive care.

The teenage girl looks bored.

Commercial.

On the big screen, the camera fades in on two young looking twenty-five-year-old girls standing next to a gigantic, in-ground, empty water tank. They smile as Mandy says, "Sea World used to be a fantastic place to go before it closed. They had killer whales and other stuff until they all died."

Then the twins are standing next to a four-story

concrete building that says Literature. "This is the University of California, San Diego, campus. UCSD had always been considered a party school until it was converted into a homeless camp. Our names are Mandy and Candy Cook, and we are ready to commit suicide."

Mandy and Candy are standing outside of the San Diego Museum of Man. As the camera pans out, Candy says, "This museum opened in 1915 as part of the Pana-ma-California Exposition. We used to like to come here to people watch."

While the twins enter a split-level Hacienda style house, Mandy says, "This is where we live with our mom. Let us show you around."

They do so, and finally up in their room, Candy says, "This is our room. We share that one bed there. We don't mind sleeping together. We do everything together. We even shower together."

Phil's voice sounds a little tight as he says, "We will get up close and personal with the Cook sisters right after these commercial messages."

I adjust the position of the second-in-line. I don't want to know anymore in-line's names.

The teenage girl in the audience is picking her nose around her nose ring. Gross.

Commercial.

I am standing by the snack table watching our security guard, who is an off-duty policeman, eat three donuts in a row. Wish I could do that.

Before the accident, I hated tormenting my sister. For me, it had to be a game. One our dad really enjoyed. Although Roberta didn't like it either, she knew it was necessary and that I had to do it to avoid beatings.

I was the stronger one, with my hair cut short and out of the way. Dressed in a t-shirt with my camouflage pants and military style boots, I was a bad ass.

My sister, dressed in some frilly outfit, was no contest for the various ways that I could take advantage of her. I squirted her with the hose. I pulled on her long wavy hair. I would dump out her favorite perfume into the toilet. I would trip her. Push her out of the car. Tear the heads off her dolls. Hide her shoes.

My sister would start crying and say, "Stop it, Ricky."

I would laugh and say, "I'm a man."

On the stage, Phil, Mandy, and Candy are sitting in chairs facing the television cameras. The girls are dressed in identical blue dresses with calico ribbons in their long blonde hair.

"Hello, everyone. I am Phil Ebenezer. I have a PhD in clinical psychology. Now girls, tell me why you want to end your lives."

The twins speak at the same time, "Growing up, we were abused."

"I see. And who was the abuser?"

"Our dad."

Phil leans closer to the twins before he asks, "Is that why you live with your mom? Because she divorced him."

"No. She killed him."

"What?"

"Yeah. He went out to get some bread during one of the riots. You know, just to do a little looting. Mom followed him with her gun. Shot him dead. Two shots. Bang. Bang. Blamed it on the rioters."

"I see. You were abused, but that abuse was

avenged. So, what is the problem now?"

"Mom got a boyfriend, and then he abused us."

"And what happened to him?"

"Oh, mom killed him, too. Same way."

"Of course. Once you have a good thing going, why change it. So now what is the problem?"

"Mom came home with another boyfriend. Abused us. Killed him."

"So how many times has this happened, exactly?"

"Seventeen. So far. She came home with another guy yesterday, but he hasn't touched us yet."

"Maybe she warned him? Or maybe he is different?"

"Doubt it."

"So why do you want to die?"

"Because we are trapped. We see a pattern here, and we don't think it is going to change."

"So why don't you just leave? Move out."

"Where would we go? We don't have any place else we could go. There are no jobs anywhere. We couldn't pay rent even if we could find a place, which we can't. We tried."

"Really? Two beautiful twenty-five-year-old twins with long blonde hair that do everything together, even shower together. And there isn't anything you could do to earn money?"

"And not be abused?"

"Ah, I see your point. Well, are you ready for the LIVE portion of our show?"

"We are."

"All right then. Let's do it. Don't forget to stay tuned after the show for your XCAL 1 evening news, the only official state newscast. Remember folks, if you didn't see it on XCAL 1, it didn't happen."

Commercial.

"Welcome back. If the audience for this show is anything like me, I'm glad there is more time for you two beautiful young ladies. When you two shower together, does anything else happen?"

The girls sit silently.

"No? Too bad. Well, your mom sure sounds like an interesting lady. Not that I would want to get on her bad side."

Silence.

"Did you two ever get a chance to go to Sea World before it closed?"

The girls answer with one voice, "We did. Twice."

"Yeah. They kind of got a bad reputation there for a while. Rumors that they were mistreating the orcas."

Silence.

"But I guess they weren't."

Silence.

"Mistreating the orcas, I mean."

Silence.

"I'm sure the audience is loving this great conversation. Can we do a close up or something as we go to commercial? Be right back."

I direct two stagehands to pick up and carry off-camera the pole holding the rope that is between the second in-line and the third. The third looks nervous, so I go over and reassure him that everything will be okay.

The teenage girl in the audience is chewing gum with exaggerated jaw movements.

Commercial.

Brian escorts Mandy and Candy out. I place them one behind the other. Mandy is in front. Candy is in back, her front pressing into Mandy's back. Candy puts her arms around Mandy. Mandy places her hands on Candy's arms. I study their necks briefly. I adjust their position. I pull back to see their faces and their trusting, deep blue eyes. I check the sister's positions by looking up the line, then down the line.

I fuss for a bit, then say to both, "You don't have to do this. Just step away, and the star won't hurt you."

I walk back to my starting position, check that the doc is ready, cock my arm back, and throw the star. The star does its thing with the first in-line, the rope and the second in-line. It flies on toward the twins, grazes Mandy's neck first, then Candy's. Their bodies shudder. Together they fall in a heap to the ground, blood streaming. The blood is soaking into their blonde hair, turning it red.

The doctor rushes over. He stares down at them. He adjusts Mandy's dress to better cover her legs. It has risen almost all the way up as she fell. After four long minutes, he gives one thumb up. The crowd stays silent. After another two minutes, he gives the second thumbs up.

I am still standing where I began, my heart heavy. The Cook sisters are lying dead on the ground, their deep blue eyes now dull and unseeing. I bow my head and place my hand over my eyes. The crowd is going crazy with shouts and cheers.

Maybe they should have sent their mom out into the riots to do the shopping. Or gotten her to change her taste in men.

The teenage girl in the audience is popping three-foot bubbles with her gum.

Commercial.

I feel sorry the first in-line got hurt, but it wasn't my fault. Brian insisted and I tried to warn him. Also, I was a bit freaked out about Mandy and Candy. Was there no other choice for them but death?

Season Two, Episode Eight

CAPPING S'ERS
XCAL - 1
10-11 pm
New "Caroline Jackson"
S2/EP08, (2018), The latest installment of the weekly show that highlights an individual who desires to commit suicide. With an assist from thrower Ricky Fordham, the individual may or may not die.

Brian offered a 250,000 California dollar reward for whoever could find a star for him. I don't know if any others exist or not, but I have never seen or heard of any. I threw away the box it came in long ago, but with the star's help, I can remember the return address on that box in an instant. But I didn't tell Brian that.

No other real star showed up, but there were a lot of pretend ones. Some of them looked darn good. Better than mine. The problem was, they didn't know what kind of material to use. Steel, aluminum, plastic, glass? They tried everything, but none of it worked. I never had the star analyzed (despite Brian's insistence) and I didn't recognize what it was made of either.

Most of the fakes were rejected just from looking

at them, but there were a few that Brian had me try. Not even close. And then he tried them himself, just in case I was making the others fail on purpose. I don't think Brian trusts me.

Brian also told me that the Governor wants one, although he doesn't know why. I know why. How powerful of a political tool would it be if you could know someone else and all their thoughts, deeds and secrets; completely, instantly?

Sitting in my trailer, I reflect back to when things started to happen for me.

I saw a poster for the upcoming Fourth of July festivities that would take place in the park square of the town I was then living in. The town's mayor oversaw the event, and although I had never met him, he knew me, though not in a good way. He was a big burly man with a deep voice and an enormous beer belly. I approached him about letting me do a throwing demonstration during the celebration, but considering my reputation, I think he was afraid that I was going to wind up killing someone or something. It took a lot of persuading and a small bribe, but I got him to agree.

I was so nervous that I don't think I slept for a week beforehand, but finally the big day arrived. They cordoned off a thirty by twenty yard space for me. Smaller than I was used to but considering all the different places I had to practice in these past few years, that wasn't too big of a problem. It required some adjustments, and there was zero time to practice. There was a chalked out area for me to throw from. All around the perimeter of the whole thing were sawhorses holding signs that said, 'Danger. Stand well back.' They even erected a wood wall at the far end, so the star wouldn't fly off into the crowd.

I had arranged for my sister to be there. She

had never seen me throw before. Her arms were twitching, her head moving side to side, and her pale green eyes had never looked more alive.

I set up two wooden poles to bounce from, another pole with an arm to hang a rope from and one final pole. The final pole was meant to stop the star. If I had it figured out correctly, the star would impact that final pole and get stuck there. I had never used a final pole before, but I thought that I had every contingency covered. I was wrong.

I stood ready to throw. There were probably a hundred people watching. A low murmur rippled through the crowd. People were pressing forward, crowding the sidelines, ignoring the signs. A reporter from the local paper was there, standing with a pen, note pad and a camera around his neck. I wiped my sweaty hands on my jeans with the holes in them as I prepared to throw.

I extended out my left arm with its mangled hand. The hand felt like someone had stuck a knife in it. My right hand was itching like crazy. I cocked my right arm back and let the star fly. It flew straight toward the first pole, ricocheting off with a loud *thunk*, a little chip of wood flying off from the impact.

The star flew toward the second pole, again a *thunk* and a chip. The star cut the rope perfectly, the weight at the bottom falling down to earth with about three feet of rope falling on top of it. The star flew on to the last pole and impacted it.

Everything would have been okay if it wasn't for that, where the star impacted the final pole, there was a loose knot. The idea was for the star to impale itself in the pole and no one would get hurt. It didn't. To my horror, the star hit the pole and spun on, taking the loose knot with it. The star even seemed to gain speed as it shot off through the crowd, people diving and dodging all over, and on toward the bandstand.

Fortunately, the band members were not playing

at the time. They had joined the crowd watching my throw. The star crashed into the band's gear, sheet music flying everywhere, and it eventually came to rest, stuck inside a tuba.

Well, you can imagine the newspaper story that came out about that. About how I almost killed a tuba player. It was on the front page! The tuba player would have been all right, but the musician that would have been sitting in front of him would have lost his head.

After that publicity, my fame grew, and other towns within the county wanted a demonstration of my star skills. There were no more mishaps, and I increased the number of poles per throw from three to four and the number of ropes from one to three, although I think most people showed up to see if I really would accidentally kill someone that day.

The newspapers were helping my career quite a bit. Starting with "TEENAGER NEARLY KILLS BAND" to "AMATEUR NINJA THROWS DEADLY STAR" to "STAR THROWER TO ATTEMPT NEW RECORD," the headlines kept bringing the people in.

By the time I was nineteen, I was getting 500 California dollars per demonstration and was performing in five counties. I gave half of the money to my sister. Well, not exactly to her. She couldn't do anything with it herself. I either gave it to her caretaker, or I spent it on her directly. Like for a new blouse or coat. I hoped her caretaker spent the money I gave him on her, but I doubted it.

By the time I was twenty, my act was getting stale. Cutting a rope just wasn't that interesting, regardless of how many poles were involved. I wasn't getting any repeat business, and even I was getting bored with it all. I needed something new.

"Welcome, California, to the latest episode of *Capping S'ers!*"

I look at the audience. My sister is still absent. Above where she would be, I see a lovely couple with the girl's hand buried beneath the blanket covering the man's lap. Sexy.

"Tonight, we are doing something unique and different. Our S'er is Caroline Jackson. We have a secret surprise for Caroline that we will reveal later in the show. But for now, we are going to visit Caroline in her hometown of San Francisco. We are going to interview her live in our studio, and then LIVE we will watch the Capp and see if Caroline becomes our latest S'er. Stick around, folks. We will be right back after this commercial break."

I step onto the stage floor and wave. The crowd goes crazy. The lovely couple in the audience pulled the blanket up to their necks. Funny. It isn't even cold out tonight.

Commercial.

While playing the *Capping S'ers* theme music, the camera focuses in on a pale thirty-year-old woman standing next to a sign in the shape of a ship's wheel. The woman smiles as she says, "Fisherman's Wharf used to be such a great place to shop and eat."

Then, the woman is standing next to a street sign that says Post and Stockton. "This is Union Square. It has been a gathering place since the American Civil War. It still is with demonstrations and riots nightly. My name is Caroline Jackson, and I am ready to commit suicide."

Caroline is standing on the sidewalk of Mission Street. As the camera pans out, Caroline says, "This is the Academy of Art University. This is where I used to go to school."

Next, Caroline enters a five-story apartment

building. She says, "This is where I live. Let me show you my apartment. It's on the fourth floor."

The camera follows her up the stairs and inside the two-bedroom apartment. Caroline says, "I have the bedroom on the right. My roommate has the one on the left. A third person sleeps on our couch most nights but doesn't pay us any rent. We all share the kitchen and one bathroom."

"We will get up close and personal with Caroline Jackson right after these commercial messages."

My cue sounds in my ear, but I am in deep conversation with the second-in-line. Where the lovely couple in the audience were sitting, their seats are empty. Guess they had to leave for some reason.

Commercial.

Phil is staring at Caroline. Caroline is wearing a smart, one-piece jumpsuit.

"Hello, everyone. I am Phil Ebenezer. I have a PhD in clinical psychology. Now Caroline, tell me why you want to end your life."

"I'm fine. There's nothing wrong with me."

"I see. Then why are you here?"

"I just love the show. My friend Dwaine and I talk about nothing else."

Phil picks up his 3 X 5 card and kisses it before he speaks, "Well, I'm glad you love the show. But there must be something wrong with you if you are willing to end your life."

"Oh. There is. There is."

"And what is that?"

"I'm depressed."

"Go on."

"I can't think."

"And?"

"And I walk around in a fog all the time."

"Okay. That's good. Well, we do have a surprise for you."

"What's that?"

"Your best friend, Mr. Dwaine Hoffman is going to be an in-line on your Capp!"

"No way!"

"Yes, way. Ricky has been working in secret with Dwaine for weeks now getting him ready."

"Wow! That is just awesome."

"So, are you ready for the LIVE portion of our show?"

"I am."

"Don't forget to stay tuned after the show for your XCAL 1 evening news, the only official state newscast. Remember folks, if you didn't see it on XCAL 1, it didn't happen."

Commercial.

"Welcome back everyone. We are still here with Caroline, and we have just over ten minutes to kill. So Caroline, I'll start off with the obvious, you were an art student."

"Yes. The school closed before I could get my degree."

"That's too bad. What kind of art did you study?"

"Ceramics."

"So, you used a wheel and made bowls?"

"No, I used a slab roller and made tiles."

"Well, I don't know what a slab roller is. Did you still use a kiln?"

"Of course."

"So, what good is a ceramic tile made from a slab roller?"

"Well, the tile could cover a floor, become a kitchen or bathroom back splash or even be hung as a decoration."

"Hung like artwork?"

"Yes. Like artwork. Like an artist. Like art school. Ceramic tile, even if it serves a useful function, is art."

"If you say so. So, did you paint on your tiles?"

"I paint with glaze."

"Paint with glaze. I don't know what that means either. So, are you a painter or not?"

"I am an artist who works with clay. I sculpt; I paint; I etch. I use fire that transforms dirt into beautiful pieces of art."

"Sounds like you are full of yourself to me. Ah, I see we are out of time, so we won't get a chance to hear what else Caroline can do with her fired dirt. We'll be back right after this."

In the seats the lovely couple vacated are two young men, giving each other high fives.

Commercial.

I step into camera range and wave to the crowd. There are loud shouts and whistles. Brian escorts Caroline out. I study Caroline's neck. Looks fine. I see her face and her lively steel colored eyes. I check Caroline's position.

I fuss for a bit then say, "You don't have to do this. Just step away, and the star won't hurt you."

I walk back to my starting position, get a nod from the doctor, cock my arm back, and throw the star. It does its thing on the first in-line and then cuts the rope. The second-in-line, Dwaine Hoffman, who I worked with for weeks trying to get him to hold still, flinches, so the star misses him and continues straight on into the far wall. Caroline is standing there, unhurt, crying. Dwaine looks distressed. I walk away in disgust. I point back to the stage where Brian is standing with Phil and shout, "Never again!"

The music starts up. The star is stuck in the far wall. The crowd is stunned silent until the 'boo's start. The two young men are being escorted out by Capping S'er security guards.

Commercial.

Talk about a disaster. What a screw up it was putting that Dwaine character in instead of one of the regular in-lines. Totally messed up the Capp. I wonder if Caroline will be on again or not. Like they did with Sally. Brian has such stupid ideas. "Have to keep it fresh and exciting," he says. I know a way to keep it fresh and exciting. Just let me do my throws. Longer and more complicated throws is the key, not this stupid stuff Brian keeps wanting to do.

Season Two, Episode Nine

CAPPING S'ERS
XCAL - 1
10-11 pm
New "Nick Newcomb"
S2/EP09, (2018), The latest installment of the weekly show that highlights an individual who desires to commit suicide. With an assist from thrower Ricky Fordham, the individual may or may not die.

As the limo pulled into the studio lot today, I couldn't help but notice that there were two sets of noisy protesters flanking the gate. The group on the left held signs that read "No More S'ers" and "Kill Ricky Instead." The group on the right had signs that read "Need More S'ers" and "Make Ricky Queen." I guess a person either likes this show or hates it. You certainly can't please everyone.

It may sound strange because it had been so long, but I miss sleeping with my twin sister. Nighttime, when it was just the two of us, was the time we connected and reconciled all the crazy things that happened during the day. My sister would tell me that she understood that I did what I had to, so I wouldn't get beaten by our dad. I would tell her that I was not jealous of her receiving all our mother's attention and love, even though I was. Nighttime was our time. But after the car accident, she got her own room with a hospital bed. I would lie alone in our bed, not sleeping, listening to my dog snoring outside, dreaming her doggy dreams. These days, I am still not sleeping, but there is no sister and no dog. Only me.

While waiting to go to makeup, I think back to when I came up with the idea of using people instead of poles. I would keep the ropes. I thought that people liked seeing them being cut and dropping. It showed how sharp the points of the star were. But how much more exciting would it be if the star bounced off a person instead of a pole. Wow! That would draw the crowds in.

But how could I bounce a star off a person without hurting them? Because I didn't want to hurt anyone. I also didn't want to dull the points because then the star wouldn't be able to cut the ropes. And even if I did, as fast as the star was rotating, it would hurt like hell if it hit an unprotected person.

I could dress them in a suit of armor, but I didn't see how I can get a reliable bounce out of it. The person, of course, was going to have to hold still. They can't move or flinch. But where was I going to get a suit of armor? And where on the suit could I get a reliable surface to hit where I can get the same ricochet every time? And where would the danger factor be if a person was dressed in armor from head to toe?

Okay, forget the suit of armor. I still needed something that would protect the person and, at the same time, give me a surface to bounce the star off of. Maybe armor on just part of the body. It would have to be on the outside edge of the body, like an arm or leg. An arm could be held in tight against the body. Armor could be placed on the outside of that. But people have different size arms. The difference between a man's arm and a woman's is huge. And some guys have well-developed arms, and some don't. Also, an arm would be the first thing to move if the person panicked. A leg would probably be more stable, less likely to move. But again, different size legs would have different curved surface areas. I would need volunteers with identical body sizes. The other problem with the leg is that it is too far down. I needed more height than that for my throws.

What about the neck? It would be easier to find people with the same or similar neck sizes. I could make the armor go all the way around the neck, giving more protection and giving me two sides to bounce off of. Because the star would be closer to the head, it would be a more dramatic throw. Make the neck armor out of metal, silver or gold-plated, so it looks pretty. Put some carvings or designs on it to make it more attractive and tribal looking. Like a piece of jewelry. Who knows, I could be starting a whole new fashion trend. But leave the striking area blank, both on the right and left sides, clean and smooth. That way I'll have a good striking surface, and my throws could arc around either clockwise or counterclockwise depending on which side of a person I hit. Yeah, that should work.

I thought it would be hard to find someone to volunteer to stand perfectly still while a lethal weapon was thrown at their neck. It wasn't. There are a lot of crazy people in the world, and most of them seem to have a death wish. All I had to do was run an ad in the paper, and I had more than enough volunteers. I only needed three, at first.

Making the neck armor was the hard part. It

was way more money than I had. I tried borrowing the money, but when I explained what I wanted it for, I got laughed at. I went to work driving a forklift and loading trucks for intrastate commerce.

I was saving every penny I could, but it still took nine months before I had three pieces of neck armor. I had to acquire them one at a time. No volume discount for custom work. No fancy carvings. Silver plated (cheaper than gold). I painted the throat of each a different color—one red, one blue, and one green, just so I could tell them apart.

I had never practiced with a person in neck armor before (duh, no one else ever had either), so I attached one to each of my three volunteers and off into a field we marched. It didn't go too badly, although one of my volunteers quit after losing most of an ear. It was his fault. He moved. They were nervous at first and did a lot of jerks and other movements, which would upset the throw. By the time it reached the second or third in-line, the star was either not even close or had them jumping out of the way.

Eventually though, the person who was first in-line settled down, then the second in-line had to get use to the strikes against their neck, and finally the third in-line. Getting to the point where I could consistently make a throw and hit all three in-lines every time, without them moving, took months. I had the ropes being cut between the first and second in-line and again between the second and third in-lines. I felt it necessary to show that the star was deadly, not just some harmless piece of plastic or something. After the third in-line, I had a post that would catch the star. I found that a four by six piece of lumber worked better than a round pole. And one with no knots in it.

I also discovered that during the times when we went a little late in practice, and it was getting dark, the spark given off by the star hitting the neck armor was quite bright. I thought it would be awesome to someday do a night throw where all you see would be the star heading off into the darkness, then *thunk* and a flash of light, and then another, and then another. Maybe set the ropes on fire too, so they could be seen when they were cut.

My first public throw with real people in neck armor was a sellout. There was even a local TV news camera there. Definitely was a good idea to change up the act. I admit I was nervous, but the throw went off perfectly. It was even featured on the 11:00 o'clock news.

It wasn't until my third people throw that there was a problem. I had everything set up—all the people in place, ropes ready, final square post in position. I was standing with my left arm extended and my right arm cocked, visualizing how it would go—when a teenage girl ducked under the sawhorse barrier, ran over, and stood in front of the first rope. She stood there, ramrod straight, arms down at her sides, her body quivering.

I froze in my pre-throw stance as I watched her. When she still hadn't moved after a minute, I yelled over to the first in-line to relax and open his eyes, and then I walked over to her.

"What do you think you are doing?"

"I want to be part of your throw."

"You can't. You aren't wearing any neck armor. You would have been killed if I had made my throw."

"That's okay. I want to die."

It was a hot day. I could feel the sun burning down onto the back of my neck. I was sweating.

"Why?"

"My stepdad raped me, and my mom just let him. Twice."

"Well, I can't help you with that. You should go see a counselor or something."

"I did. He wants to see me once every week for 300 California dollars a session. My mom doesn't have any money, and the state won't pay because there is no court case with a conviction."

"You didn't press charges?"

"I did. But it was just my word against his, and my mom said that I wanted it. That I seduced him. Now my boyfriend won't touch me, and I just want to die."

She was crying.

"Well, I still can't help you. Life sucks, okay? We all have our problems, so just deal with it and move on. You think that my life is a bed of roses? I've gone through some shit you wouldn't believe. Now get back into the crowd. I'm not going to throw until you do."

She stood there for a few minutes, staring at me defiantly. I regained my spot and stood there with my hands and the star at my side. The pain in my left hand intensified and I desperately wanted to scratch the itching in my right. She finally sighed and rejoined the audience. I saw that the first in-line was ready again, his eyes closed and his body rigid like it was always before a throw.

I went into my stance, left arm straight out, cocked my right arm, visualized, and threw the star. It hit the first in-line in the neck armor. *Thunk*. A spark. Perfect. It flew toward the first rope. The girl ducked under the barrier and ran toward that first rope. She was hit in mid stride by the full force of the star. It ripped into the side of her neck. Her body shuddered. A point caught in her Adam's apple, ripped it out and tossed it to the side. She collapsed; the star stuck in her spinal cord at the back of her neck. She was dead before she hit the ground, her head nearly chopped off, but her heart kept pumping, and blood flowed over the ground. The crowd gasped as the camera rolled, recording everything. A few people fainted. I had flashbacks to my mother's death. It's taken me years to get over that. I didn't want to be locked up again. I threw up.

"Welcome, California, to the latest episode of *Capping S'ers!*"

In the audience is a girl whose face is painted in *Capping S'ers* colors, her right fist pumping the air, wearing a t-shirt with my portrait on it bearing the caption, "Leave no S'er alive." What is that supposed to mean? Kill them all? Even if they step away?

"Tonight, we are going to meet a very special person. His name is Nick Newcomb. We are going to visit Nick in his hometown of Los Angeles. We are going to interview him live in our studio, and then LIVE we will watch the Capp and see if Nick has the balls to die. Stick around, folks. We will be right back after this commercial break."

I step onto the center of the stage floor and wave. The crowd reacts. I had spoken to one of the security guards on the way over from my trailer and was told that before the police could arrive, the protests had turned violent. Thirteen people dead and fifty-five injured. The girl with the t-shirt is doing high kicks in the aisle.

Commercial.

On screen is a beefy forty-year-old man standing next to a sign that says Pawn Shop. The man smiles broadly as he says, "This is my favorite place to offload stolen goods."

The man is standing next to a street sign that says Hyde Park. "This is one of the oldest neighborhoods in South Central. My favorite tattoo parlor is just around the corner. My name is Nick Newcomb, and I am ready to commit suicide."

Nick is standing on the stage of the Hollywood Bowl. As the camera pans out, Nick says, "I used to sneak in here for concerts all the time. Before I went to jail."

Nick points at a sleeping bag laid out in a

cardboard box. He says, "This is where I sleep."

The camera pans to the right and shows a sidewalk crowded with similar bedding and pans to the left to show a sidewalk packed with more of the same.

"We will get up close and personal with Nick Newcomb right after these commercial messages."

The girl in the audience is gesturing with her arm as if she was throwing a star.

Commercial.

Phil and Nick are waiting. Nick is wearing torn blue jeans and a sleeveless t-shirt. He has massive arms.

"Hello, everyone. I am Phil Ebenezer. I have a PhD in clinical psychology. Now Nick, tell me why you want to end your life."

"I'm bad. I've been really bad."

"I see. What did you do?"

"Well, I started out just doing little stuff, you know. Pickpocketing. Purse snatching. Breaking and entering. But the last B&E I did didn't turn out so well. I didn't think anyone was home. Then this dude shows up with a pistol and goes all Dirty Harry on me. It was self-defense. I had no choice."

Phil gets his 3 X 5 card and waves it at Nick as he asks, "So you killed the dude?"

"Yep. Had to."

"And what about the wife?"

"Yeah. She had to go, too. Came out when she heard the noise."

"And the two kids who were asleep in their bedroom?"

"Well, I was already there. Had to make a clean sweep of it. You never know. Maybe they were just pretending to be asleep. I'd been making a lot of noise."

"So why are you on the show?"

"Duh. My trial is in two weeks and if convicted,

they are going to put me in prison, man. For life. Have you ever been in a California prison? Man, I don't want to go there."

"So, you would rather just end it now? Kill yourself to avoid a lifetime in prison?"

"I would."

"All right then. The officials let you out to come here on the show, so they must be okay with it. I hear all the prisons are overcrowded anyway. Okay, let's do this."

Commercial.

"We are back with Nick. We still have some time to kill. Forgive the pun. So, Nick, what is your favorite thing to steal?"

"Money. If I steal money, then I don't have to fence it. That guy cheats me every time."

"I see. Where do you get most of your money?"

"Well, I always pick a nice house. One with lots of curb appeal. I pick them because they must have money. Houses are expensive to upkeep, so if it is kept up, they got money. So, I pick them."

"And what do you do after you pick them?"

"Well, I like to case the place during the day. I pretend I am the meter reader. Everyone always ignores them. Except maybe the kids. Sometimes." Nick appears to run out of steam.

"Go on. You are casing the joint during the day."

"Yeah. I am looking for the easiest way to break in. I like the place to be occupied, otherwise if they were on vacation, they might have taken their money with them. Windows are the best. Low windows or windows in doors." Nick winds down again.

"Then what do you do after you figured a way in?"

"Oh, then I figure out an escape route. I like to do that while it is still light out. I like lots of bushes and stuff. Maybe even a tree. I must figure out the escape route beforehand. It is too hard to try to do it in the dark and on the run." Nick is out of gas at this point. He covers his mouth as he coughs.

"Nick, are you feeling okay?"

"Yea man. Never better. Why?"

"No reason. Well, there you have it. How the mind of a criminal genius works. The Capp is coming up."

The girl in the audience is showing off her t-shirt to the camera.

Commercial.

Brian escorts Nick out. I study Nick's heavily tattooed neck. I pull back to see his face and his unrepentant gray eyes. I check Nick's position. I fuss for a bit, then say, "You don't have to do this. Just step away, and the star won't hurt you." Nick coughs in my face.

I walk back to my starting position, check with medical, cock my arm back, and throw the star. The Capp goes as normal. The star flies toward Nick, grazes his neck. His body shudders. He falls to the ground, blood streaming. Doc runs over. I watch the ever-increasing pool of blood but then glance up.

I just catch the third in-line stepping away, and the star penetrating the bleachers where the audience watches in horror. People dive for cover. One spectator sticks his neck out. The star bounces off an empty seat and changes direction. It doesn't travel very far until it hits someone's arm. He screams in agony as the star has penetrated to the bone. His nearly severed arm hangs useless as he stumbles out of the stands and starts running out of the building. Before he hits the exit door, he is tackled by a paramedic who starts applying a tourniquet.

The doctor gives a thumbs up. The *Capping S'ers*

theme music starts up. I walk over to where the screaming spectator is and jerk the star out of the bone.
The other in-lines are still at attention. The third
in-line has fled out the door. Brian is in hot pursuit.
Nick is lying dead on the ground, eyes open. The crowd
is going crazy with extra shouts and cheers.

Nick deserved to die. Good riddance. At least I
saved the state the cost of a trial.

The girl in the audience is bent over and throwing up. I head back to my trailer.

Commercial.

God, what a mess. I hardly know what to think.
This show is going totally nuts. People at the gate
killing themselves, an in-line breaking rank and
running away, an audience member nearly losing an arm,
and worse of all, my throat is a little scratchy like
I'm getting a cold.

Season Two, Episode Ten

CAPPING S'ERS
XCAL - 1
10-11 pm
New "Mary Butler"
S2/EP10, (2018), The season 2 finale of this weekly show that highlights an individual who desires to commit suicide. With an assist from thrower Ricky Fordham, the individual may or may not die.

Even though I quit being interviewed by Phil after the second show, Brian still had me do the talk show circuit. I can't say I enjoyed it. I don't like talking about myself, or the show, so I was reluctant, but I did it. Brian said it was in my contract, which I still haven't read. They all asked the same questions, made the same comments, and I gave the same answers.

They would ask me stupid stuff. How did you get so good at Capping? Practice.

What was your scariest moment? The first time I threw before an audience.

Do you ever get nervous before a show? Yes, always.

Who is your favorite S'er? I don't have a favorite. I don't know any of them.

Do you watch the video package or interview? Yes. Brian makes me. Why is that? Because I missed my cue the first time I tried to avoid it. Why did you try to avoid it? Because I don't want to know them. Why not? I just don't.

Do you and your in-lines hang out? No. Why not? I don't know any of them either. Why not? I don't know. I just don't want to.

Do you have a special someone? No. Why not? Well, the show keeps me pretty busy. But surely there is time for romance? No. There isn't. I practice an awful lot.

Most of my answers are lies. For example, I never did tell the talk show hosts or anyone else the real reason I don't talk with the in-lines.

It was because of Shirley, early in season one, a back-up in-line. Our only female in-line. She came up to me one day at rehearsal while we were on break. I was reaching for another donut (it was not a dress rehearsal) when she said, "Why don't you talk to the in-lines?"

"What?"

"The in-lines. You never talk to us other than 'stand here' or 'stand there' or 'don't move.' Why is that?"

"I'm talking to you right now."

"Only because I started it. You are like a God to us. We put our lives in your hands every time you throw. What if you missed?"

"I never miss."

"Not yet. But you could. Then we would be dead too."

"Maybe that is why I don't talk with in-lines."

"Look, I'm not the kind of girl who waits around for other people to make their move."

"Obviously."

"Let's go out. Tonight. After rehearsal."

I stared at her before answering. She looked

beautiful in her black leather one-piece suit (the in-lines always must dress for rehearsal). I wished I could look that good. And I have never seen anyone who wore their neckwear as elegantly as she did.

"Go out for what?"

"A drink. Just as friends."

"Okay."

We went to Mario's that night. We talked and ate and drank until I noticed that we were the only ones left in the place. I was a celebrity, so they weren't going to kick us out, but I knew we were several hours past closing. Shirley was so easy to talk with that we agreed to do it again the next night. This was before the show had bodyguards for the in-lines.

The next night was even better. We ate quickly and went back to my place. On our first date, she had accused me of never being in an adult relationship. Of being afraid of one. She may have been right, but we certainly started one that night.

When I woke up the next morning, the bed was empty, but I could smell bacon and eggs being cooked in the kitchen. I hardly ever used the kitchen. My usual breakfast was plain burnt toast. Always has been.

"Where did you get the food?" I wanted to know.

"There is a cute little grocery store just around the corner."

"There is? You shouldn't be out alone. It is too dangerous."

"Don't worry. None of the bad people get up this early." She was right about that. The daily riots usually didn't start until after two in the afternoon.

We enjoyed the food and the morning and parted with a kiss. As I gazed into her light brown eyes, we promised to talk more at the studio. I thought maybe adult relationships weren't so bad after all.

I believe that this was the only time I was ever glad to be heading into work. When I got there, I didn't see Shirley. I asked Brian about her, and he replied, "Didn't you hear? She was killed this after-noon. A home invasion."

I was stunned, "Robbery?" We had shared a bed just hours ago.

"The police didn't think so. Not based on what was written on her wall. In her blood."

"What was written on the wall?"

"*Capping S'ers* is death."

So that's why I don't talk to in-lines, or anyone else, if I can avoid it. Because just like S'ers, in-lines die too.

I remember that on this one talk show, they had a nuclear physicist who claimed that what I did was impossible and therefore must be faked. He had all sorts of diagrams and formulas that "proved" it. Especially since I didn't use any aids or tools. I just eyeballed it before I threw. If you ask me, all he "proved" is that there is no such thing as bad publicity.

Once the media found out that I had killed my mom, they went nuts over that. Those records were sup-posed to be sealed, but somehow, they found out anyway.

Did you kill her on purpose? No. Is that why you don't mind killing S'ers? Because you already killed before? Would you have killed your dad the same way if you had a chance? Do you plan on killing anyone else? Besides S'ers, that is? I stopped doing talk shows. Was my dad still alive? I didn't think so. I had heard that he drove his big rig off a bridge. On purpose, I hoped. With what he had done to my sister and me in his thoughts as he died, even better.

I know he beat up on my mom, but then she passed it along. Did that make her a victim or an abuser? I don't know. Do I regret killing her? No, my only regret about killing her is because that action was what kept my sister and I apart for all those years.

Waiting for makeup, I remember how after that teenager ran into the path of the star, I swore never to throw again. Two people were dead because of that star. I dismissed my volunteers. I took the three pieces of neck armor that had taken me so long to acquire and pounded on them with a sledgehammer. Tears flowed out of my eyes as I pounded and pounded, and I had no idea why. I wasn't being a man, but I couldn't help it. I went back to work driving a forklift and loading trucks for minimum wage, although on most days there was nothing to load. But I couldn't bring myself to toss out the star. I dug a hole in the back yard of the home I was staying at and buried it.

The incident was ruled an accident. Her name was Kathy Lyndhurst. I had only known her for five minutes, but she would haunt me for the rest of my life. I will never forget the look on her face at that moment when the star struck her. So like my Mom's. Did she still want to die right then? I don't think my Mom did. Was Kathy happy to end her life so dramatically? On camera, videotaped, immortalized forever? Or did she realize, in that final moment, that she was making a mistake? I don't want to think about or remember any of it, but I do. I can't stop thinking about her. About how her eyes opened so wide at the moment of death. Pale green eyes. I often wondered about Kathy. About Mom. About the similarities. About the differences. About me. About what I did.

About what I am.

Once my sister and I were reunited and before I became a celebrity, I talked with my sister a lot about Kathy and mom. Of course, all my sister could do was use her eyes to convey whatever emotion she was feeling. I interpreted it as sympathy and understanding.

After one such visit, as I was walking to the bus stop, in clear daylight, four guys came out of an alley. One of them had a gun. He robbed me of my wallet and backpack and then beat on me just because he could. My immediate thought was that if I had the star, I would so throw it at the guy with the gun who was now running away. I knew it would kill him when the star hit the back of his neck. I knew I could hit him, even at that increasing distance.

My second thought was how glad I was that I didn't have the star with me. It would have been in the backpack, and I would have lost it forever. My third, fourth, and fifth thoughts were amazement at how violent California had become, how close to death I had been, and how much I missed throwing the star.

So I started throwing again and it wasn't but three months later when I was approached by Hollywood. His name was Harvey Howard, and he said he was a producer. He looked the part with his flamboyant manner of dress and long stringy hair.

"Kid," he said, "I think you have a winner on your hands."

"What are you talking about?"

"Your star act. Where people can kill themselves."

"You saw the video of Kathy?"

"Yes. Very impressive."

"Kathy was an accident."

"Of course she was. I didn't say that you did it on purpose. But by using your star, I believe that you can provide a service for people."

"What are you talking about? I don't want to provide any service."

"I'm talking about a TV show, kid. One where you are the star. You do your little star throw thing, people that want to die stand in the way, and magic! A hit series! You could make millions. Just by providing an avenue for them to kill *themselves*."

What was this guy talking about? How was this legal or even just okay? I knew society had declined a bit since the borders closed, but had we really come down to this? This was a disgusting idea.

"What if I don't provide an avenue? Then there won't be any killing."

"Sure there will be. If someone really wants to die, they will do it whether you are providing the means or not. They will use a car, a shotgun, or a policeman. But they will still kill themselves. You will be providing them a way to do it gracefully, lov-ingly, and with a chance for them to tell their story. You would be giving them a chance to explain why they are doing it. What is driving them to it? And if people in the audience see that, then maybe someone else will think that their own situation isn't so bad, and they won't kill themselves. By providing a tasteful artis-tic avenue for the ones who are going to do it anyway, you will be helping other people not to do it at all. You will be saving lives. Not taking them."

"I think you are crazy."

"Yeah, crazy smart. This is all backed by the state. I've already cleared it with them. You don't have to worry about being accused of murder or anything because you wouldn't be doing anything wrong. If they are not restrained and have full freedom to change their mind at any time, you're in the clear. The state will even sign a waiver for you, so it is all nice and legal. This can be a big deal. The TV coverage will blanket the whole state. California needs you, kid. What do you say?"

This guy was serious. Would a TV show like he was describing ever get on the air?

"Why does California need me?"

"These are hard times, kiddo. Quality enter-tainment will help keep people from worrying about their own problems all the time. Keep them inside and off the streets. Less riots. Less property damage. Less overwhelmed police force. You will be doing a world of good. You will be a hero, and the audience will love you!"

I still can't believe it. Such a thing would never happen.

"No. I'm not going to help people die."

"I can offer you money. Lots of money. More California dollars than you ever dreamed of."

"No. I won't do it," I said as I walked away.

Harvey kept pestering me, and I kept saying no. This went on for months. Harvey kept trying new angles. Promising fame and fortune. Telling me that my "art" shouldn't be kept hidden. That I should be using my "talent" for good.

I never would have said yes if he hadn't told me that they could fix my sister.

"Welcome, California, to the final episode of season two of *Capping S'ers*!"

Sitting where my sister used to sit is an elderly man in a wheelchair. I watch him for more than a few minutes when, from under his blanket, he pulls out a pistol and starts waving it in the air. Whoa, what is that for?

"Tonight is the finale of season two, and boy do we have a show for you. Ricky Fordham has been using her creative genius and has come up with a never seen before performance you won't want to miss. Oh yea, we also have an S'er. Her name is Mary Butler. So, after these commercials, we will visit Mary in her hometown of San Jose. Then we will interview her in our studio, and then LIVE we will watch the Capp and see what Mary does. Stick around, folks. We will be right back."

The audience seating has doubled in size from the previous show. On the stage floor, the first and third in-lines are facing the audience while the second in-line has his back to the audience. The elderly man in a wheelchair points his pistol at me. I run to the snack table but can't find Brian. Where did all the security guards disappear to?

Commercial.

On screen, while playing the *Capping S'ers* theme music, the camera fades in on a rail thin twenty-two-year-old woman standing on the sidewalk outside the Hotel De Anza. The woman smiles timidly as she says, "At ten stories, this hotel was, for a long time, the tallest building in downtown San Jose."

The woman is standing outside of the Lick Observatory. "This was the world's first permanently occupied mountain-top observatory. My name is Mary Butler, and I am ready to commit suicide."

Mary is standing by a fountain. As the camera pans out, Mary says, "This two-point-two acre park is the oldest public open space in California."

Next, Mary is outside of a brown stucco house. She says, "I live here with my grandparents. But they are taking a nap, so we can't go in."

"We will get up close and personal with Mary Butler right after these commercial messages."

The elderly man in a wheelchair is flanked by *Capping S'ers* security guards. The pistol is not in sight. Thank God. I guess Brian, or someone, saw him as well.

Commercial.

I am at the snack table wishing there was some hard liquor, but there isn't. I sure could use a drink. Or a joint. Phil and Mary are on stage. Mary is wearing a red tent dress.

"Hello, everyone. I am Phil Ebenezer. I have a PhD in clinical psychology. Now Mary, tell me why you want to end your life."

"Well, Phil. I have an eating disorder."

"So how does that work?"

"Well, I eat. But then I panic that maybe I ate too much. I am deathly afraid of gaining weight and getting fat. So, I throw everything up."

"You don't like your body?"

"No. Do you?" she asks as she stands and pulls the tent dress over her head. She is nude underneath.

"Well. I don't like how your ribs stand out, but your tits are nice."

Mary starts crying, "See what I mean? I have a horrible body. I just want to end it all."

"All right then. Put your dress back on and then let's do this."

Commercial.

"We are back with Mary." She is dressed again. "Mary, we have some time so, in your video, you went to Lick Observatory. Do you like star gazing?"

"Yes. It is free and open to the public. I can see all the wonderful stars. And planets, too."

"Do they have any special programs there?"

"Well, they have tours every hour on the half hour. You get to see the telescope. It was the world's biggest at the time it was installed. They have videos on space exploration. And the view from up there. Amazing. As long as you can handle the drive up."

"Okay, enough about that. Let's talk about something else. You say you live with your grandparents. Tell me about them."

"Well, they are both retired. They are in their eighties. Grandpa was a railroad engineer, and grandma was a schoolteacher."

"Well, it's a good thing that gramps retired because there aren't any trains running now. What did your grandma teach?"

"Everything. She taught her whole life. When she started, it was in a one-room schoolhouse. Later she taught English and History. I learned a lot from her."

"Like what?"

"Oh, just things about life."

"Didn't she teach you about nutrition and eating properly?"

"She did. And I do eat properly. I just can't keep it down because I am afraid of getting fat."

"Okay. Brian is signaling me that we still have six minutes to go. Don't forget to stay tuned after the show for your XCAL 1 evening news, the only official state newscast. Remember folks, if you didn't see it on XCAL 1, it didn't happen."

Commercial.

"We are back with Mary, trying to fill the last four minutes of our interview time. Is there anything else you can tell us about your grandma?"

"She was very beautiful when she was young."

"We all were when we were young."

"Not me."

"Come on. I bet you were a very cute baby."

"Well, yeah. Back then. A bit chubby. A porker, actually. Not now."

"What are you? Obsessed over this weight thing? God, no wonder you want to kill yourself. Are you ready for the Capp or not?"

"I'm ready."

"Fine. Brian is just going to have to deal. We will be back with the LIVE Capp right after this."

I am running back and forth between the three in-lines, frantically adjusting each one. The space by the guardrail where the elderly man in a wheelchair was is empty.

Commercial.

I stand nervously where the second pole with the

rope had been, and the in-lines are standing at attention. I hope this new Capp goes okay. Brian escorts Mary out. I study Mary's scrawny neck. Her jugular vein is nearly popping out of her skin. I check Mary's position by looking up the line, then down the line.

I fuss for a bit then say, "You don't have to do this. Just step away, and the star won't hurt you."

I walk back to my starting position, get the ready signal from the doctor, cock my arm back, and throw the star. It flies straight at the first in-line, who's side is turned toward me. With a *clang* and a spark, the star bounces off the front of his neck armor and continues further on.

The star cuts the rope as it passes by on the way to the second in-line, who's back is to the audience. The star bounces off the front of his neck. It flies on toward Mary, grazes her neck. Her body shudders. She falls to the ground, blood streaming. The star bounces off the front of the third-in-line's neck armor. It continues on to plant itself in the final post.

After the doctor gives his thumbs up, the *Capping S'ers* theme music starts up. I am standing, relieved, at my starting position. The Capp went well, even with the changes. The in-lines are still at attention. Mary is lying dead on the ground, her dark green eyes staring off into the distance. The crowd is going crazy with shouts and cheers.

Commercial.

I miss Shirley. It was only a two-day romance, but her death affected me deeply. I should have left the star buried in the ground. I have caused so much death. All because I wanted my sister to be whole again.

Season Three, Recap

CAPPING S'ERS
XCAL - 1
10-11 pm
New "Season 3 recap"
S3/EP11, (2018), Season 3 is recapped in this show that highlights an individual who desires to commit suicide. With an assist from thrower Ricky Fordham, the individual may or may not die.

Season three with its ten shows seemed to go by in a flash. First was the off-season break, where Brian kept me busier than ever with supermarket openings, celebrity interviews, and all sorts of marketing and promotions. If I had one more camera flash in my face, I would have screamed. The show was getting huge. I was an A-listed celebrity. I was forced to ride in limos, attend night clubs, and have affairs. The more publicity the better. I didn't need reservations anywhere in town. The mayor gave me a key to the city. I got a star on Hollywood's Walk of Fame. People recognized me even without the makeup and the cat woman suit. I could get anything I wanted if I let them take a selfie with me.

At first, they said that my sister's surgeries were going awesome, then great, then acceptable.

I haven't seen any change or improvement in her. Instead, I think that I see more tragedy in her eyes than before. Are they helping her, or are they just pretending, to keep me happy and on the show? I don't know. I am having deepening doubts about the show as it is. I don't know how much longer I can be providing an avenue for people to commit suicide without it stealing my soul.

Season three is over, and I am chilling alone, watching the season three recap show. As I watch, my mind, as always, drifts off at times to other matters.

"Welcome, California, we have an extra special show for you tonight. It is a recap of all the highlights of season three of *Capping S'ers*!"

I sigh.

"Tonight, we will discuss each show of our ten-episode season three. We will also look forward to season four and what new and exciting things we can expect then. We will get started right after these commercial messages. Stick around, folks. We will be right back."

There are several imitators of our show, but none of them are any good. First off, they don't have the star. No one else has ever stepped up to say they have one, so the imitators try to make one without a prototype. They can't get the weight light enough so the star sails like mine does. Also, they don't have my years of practice. They can't do what I can do.

I did hear about this one guy in Oakland, though. Apparently, after one of my shows, he lined up four of his buddies on the sidewalk. Three of them had on neckwear and one didn't. He then ran down the line with a machete.

He hit the first guy's neckwear with the machete. *Clang*. A spark. He hit the second guy's neckwear with the machete. *Clang*. A spark. He hit the third guy's bare neck with the machete. He bled out. He hits the fourth guy's neckwear with the machete. *Clang*. A spark. He didn't even need to cut rope or have a final post.

The second time he did this on a city sidewalk, he was arrested and charged with murder. He is currently awaiting trial. How is what he did any different from what I am doing? Is it because I do it on a TV show? Is it because I throw a star instead of using a machete? Is it because my S'er can just step away? His probably could as well. Is it because I have a letter from the state saying that it is not murder? Maybe. But even if I am not violating man's law, what about God's law? What aspect of what I do is morally correct? How am I any different from that man in Oakland? I am afraid that I am not any different at all. And now that I know how the Governor really feels about that piece of paper saying I will never be charged with anything, maybe I am more at risk than I want to be.

While playing the *Capping S'ers* theme music, the camera fades in on Phil standing on stage. "Hello, everyone. I am Phil Ebenezer. I have a PhD in clinical psychology. On our first show in season three, we had an S'er named Gabriella Patrick. She lived in Los Angeles. She was a rape victim. Very pretty girl. No one should be violated like that. We should find the guy, bring him on the show, and rape him. See how he likes it. She had a lot of trauma. Nightmares. She had to quit her job. Couldn't find another one. She lived alone because her roommate was killed in a mugging. She said she was afraid to go outside. We had to send two bodyguards to help get her to the studio. But the Capp was successful, so she doesn't have to worry about any of that now. We'll talk about episode two right after we show the Capp."

All I ever wanted was to be left in peace. I don't need love and affection, not really. My dad didn't want me unless he changed me. My mom went crazy after I destroyed the daughter she did want, so I ended up killing her. Did my sister love me? How could she? I tormented her when we were young, then destroyed her body in that car wreck. I liked it when Irene watched me throw, but I was just a kid and didn't know any better. I liked the attention of having an audience at first, but the fan's love and hate quickly got overwhelming and smothering.

I never stay with a sex partner for more than a day or two. After that, they seem to think they own you.

Let's go hang out with my friends. Let me introduce you to my parents.

I enjoyed my two dates with Shirley before she was killed. I felt real passion and desire for the first time. But she died because of the show. Because of me. How many people were dead because of me? Dare I feel passion and desire again, or will that person also die?

I don't know how I will ever find my 'field behind the barn' escapes now. I tried a couple of times to find a place where I could do throws just for myself, but it always attracted a crowd, which soon turned into a mob. I am a victim of my own success. Paparazzi follow me everywhere, snapping at least 100 pictures if I just peek out the window. I don't dare go out. Since when is what I do so newsworthy? And why?

"Hey, California. I am Phil Ebenezer. I have a PhD in clinical psychology. On our second show in season three, we had an S'er named Steve Kelley. He lived in Sacramento, the former state capital, before coming on the show. He, poor guy, lost everything in one month. Talk about having a shitty month. Can't blame the guy for wanting to end it all. In one month, he lost his wife and two kids in a house fire. He lost his job and his pension when his company went under. He lost his house, of course. I think I already mentioned that. He was living on the streets. He lost his car when a drunk driver ran a red light and crashed into it. He lost a leg when he was pushed through a store window during a riot on the street he was living on. He lost all his money when his bank closed. And after coming on this show, he lost his life. Poor guy. He had a hell of a bad month. We'll talk about episode three right after this Capp."

I have developed an after-show routine. After a Capp, I head straight home. The rest of the crew and in-lines go out and party till dawn. I go home with my two bodyguards. One stays in the lobby of my building. The other stands guard outside my door after checking that my rooms are safe. I go in, lock my door, and flip the deadbolts. I go into my bathroom and, fully clothed, climb into a corner of the shower. I close the shower curtains.

I don't turn on the water. I am not crazy. But it takes me about twenty minutes of shivering with my head down before I can calm down enough to climb out and do anything else.

When I go to bed, it takes me another hour or more to go to sleep.

I keep seeing their eyes.

Starting with my mother and her mean brown eyes,

who I killed in a fit of anger. Was she a victim of abuse or an abuser? What drove her to be so mean to her own children? What happened to her motherly love? Did my dad beat it out of her? She couldn't fight him, so she took it out on my sister and me? She could have broken the chain of abuse. Couldn't she?

Then Kathy Lyndhurst with her pale green eyes; a rape victim whose mom didn't believe her.

Next in the parade is Dawn Adams with her terrified hazel eyes, who got pregnant, then embarrassed on the show.

Ivory Beck with her quiet determined pale green eyes, who was tricked into having sex so the man could win a bet.

Rob Bennett comes next with his calm resigned pale blue eyes, who had lost everything.

David Miller with his lazy dark brown eyes, who had chronic depression.

Janet Forbes with her teary amber eyes, who killed a mother and two children in an automobile accident.

Lucy Doyle with her distant tired dark brown eyes, who was abused by her husband.

Herb Jones with his accepting copper eyes, who had terminal lung cancer with six months to live.

Next to march by is Amanda Hart with her faith-filled gray eyes, who wanted to join God.

Mathew Morgan is next with his resigned hazel eyes, who had hypercortisolism.

Mandy and Candy Cook with their trusting deep blue eyes, who were being sexually abused by their mom's boyfriends.

Nick Newcomb comes next with his unrepentant gray eyes, who killed a family in cold blood and then was afraid to serve time for his crime.

Mary Butler with her distant staring dark green eyes, who had an eating disorder.

Even Shirley with her loving light brown eyes is

part of the parade. While I did not kill her directly, she did die because of the show. So I am still
responsible. If there had been no *Capping S'ers* television show, she might still be alive. Shirley had done
nothing wrong. She didn't want to die. I'm sure she
fought her attacker aggressively. She wanted nothing
more than to live life to its fullest. What would she
think, I wonder, that she is part of my parade of eyes?

I feel the weight of all those eyes. It weighs
me down until I feel I am about to be pressed out
through the bottom of the mattress. After the parade
of eyes comes the smell. The smell of freshly spurting
blood. Their blood all smells the same and different at
the same time, each one combining with the group before
to become one giant stink.

Lastly is the chorus line dance. While the
Capping S'ers theme music plays in my head, and the
Capping S'ers flags wave in the background, I see their
eyes as they looked at me when I studied their necks.
Then the smell of their blood, the fall of their
bodies, and then the look of their eyes after they bled
out. Then the next one who died at my hands. Then the
next, and the next, and the next. After every show,
the dance takes a little longer, and the weight is a
little heavier.

That is my after-show routine.

"Welcome back. I am Phil Ebenezer. I have a PhD
in clinical psychology. On our third show in season
three, we had an S'er named Frank Peterson from Long
Beach. My hometown. He was a poor lost soul. I mean,
the guy felt he had no purpose in life. He kept going,
'Why am I here?' I don't know. Because you are? Now
make the best of it. Not this guy. He said he was a
failure at everything he tried. And brother, he tried
them all. He had a list of jobs that he had failed at

that was a mile long. Barber, fork-lift driver, dog walker, accountant, janitor, and vice president, just to name a few. Anyway, he was successful at not stepping away during the Capp, so he isn't such a loser now, is he? We'll talk about episode four right after showing this Capp."

Meanwhile, I was becoming even more famous. I moved out of my condo and into a mansion that the studio let me have for free. Me, all alone, rattling around that big empty place. I tried to accept being a celebrity by having friends, throwing parties, and cutting in line at clubs. There were people throwing themselves at me. I even let myself catch a few. Before long, there were people living in the mansion that I didn't know and would rarely see. All for the free booze, drugs and sex. I could hear them at night.

I remember the first time I had sex with a boy. He did all the right things. He touched my breasts, kissed my nipples, played with me down there, put his thing in me and moved it in and out until he came. It was like watching a movie about someone else. I enjoyed the kissing part. When we first started doing that, I got warm and my lower parts got tingly. But despite how long we kissed for, the passion never grew past that. After a while, even the kissing got tedious and boring.

Even though I was not responding to the guy's lovemaking, he never noticed. He just went on doing his thing, enjoying every minute of it. After he came, he fell asleep on me. I definitely did not enjoy that. He was heavy. And sweaty. And hairy. He kept wanting to know if it was good for me.

I assured him it was.

He kept wanting to know when we could do it again.

Never.

Thankfully, I transferred to another foster home soon after that and never saw him again.

The first time I had sex with a girl, it was kind of the same thing. She touched my breasts, kissed my nipples, played with me down there, put her fingers inside of me and moved them in and out. I then did the same things to her, but it was still like watching a movie. The kissing was good at first, but the passion never grew. No way was I close to the groaning, grunting, and head tossing like you see in the porn videos.

Overall, I would say I liked being with a girl better. At least a girl wasn't oblivious to what I was or was not feeling. A girl didn't fall asleep on me. A girl wasn't sweaty and hairy. And a girl wasn't too demanding later.

Usually.

"We are back. I am Phil Ebenezer. I have a PhD in clinical psychology. On our fourth show in season three, we had an S'er named Melissa Ruby from San Francisco. She was on the show because she had lost custody of her kids. She had gotten drunk and did some stupid stuff. So, she lost custody of her three kids forever. She was complaining that she can't have her old life back. She ruined it forever, all because of a few stupid moments. Said that since she couldn't have her old life back, she didn't want to go on living. So, she came on the show, became an S'er, and got her wish. We'll talk about the next episode right after this."

I can't say that everyone was a fan of the show. It wasn't long before I started receiving death threats from friends and families of S'ers who had died. It bothered me at first, and I even tried reasoning with the early ones.

I told them that they could step away. That they didn't have to do it. Anything they did after that wasn't my fault. What if they had stepped back, walked out of the studio, and got hit by a bus? Would that be my fault too?

"To resume our show, I am Phil Ebenezer. I have a PhD in clinical psychology. On our fifth show in season three, we had an S'er named Pamela Burnett. She lived in Oakland. Her problem was that her house burnt down. Now compared to some stories we have heard on this show, that doesn't seem like a very big deal. Of course, having all the rest of her family still inside while she watched it burn from the street probably didn't help. Also, how about the way those arson investigators talked to her? Downright insulting, that was. Oh well, maybe she did do it. Either way, she didn't want to go on living, so she came on the show, and now she is dead too. Good riddance, I say. I didn't like her. We'll talk about episode six right after airing the Capp."

One night, early in season two, before I had bodyguards, I heard a hammering at my front door. Maybe I wouldn't have opened it if I hadn't been half asleep, but open it I did. I had just unlocked the deadbolt and turned the handle when the door flew open, slamming into the wall with a boom and knocking me backwards. I fell on my ass as a man rushed in and stuck a gun in my face.

"I'm going to kill you!" he shouted.

"Wait. What?"

"I'm going to kill you," he repeated.

"But why?"

"Because you took away my wife. Killed her on that damn TV show of yours."

"I don't kill people. She volunteered to be on the show. Probably months in advance. Where were you when she did that?"

"We've been separated. For a while." He started crying and said, "How am I going to live without her?"

"Well, if you have been separated, for a while, you are already living without her. Aren't you?"

"Yeah, but I don't like it. I'm not happy."

"So I've gathered."

After a moment of silence, I added, "You should find a good therapist. Someone who can help you cope with your loss."

"Maybe I should just go on that show of yours. Just end it all."

"Well, you could apply if you like. If you want, I can put in a good word for you."

"You would do that? After I busted in here and all?"

"Sure, why not. Anything for a friend."

"Well, thanks. That's right big of you."

He stood there looking at me still on the floor.

He started walking toward the door. "I guess I'll be going now."

"Okay. See ya."

I went over to the door, locked it, and leaned against it, breathing a sigh of relief. It was the very next day when I told Brian that I needed a bodyguard, and more deadbolts.

However, I found out that generally once someone makes up their mind to avenge something, it is hard to convince them otherwise. I don't know if my bodyguard ever saved my life or not. There were only a couple times when shots were fired in my direction, and I was hustled away. Were those shots fired at me? I don't know.

Hollywood has a lot of violence, and it seemed to be getting worse. I took to staying home more. Ordering pizza in and watching TV. Locking myself in.

"Hello, everyone. I am Phil Ebenezer. I have a PhD in clinical psychology. On our sixth show in season three, we had an S'er named Liz Russell from Anaheim. This middle-aged single mom came on the show to kill herself because she had an overwhelming desire to kill someone. It didn't matter who. She had no one in mind. She just felt this overpowering urge to kill. Wonder what was driving that? I blame it on the evening news. All the violence they show on that. Riots, murder, and such, every single night. Why, it would drive anyone to have those urges. Sometimes, even I get the urge to wring someone's neck. Like every time I do an interview. Oh well, she came on the show and did a successful Capp, so she is not killing anyone now. So this show did save someone's life. It could have been yours. We'll talk about episode seven right after this."

I sometimes worry about how violent California is becoming. Every day you hear about more riots, more murders, more home invasions, more hit and runs, more robberies, and more looting. I never leave my mansion anymore. I have three bodyguards now. I ordered everyone else out.

The guards are quiet, and they tend to hang out in the kitchen, a room I seldom use. My voice echoes when I speak, which is also rarely. Mainly it is the slap of my bare feet on the marble tile that is the only sound to hear.

I sometimes wonder if *Capping S'ers* is making things worse. Is our weekly display of blood and death saying that this type of behavior is okay off the show? Am I becoming a role model for criminals and insane idiots? Is this show driving social behavior or reflecting it?

"Now, back to it. I am Phil Ebenezer. I have a PhD in clinical psychology. On the seventh show in season three, we had an S'er named Stuart Hill from Los Angeles. This character had a philosophical desire to die. I mean, he had it all figured out, with pie charts and everything. He wasn't depressed or had anything wrong with him. For him, it was all about control. He knew he was going to die someday. This way, it would be on his own terms. Not some random event. He had put all his affairs in order before he came on the show. He was ready to go. And now he is gone. Good riddance. We'll talk about episode eight right after this Capp."

I get lots of fan mail. I don't remember most of them. A lot of them are death threats. That and marriage proposals. I do remember this one, however, because it was the shortest one I ever got:

> *Dear Capper:*
>
> *Thanks for killing my brother. We can use the money.*
>
> *Sincerely,*
>
> *George Jones*

Another letter I remember because it was so creepy:

Dear Ricky,

You don't mind if I call you just by your first name, do you? I feel I know you so well even though we have never met. I have spent so much time praying for you that I can feel our souls touch.

I want you to know that I forgive you. I know that you didn't kill our son because you are a bad person. I don't get that feeling about you at all. I think you were just an instrument of the devil, and you just could not resist the temptation. The temptation of money and fame. I forgive you for not being able to resist. I also have temptations. The temptation for revenge is one. It is very strong. But I ask God to free me from this temptation, and he does. Every day.

You too must pray. You must pray for strength, courage, and forgiveness. I will help you pray. Just give me your address, so we can meet, and we will kneel together and pray for the strength and courage to resist temptation. We will pray together for forgiveness for our sins. And together, God will deliver us from evil!

I pray that this message reaches you, and you hear, and you obey.

God Bless,

Pastor John

"And, we are back. I am Phil Ebenezer. I have a PhD in clinical psychology. On our eighth show in season three, we had an S'er named Gregory Sherman.

He lived in San Diego. He was a certifiable paranoid schizophrenic. Had all the symptoms. I have a PhD, so I should know. We let him rant and rave for a while. Talked about the voices in his head. How everyone was out to get him. Accused me of being a spy. He was off his meds, obviously. When it got to be time, he came out, and we Capped him. Kind of boring, actually. We'll talk about episode nine right after we show this."

I try to visit my sister every day. I sit by her side and hold her hand. I tell her about the show. They say they have it on the TV for her but, of course, she can't tell me what she thinks of it.

I tell her how the Capp went. What new element I want to insert that Brian keeps turning down. Or what level of difficulty I want to reach but will never get the chance. Longer Capps, more in-lines. For me, it is all about the challenge of the throw. But eventually, I talk about the S'er. What they looked like. How they reacted to the setting. How they died. Their eyes.

My sister's condition has worsened as the sur-geries continue, one after another. She never seems to recover from one before she has the next one. Then the infections, organs failing, and heart stopping. They aren't fixing her; they are killing her. And again, it is all my fault.

Eventually, the doctors tell me there is nothing else they can do for her. That she can't be fixed. She is in a coma, being kept alive by machines, and they want me to say it is okay to pull the plug.

Before she slipped into the coma, I listened to her moans, and I looked into those pale green eyes. Even then, she seemed to be pleading with me to let her go. Or so I thought. I held her. I cried. I had caused her all this pain. I had destroyed her body, first with the car wreck, and now with these wasted medical procedures. They knew they couldn't fix her as they promised. They just said that to get me to do the show. Besides all the other lives that I have had a hand in ending too early, I can add my sister's.

I wait until we are alone, and I pull the star out of my backpack. I take my sister's hand and cut into it with one point of the star. I watch as her blood covers the point. I hold my sister's fingers on that point while I grasp a different tip.

I am in my sister's mind. I feel what she felt growing up, being mad at me for tormenting her, but also understanding that was how things had to be. I feel how she felt in bed at night, giggling and pretending to be asleep as I stroked her arm and cheek. I feel everything her body felt crashing around inside that car. I feel as trapped as she feels, stuck in a body that won't respond to her commands but with a mind that can't stop trying. I share her pleasure in watching animals on TV, running free and living their lives with no restrictions. My arms hurt as hers did when my dad smashed them with my baseball bat because she couldn't hold onto a glass, and it broke when it hit the floor. I feel the pride she felt when she watched me throw the star for the first time and later got my own TV show. I feel the sadness she feels when an S'er dies. I understand as she understands that this was something else I had to do, like when we were kids and I tormented her. And while she knew it was impossible, she didn't blame me for wanting to fix her. But most of all, I feel the forgiveness that she feels toward me. She doesn't hold me at fault for the car wreck, or for her broken body, or for anything else.

And I desire, as if it is my own wish, her desire for it all to end.

My sister, lost in her coma, strapped in a hospital bed, confined to a wheelchair for years, unable to communicate except with grunts, groans, and her eyes, has set me free. It is time for me to do the same.

I tell them to pull the plug and watch as she takes her last breath.

Did I just kill someone else? I suppose I did. But I know, this time, that what I did is fulfill the wishes of someone who wanted—and had a good reason—to die. I don't have to mourn my sister's death. I can, instead, celebrate her freedom, attained at long last. That certainly is better than what I experience on the show. Am I doing the same there or no? Freeing someone? Should I be celebrating? How can I tell?

And who am I going to make my confessions to now?

"In case you have forgotten, I am Phil Ebenezer. I have a PhD in clinical psychology. On our next to last show in season three, we had an S'er named Ginger Smith from Santa Ana. This poor girl had some terrible parents. She felt that she couldn't live up to their standards. They kept telling her she should achieve this, or strive for that, and what a failure she was. She was so confused that she didn't know what she wanted. She didn't know what to do or what would work. She became so frightened of failure that she froze and stopped moving. Stopped talking, too. Made for an interesting interview. Her brother told us all about it. We had to carry her to her spot in the Capp, but she stood there okay. Didn't move. Didn't step away. After the break following the Capp, we will talk about the final show of season three."

"Brian, I want out."

"Out? What do you mean, out?"

"Out. Out of the show. Out of killing people. Out of my life."

"Well, you can't get out. You're in too deep now. What about the mansion? Your friends? What about me?"

"You can have the mansion. That was all your doing. I don't have any friends, not really. Move me back into the condo. And you? You can go to hell."

"What about the Governor? He is depending on you."

I hesitate before I respond in a reduced voice, "I guess he can go to hell too."

Brian chuckles, "Bad attitude. How about a little vacation? A little R and R is all you need. Pick a place. Rest up. Get refreshed. The show will pick up the tab. We will move you while you are gone."

I stare at Brian for a few minutes. "Okay," I agree. "I don't care where. Send me someplace where they don't know me."

"No problem, friend. I'll make all the arrangements."

"Hello, everyone. I am Phil Ebenezer. I have a PhD in clinical psychology. For the final show of season three, we had two S'ers. We didn't put them together butt to cheek like we did the twins in episode seven of season two. Instead, we had the first S'er, Vickie Thomas from San Jose, in the rope's position between the first and second in-lines. The second S'er, Thomas Summers from Los Angeles, was positioned in the normal S'er spot between the second and third in-line. Hey, they both have Thomas in their name! Isn't that funny? Anyway, first time we ever tried that, and it presented no problems at all. Just made the line a little longer. Positioned the final post a little closer to the audience, but they seemed to love it.

Vickie Thomas spent the whole interview chanting. Really couldn't understand a word she said. My 3

X 5 card claimed that she was starting a new religion. Was going to be another Jesus Christ. Don't you have to perform a few miracles first?

Thomas Summers was the kind of S'er I can understand. He had cancer when he was younger. Supposedly got cured. It took years. Well, after eighteen months of being cancer-free, it came back. More aggressive. More advanced. It was terminal. He was dying and was tired of living in pain. Glad to help him along. Like I said, the Capp was perfect. The audience loved it."

I get ready to turn off the TV.

"Right now, plans are being made for season four. Big plans. I don't know what they are yet, but I'm sure they will be big. See you next season, everyone!"

Brian did make all the arrangements. During the ten-week break after the conclusion of our third season, he shipped me off to Crescent City. It is a town tucked away in the upper left-hand corner of the state. It is about as far away from Hollywood as you can get. I didn't think he would be able to find any place where I wasn't known, but I ended up in a little cabin in amongst the redwood trees. This place had no phone, no radio and no television. Very quiet. Very peaceful. Very empty. It was a short drive to town and the beach, and the people there didn't recognize me, or at least, pretended not to.

Northern California always had that 'State of Jefferson' kind of attitude. I didn't see any violence up there. No riots or murder or looting. I wondered if my TV shows were even broadcast up there. And what about across the border? In Oregon? I knew the roads were barricaded, so there was no traffic between the two states. But what if I started walking north through the woods? Was every inch of the border guarded? Or was there a wall, like there was with Mexico? What was life like in Oregon? Was there the same level of violence? Economic depression? A TV show like mine? Was there a star somewhere in Oregon? Or some other state?

I spent two weeks staring at the trees and reviewing my life. Was mankind better or worse off for my having been born? Had I used my talent for good or evil? Was I an angel of mercy or the devil of death?

Why do people want to kill themselves? Why do so many of them want to be S'ers? What was so horrible in their lives that they couldn't stand it anymore? Was suicide the best way to deal with their problems? Even though I didn't want to listen to the S'ers as they told their stories; I had. From what I had heard, it seemed like most of them just wanted someone to talk to. They just wanted their story told. They just needed a little sympathy, not death. Was there a chemical imbalance that was making them do it? Could they be 'cured' with some drug? What if my show offered counseling instead of death? Would anyone watch that?

Was *Capping S'ers* a good thing or a bad thing? We helped the families left behind with money. Was that enough? Was it even needed? If the S'er had jumped out of a window instead, the families would not have gotten anything. Does that mean the show was doing good? Does that mean the show was right? Did some people watch the show and decide they didn't want to die? Or had we glorified killing yourself so much that even more people want to do it, and do it on air?

And what about picking which S'er goes on the show. Weren't we picking who was going to live and who was going to die? Were we playing God? What about the ones not picked? Did they wind up killing themselves anyway, or were they somehow saved? Did anyone ever check up on them and see? What effect did the S'er's death have on their families and friends? What about that impact? We don't even talk about that on my show. They did it one time but decided that it was too boring. All that crying and stuff. Did I just come up with a great idea for a spin off?

Obviously, I had more questions than answers. Actually, I didn't have any answers at all. When the two weeks were up, I was no closer to knowing what I was doing than I was when I first got there, so I began the long trip back. My sister was gone. What motivation do I have to do the show anymore? Was I quitting? To do what? Or was I going to keep doing it because I didn't know what else to do?

Season Four, Episode One

CAPPING S'ERS
XCAL - 1
10-11 pm
New "Jacob Bryan"
S4/EP01, (2019), The premier of Season 4 of the show that highlights one individual who desires to commit suicide. With an assist from thrower Ricky Fordham, the individual may go through with it or not.

When I got back to Hollywood was when I heard about Sally. Sally was the girl who was on the last show of season one and had backed away but came back and told me about getting paid, so I ended up not doing that show either. So basically, she had been on the show twice and was still alive.

Well, she used to be still alive.

According to Brian, the network was airing a two-hour special showing memorable Capps of the past when a mob attacked her in her home and killed her. The mob was angry and felt cheated that she hadn't died during a Capp, so they killed her themselves. One of the leaders of the mob was quoted as saying, "She wanted to be dead. Now she is." The studio was letting the surviving family members keep the show appearance money.

How nice of them.

I must get off this show. Whether the show is good or bad. Whether I am killing people or saving people. I must get away from all those eyes. I can only think of one way that would free me once and for all. It may be wrong, but I must do it.

Since the beginning, I tried to hold myself apart from the show. I didn't want to know the S'ers. I didn't want to know their names. I didn't want to know their stories. I only wanted to do a throw. That was all I wanted. But I do know all the S'ers. I do know their names. I know their stories.

The Capps are set in stone. The number of in-lines doesn't change. Their positions are always the same. There is even tape on the floor now, so I don't have any challenge at all anymore. I feel like the show is engulfing me, swallowing me up a bit at a time, and I have lost all interest in it. I must escape, and I must do it soon.

Before I go insane.

"I want to do a bigger Capp. The biggest ever. And I want to dedicate it to Sally."

"How many S'ers?" asks Brian, intrigued.

"Three. Make it a two-hour show. I want five in-lines. That's never been done before. People say it can't be done, but I feel that I can do it. I know I can do it. We can have a first, an S'er, a second and third, another S'er, a fourth, an S'er, a fifth, and then the final post. We'll have to do it outside. There's not enough room in this studio. And let's do it at night, so the audience can see the sparks fly."

"Wait. With that kind of lineup, we could have four S'ers. One between each in-line."

"Sure," I agree. "Four. Whatever you want. And I want to do the whole season in a week. A show every night. So it's over in a week, not ten weeks."

"Why a week? What happens after that?"

"We take a two-week break, then we start a new season. Sixteen shows. The whole nine yards."

"Why a week?"

"Well, I met a girl…" I lie.

"Okay, I get it." Brian is sneering. "But one week is not enough."

"Not enough what?"

"That's not enough to make the network give up a ten-week schedule. Do you know how much advertising revenue they would lose over that period? A ton."

"Then let's go bigger."

"Bigger how?"

"I don't know. But I still want to do it in a week," I insist.

Brian speculates, "How about we start with one S'er on Monday then add one more per day. We go to two, three, four. Why we would end up on Sunday with seven S'ers and eight in-lines. That's fifteen people. And that would be," Brian calculates in his head, "twenty-eight S'ers in all for the week. The network would exchange ten S'ers for twenty-eight. Plus add in all the hype about the difficulty factor."

"I can't. Fifteen is impossible. Why, with a ten-degree deflection for each in-line, start to finish the star would make an eighty-degree turn. Even I can't do that."

"Because it is impossible is why you have to do it. Why else would the network agree to the change?"

"Will they agree to a one-week schedule? Trying to do it over ten weeks will lose all the excitement. It has to be just one week to keep the hype rolling."

"What are you going to do next season? After a seven S'er Capp? How can you top that?"

"Don't worry about that. I will come up with something."

"Okay. I like it. When can you be ready by?"

"I'll need at least three months for set up and practice. We'll need more in-lines. And more S'ers."

"Don't worry about getting more S'ers. We have way too many applicants already. You're talking about making TV history here. Yeah, we'll have plenty of S'ers."

"What are you going to do about airtime?" I ask. "Each S'er takes thirty-five minutes: five for flavor and thirty for the interview. If you added thirty minutes for each S'er, then by Sunday, the show would be—"

"Four hours long. No. No one is going to wait around for four hours for a thirty-second Capp. It doesn't matter how historic. We'll add fifteen minutes for each additional S'er, so on Sunday, the show will be… two and a half hours. Yeah, that will work. We'll just cut down on the interview time. Phil seems to be having trouble with that part of it anyway."

"Okay. I'm willing to try. I'll even slip up a little on Saturday night, so it will look like a certain fail on Sunday."

"Okay. The network won't be easy to convince. They will have to reschedule shows. We'll need lots and lots of hype. Okay, let's do it. Hey, maybe I can even get the Governor to come back for another visit on the final show. He would love it."

"Ah, great. Thanks, Brian."

I spend my every waking moment of those three months working on bigger Capps. It is the start of a new season, so two of my five in-lines are new, plus I am adding five more. It takes a while to settle them down and get them to trust me. The hype by the network is incredible. It seems like they are running promos for it at every commercial break all day long. It isn't until three days before that fated week that I get a seven S'er Capp that works. I am especially interested in where the star ends up on the final post. The height and placement are crucial if what I have in mind is going to work.

I am standing by the bleachers. They added another section but still had to turn away almost all of the huge crowd of people who wanted to get in to watch. I heard that tickets that were free for our very first season are now costing over 5,000 California dollars each. Not sure who is getting the money. Maybe Brian? Every person in attendance is wearing neckwear. They doubled the number of spotlights. There must be at least a hundred *Capping S'ers* flags ringing the bleachers.

"Welcome, California, to the start of season four! If you have been following all the hype and advertising about this show, and I assume you have been or else you wouldn't be here, then you know we are deviating from our normal Sunday night, ten-week season. This season is one week long, with a new show every night. As the week progresses, the shows will get longer, there will be multiple S'ers, more in-lines, and the Capps will get more and more dangerous. Yes folks, by the time this season is over, you will have seen things that have never been seen before! It will thrill you and, yes, even shock you. Welcome to *Capping S'ers* season four!"

The spotlights go crazy. I notice a toddler sitting on his mother's lap chewing on a plastic replica of the *Capping S'ers* star.

"Today is Monday. The first day of the new season. For this show, it will be our normal sixty minutes. We are in our normal time slot, just on a different day, and we will have just one S'er. His name is Jacob Bryan. We are going to visit him in his hometown of Riverside. We are going to interview him live here in our studio, and then LIVE we will watch the Capp and see if Jacob does commit suicide or not. Stick around, it is going to be a GREAT show. We will be back after the commercial break."

I look at the stage floor. It is the usual line up for a Capp, three in-lines and one S'er. The toddler in the audience is sucking on his thumb, and his mom is holding the plastic replica of the star.

Commercial.

They doubled the size of the big screen at the back of the studio. It is massive. On it, while playing the *Capping S'ers* theme music, the camera fades in on a thirty-five-year-old man standing on a sidewalk next to an arched entry that reads Mission Inn. He is frowning as he says, "The Mission Inn is the largest Mission Revival Style building in the former United States. My girlfriend and I used to stay here often when we were together."

The same man is standing outside a building with a large aqua sign that says, California Citrus State Historical Park. "This is the birthplace of California's citrus industry. What is left of it, anyway. My name is Jacob Bryan, and I am ready to commit suicide."

Jacob is shown standing next to barricades and a gate blocking the entrance to a parking lot. He says, "This was the UCR Botanical Gardens. It is closed now, but it used to be forty acres of unusual plants and over four miles of walking trails. All has been plowed under to erect a tent city for the homeless. My girlfriend and I never made it here before it closed."

The camera follows Jacob walking into a plain apartment building. He says, "My girlfriend and I shared an apartment here. But she is gone now."

Jacob walks down a hallway and into a room. The camera pans to show the small room containing only a couch and a small television. The walls contain no posters, pictures, or decorations of any kind. Jacob sits on the couch. He says, "I spend all my time here. I am alone now. There is no one else here."

"We will get up close and personal with Jacob right after these commercial messages."

I adjust the position of the first pole holding the rope. The toddler is asleep in his mother's lap while she is still holding the plastic replica. Business as usual.

Commercial.

The snack table is longer. There seems to be more stagehands walking around. Also, there are a lot of people standing around doing nothing. Where did all these people come from? Is Brian selling backstage passes? Some of the newcomers try to talk to me but I ignore them and walk away.

On stage, Jacob is wearing a sweater with patches at the elbows.

"Hello, everyone. I am Phil Ebenezer. I have a PhD in clinical psychology. Now Jacob, tell me why you want to end your life."

"My girlfriend left me. Now I'm all alone."

"I see. But why do you want to kill yourself?"

"My girlfriend left me. Now I'm all alone."

"Jacob, girls leave guys every day. It just happens. It's happened to me plenty of times. That's nothing to kill yourself over."

"It is for me."

"I can't believe I'm trying to talk someone out of being an S'er. No, Jacob. It isn't. Just get over it, man."

Jacob's eyes squeeze shut, "No. Don't say that. I can't eat. I can't sleep. I just want to die."

"Okay man, it's your funeral. Don't forget to stay tuned after the show for your XCAL 1 evening news, the only official state newscast. Remember folks, if you didn't see it on XCAL 1, it didn't happen."

Commercial.

"And we are back. Some things never change. Brian says I have twenty minutes to fill before we can do the Capp. So, Jacob, what do you want to talk about?"

"My girlfriend?"

"Man, you are obsessed with that girl. Get over it. No, let's talk about something else. Tell me the most amazing thing about yourself that you can think of."

After a couple of moments, Jacob confessed, "Well, I remember this one night. It was in the summer. It was hot, so I had my window open. I woke up about three in the morning because I smelled smoke. I looked out my window and saw that my neighbor's house was on fire. I quickly jumped out of bed, threw on some clothes, and went over there. I pounded on their door and yelled, and finally they all came running out. The mom and two kids. The dad was away on a business trip."

"So no one was hurt, and you saved that family's lives?"

"Yeah. No one was hurt."

"So you are a hero."

"I guess. I never thought of it like that."

"Jacob, did you ever stop to think that if you had been on this show first, before the fire, that family might all have died that night?"

"I never thought of it like that. Say, can I change my—"

Commercial.

Brian and Phil escort Jacob off the stage and into the back rooms. Brian has his arm around Jacob in a grip almost like a bear hug.

"Welcome back, folks. Sorry for the audio feed going out just before our commercial break. Technical difficulties. Ah, Jacob had to go backstage and can't finish the interview. He was feeling ill. We are going to go to another commercial and then show you some memorial Capps that have happened on this show until it is time for tonight's Capp. Stay tuned."

Commercial.

"Ladies and gentlemen, welcome to the LIVE part of the show. Let me introduce you to Ricky Fordham, our Capper."

I step into camera range and wave to the crowd. They go crazy with shouts and applause.

"Ricky has, through years and years of practice, perfected a technique of throwing a star that will allow Jacob, by simply standing still, to end his life. So, without further ado, we'll proceed to the LIVE Capp where anything can happen."

Brian escorts Jacob to where I am standing. Jacob is walking a little wobbly. I study Jacob's neck. The throbbing jugular vein can be plainly seen. I pull back slowly to see Jacob's face and his drooping, half-hidden eyes. I check Jacob's position by looking up the line, then down the line.

I lean in and whisper, "You don't have to do this. Just step away, and the star won't hurt you." Jacob doesn't react.

I walk to my starting position. Brian is still standing next to Jacob. I glance over to the medical team. They look ready. I extend my left arm with its mangled hand, the cut in my right hand itching furiously. I cock my right arm back and throw the star. It flies straight at the first in-line, then bounces off.

The star cuts the rope as it passes by on the way to the second man. Brian grabs hold of Jacob's arm. The cut portion of the rope falls to the ground. The star bounces off the second in-line. It flies on toward Jacob, grazes by him, cutting his neck in the process.

His body shudders. Brian lets go, and Jacob falls to the ground, blood pulsing from his body. I stare at the pool of blood as another *clang* is heard, then a *thud*.

The doctor walks slowly over and watches Jacob bleed out. He gives the crowd a thumbs up.

The *Capping S'ers* theme music starts up. I am still standing in my throwing spot. The in-lines are staring at Jacob lying dead on the ground. His half-hidden eyes are closed. Brian is walking back to the stage. The star is stuck in the last post. The crowd is going crazy with shouts and cheers.

The toddler is still asleep while his mom, standing up and holding him, is cheering and throws the plastic replica of the *Capping S'ers* star straight up into the air.

Commercial.

I am excited after the show. The end is in sight. If I just get thru this week, then everything will be better.

Season Four, Episode Two

CAPPING S'ERS
XCAL - 1
10-11:15 pm
New "Brenda Jones & Diana Espinosa"
S4/EP02, (2019), The Tuesday edition of the week-long Season 4 of the show that highlights two individuals who desire to commit suicide. With an assist from thrower Ricky Fordham, the individuals may or may not go through with it.

"Welcome, California, to the Tuesday show of season four! For the first time ever, we are coming to you on a Tuesday night. As the week progresses, the shows will get longer, there will be multiple S'ers, and the Capps will get more and more dangerous. Yes, folks, by the time this season is over, you will have seen things that have never been seen before! It will thrill you and, yes, even shock you. Welcome to the special Tuesday edition of *Capping S'ers* season four!"

I am standing in the shadows of the studio looking out at the seated audience. My twin sister used to sit out there. I notice a man holding a sign that says, 'Marry Me Ricky' standing next to another man holding a sign that says, 'Repent Devil Woman.'

My thoughts go back to what happened to me earlier today. After last night's show, the limo ride back to my condo, and the parade of eyes, I fell asleep at two in the morning. Three hours later I am startled awake as two men drag me out of bed, grab a robe and hustle me out the door.

"What the hell!" I scream.

In the hall, my bodyguard moves out of the way to let them by. I stare at him, "David! Why aren't you stopping them?"

He shrugs his shoulders.

"Who are you? Where are you taking me?"

"Shut up lady! Someone wants to see you."

Lady? I don't think I have ever been called that before. Don't they know who I am?

They throw me in the back of a new stretch limo and speed away from the curb.

I am terrified and stunned but all I can think to ask is, "Nice car. Where did you get it?" I haven't seen a new car in years.

They roll up the privacy glass without answering.

"Not talkative, huh?"

I am getting more and more angry as the ride continues in silence. I watch the occasional lights as we drive up into the hills. It is still dark when we finally pull onto the grounds of an expansive mansion. The place is lit up so brightly that it is almost like daylight.

Well, whomever is abducting me has taste, and money. I wonder if they also have some fresh coffee.

I am escorted into a room that looks like a library or a fancy den and left alone. Well, at least they didn't tie me up. I look around in awe. I have seen some fancy places but nothing as nice as this. It is only a few minutes later when in walks a man.

The Governor.

Aw, shit. This is not going to be good.

"Hello Ricky. Good to see you again."

"Wish I could say the same. What's the big idea? Dragging me out of bed in the middle of the night and bringing me here?"

"Yes, sorry for the inconvenience, but I have been intrigued by our last encounter."

"What about it?"

"Don't be coy, Ricky. It doesn't become you. You know what happened the last time we both touched the star."

"I don't know how to control that."

"Doesn't matter. I am interested to know what happens when three people simultaneously hold the star."

"I wouldn't know. Nothing like that ever happened before or since. It may be that it just works for us two, for some reason. Or only worked just that one time. Or,… I don't know."

"Yes, all intriguing questions. Ones I would like to pursue further."

"Well, I would love to accommodate you, but you see, I left home kind of in a hurry. So I didn't have time to pick up things for our visit."

"Oh, don't worry about that. I have had the star here for hours."

"What! Of course you have! Apparently, my condo has an open-door policy for you! You can break in whenever you like and take whatever you want while my bodyguard just stands by and watches!"

"Oh, there was no breaking in. Your doorman, who is not a bodyguard in my opinion, was quite willing to open the door for us. Oh, by the way, he has been replaced by one who is, shall we say, more suitable."

"More loyal, more likely."

"Well, like I said. I have some questions about the star."

"And I don't have answers."

"Oh, I think you do. I can't seem to activate the star's 'special features'. When I hold it with someone else; nothing happens. I think you know how it works. Which is why I had you brought here."

"I don't. What happened before must have been some kind of freak accident."

"All I ask is for you to hold the star. That's all. Then you can go home, safe and sound."

"You better let me go. I have a show to do tonight, you know."

"I don't give a damn about that stupid show! That is just something to appease the masses. Stupid, uneducated masses." He takes a deep breath. "Just hold the star, please."

In walk three men. Two are beefy; one of whom holds the star.

"John," the Governor says, "let me introduce you to our latest guest. This is Ricky. She will be assisting us today."

"I recognize her from the show. What will she be assisting us with?"

"Our little chat. Remember, that I invited you here for a little chat."

"Yes, I was wondering when we would get around to that. Are we going to be holding onto that star thing again?"

"Indeed, we are."

The Governor has us all sit on a couch, him in the middle. We each hold a point of the star. I instantly enter the mind of the Governor and can see what he wants to chat with John about and what the Governor intends for him after that interview. I can also feel the Governor's presence exploring my every memory, thought and emotion. John's presence is absent.

"See," I say to the Governor, "I told you it wouldn't work. So, I'll just be off now."

I stand but the Governor pulls me back down.

"Just a minute."

We sit there in silence until the Governor says, "I think your theory is correct, Ricky. I did cut my finger and bleed on the star before we both touched it. That, and you, are the key."

To one of the beefy men, the Governor orders, "Cut off one of his fingers."

"What!" John shouts as he jumps up.

He is pushed back down. A knife suddenly appears, and a finger falls to the floor. The Governor makes sure that some blood squirting out falls on a point of the star.

"Now," says the Governor, "let's try this again. Hold his fingers on one of the points."

This time John is accessible to both the Governor and me.

After the Governor is satisfied, he orders John to be removed and disposed of. I know what that means.

"Well, thank you, Ricky. You have been most helpful. My men will take you back now."

I don't need to ask what happened to John. I don't need to ask what the Governor plans for me. As I sit in the car, staring down at the bloody star in my lap, I don't have to ask any questions at all, because I know the answers.

I have been in the Governor's mind and it is a dark horrific place.

"This show will be seventy-five minutes long. The nightly news will be on fifteen minutes later than normal, and we have two S'ers. Their names are Brenda Jones and Diana Espinosa. We are going to visit Brenda in her hometown of Stockton and Diana in her hometown of Fontana. We are going to interview them both live here in our studio, and then LIVE we will watch the Capp and see if Brenda and Diana do commit suicide. Stick around. It's going to be great! We will be back after the commercial break."

The man holding the sign that says, 'Marry Me Ricky' and the man standing next to him holding the sign that says, 'Repent Devil Woman' are reading each other's signs.

Commercial.

On screen, while playing the *Capping S'ers* theme music, a fifty-year-old woman standing on a sidewalk next to a sign that says San Joaquin Delta College. She is smiling as she says, "Here in the Atherton Auditorium is where the Stockton Symphony used to play. They were the third oldest professional orchestra in California. There are no orchestras left in California anymore. I don't know about in other states. If there are any left."

The same woman is standing outside a building with a sign that says University of the Pacific. "UOP was the oldest chartered university in California before it closed. My name is Brenda Jones, and I am ready to commit suicide."

Brenda is standing next to a PV-2D Harpoon aircraft. She says, "This was the Stockton Field Aviation Museum before it closed. This aircraft is from World War II. Now, no one is caring for it, and it is just rusting away."

Next shot is of Brenda walking into an upscale apartment building. She says, "This is where I live. I had a house nearby, but with my husband gone and my children fully grown, this is all I need."

We see Brenda walking down a hallway and through a door. The camera pans to show the small, tastefully decorated apartment. Brenda sits on the couch. She says, "I don't go out much. I do like watching *Capping S'ers*, though. It is the highlight of my week."

"We will get up close and personal with Brenda right after these commercial messages."

I adjust the position of the second in-line. It's a woman. At least she has a top on. If it can be called that. It looks like a black leather bra. Good thing she doesn't have to move. It looks like her boobs would fall out if she twitched.

The man holding the sign that says, 'Marry Me Ricky' and the man holding the sign that says, 'Repent Devil Woman' are hitting each other with their signs.

Commercial.

Phil looks ready. Brenda is wearing a women's three-piece suit.

"Hello, everyone. I am Phil Ebenezer. I have a PhD in clinical psychology. Now Brenda, tell me why you want to end your life."

"I have terminal cancer."

"I see. I think we already did that one."

"Excuse me?"

Phil picks up his 3 X 5 card and taps his knee with it. "Brenda, I don't know what to ask you. I can certainly see why you want to die on your own terms. What kind of cancer do you have?"

"Breast cancer."

"And how long did they give you to live?"

"I'm already past that date. It is in remission now. But it will be back. I have been through this twice before. Chemotherapy. Radiation. I can't do it again. I just want to die."

"Well, shouldn't you take some time to enjoy the remission? Do something with the time that is left?"

"Like what?"

"I don't know. Something. Isn't there anything that you always wanted to do but haven't done yet?"

"No. My bucket list has all been checked off."

"What about your kids?"

"They are all grown and moved away. They don't have the time or money to come sit with me while I take six months to die. This way is just easier and quicker for all concerned. Besides, they will be grateful for the money."

"Okay, well, let's go and get on with it then."

I direct two stagehands to pick up and carry off-camera the pole holding the rope that was between the first and second in-lines. I look over to where the two men with signs were. Their seats are empty.

Commercial.

On screen, while playing the *Capping S'ers* theme music, the camera fades in on a very cute thirty-year-old woman standing on a sidewalk next to a street sign that says Spring Street. She is smiling as she says, "Cruising Spring Street used to be prime time activity here in Fontana. Held on the first Friday of every month, it was the place to see and be seen in your restored classic car. Of course, no one does that anymore with gas prices the way they are."

She is standing outside an art deco style building with an orange sign that says Center Stage Theater. "Center Stage was Fontana's premier theatrical event center before it closed. Originally built in 1937 as a one screen movie theater, it closed in the 1950s, and was then used as an Elks Lodge among various other things. Too bad it never got back to its old glory. My name is Diana Espinosa, and I am ready to commit suicide."

Diana is standing next to sign that says California Speedway. She says, "This was primarily a NASCAR track before it closed. Built on the site of the former Kaiser Steel Mill in 1995 and 1996, they left one tall chimney standing to represent the history here. Now no one is caring for the track, and it is just eroding away. You can see that the chimney has mostly already fallen down."

Diana walks into a stucco duplex. She says, "This is where I live. I used to be married, but I have been divorced now for the past ten years and live alone. We had no children."

Inside, it is a sparsely furnished home. Diana walks into the bedroom and sits on the bed. She says, "This is where I do most of my entertaining. I hardly ever use the living room."

"We will get up close and personal with Diana right after these commercial messages."

I adjust the position of the third in-line.

Commercial.

Diana is in shorts and a crop top.

"Hello, everyone. I am Phil Ebenezer. I have a PhD in clinical psychology. Now Diana, tell me why you want to end your life."

"I like sex."

"I see. I certainly don't see anything wrong with that."

"No. You don't understand. I like sex. A lot."

Phil closes his eyes as he fondles his 3 X 5 card. "So, when you say you like sex a lot, do you mean that when you are having sex, you want it to go on for a long time? Or do you mean that you want sex several times a day?"

"Can I have both?"

"Well, that's agreeable to me. Have you had a lot of sexual partners?"

"Yes. I have trouble saying no."

"Really? What's the worst line that you have ever fallen for?"

"A guy doesn't need a line with me. He just looks at me, and I can tell what he wants."

"To be honest, I am having difficulty seeing what the problem is here."

"Well, this has caused problems in my life. I married my high school sweetheart when I was young, but he got tired of coming home at night to find me in someone else's arms."

"You mean, like a different man every night?"

"Yeah. I would go out shopping, and someone would pick me up. Eventually the word got around, and I would have guys lined up at the door."

"Did you charge any of these gentlemen?"

"No. What do you think I am?"

"Okay. I can see how this might cause some problems in your marriage. What else?"

"Well, there are the diseases. I must have caught every type of STD there is. Also, now I have AIDS."

"And that is why you want to kill yourself? Because you have AIDS?"

Diana shakes her head, "No, I want to kill myself because I hate myself. I am a bad person. I know I shouldn't be sleeping with literally every guy who asks. I hate myself because I just can't say no. I just want to die."

"Okay, well let's go and get on with it then."

I direct two stagehands to pick up and carry off-camera the pole holding the rope that was between the second and third in-lines.

Commercial.

I step into camera range and wave to the crowd. The roar is deafening. I am standing in the first S'er's spot. Brian escorts Brenda to where I am standing. I study Brenda's neck. I pull back to see Brenda's face and her bright, amber colored wide-open eyes. Can't say I care for her heavy makeup, however. Or her choice of color for eyeliner. Purple. Really? I check Brenda's position, then lean in and whisper, "You don't have to do this. Just step away, and the star won't hurt you."

I move to the second S'er's spot. Brian escorts Diana to where I am standing. I study Diana's neck. A shallow cut should do it. I pull back to see Diana's face and her eyes. Clear blue. Makeup is tastefully done. She is staring at me. I check Diana's position, then whisper, "You don't have to do this. Just step away, and the star won't hurt you."

I walk to my starting position, check with medical, cock my arm back, and throw the star. It flies straight at the first in-line, bounces off and flies on toward Brenda, grazes by her, cutting her neck in the process. Her body shudders. She falls to the ground, blood streaming from her body.

I glance at the blood as the star continues to the second in-line, bounces off and flies on toward Diana, grazes by her, cutting her neck. She shudders, falls to the ground, blood streaming. I stare at the growing pools of blood as another *clang* is heard, then a *thud*.

They really need to put in a grate to catch the blood.

The doctor seems confused as to who to attend to. He first goes to Brenda, looks at her and then goes to Diana. I see Brenda raise her hand like she has a question. I go over to her and barely hear her say, "Help."

"Hey Doc. Over here!"

He has his back to me, so I yell again. He comes over and looks at Brenda. He gives the audience a thumbs up. I look down. Blood is still streaming out. I guess she's dead. He didn't check for a pulse or anything.

The *Capping S'ers* theme music starts up after the second thumbs up. The crowd is going crazy with shouts and cheers.

The seats where the men with the signs were, is occupied by two different young men who are chest bumping each other.

Commercial.

Another day closer to the end and two more sets of eyes to add to my nightly parade.

Season Four, Episode Three

CAPPING S'ERS
XCAL - 1
9:30-11 pm
New "Ming-Na Lee, Kristy Nathaniel & Karla Rojas"
S4/EP03, (2019), The Wednesday edition of the week-long Season 4 of the show that highlights three individuals who desire to commit suicide. With an assist from thrower Ricky Fordham, the individuals may go through with it or not.

I am in the makeup chair. People are fussing with my hair, lips, and eyes. Nearly every part of me is being attended to, but my mind is racing with other thoughts. I stare at the star lying on the counter next to me. All the blood has been washed off. It is clean and shiny. Just like it is at the start of any other show.

But what the hell is that thing?

I never questioned it before. I have had it so long and acquired it at such a young age, that I just accepted it.

But what the hell is it?

It is obviously alien. There is nothing like it on earth that I know of or ever heard of. So, that answers the question about other intelligent life. But that answer raises so many more questions.

How did it get to be here on earth?

What is its purpose? Is it supposed to fly? Is it an interrogation device? Is it a memory device?

What other 'special features' does it have? And how do you access them?

How did it get to be in my grandparent's attic?

Who in New York sent it to them? I can still remember the box and the return address, even without the star's help.

Did they ever use it? For what purpose?

There were no instructions in the box with it, so how did they know how to use it? If they did?

Why did they have it?

Oh my God, were they aliens?

If one, or if both of my grandparents are alien, then my mother is as well. Is that why she always acted so strange? And if that is true, I am an alien too. Somewhat diluted, maybe, unless of course, my dad was an alien as well. Are there aliens living among us?

If I am an alien, is that why I always felt so indifferent to everything. To how I grew up? To how I feel about people and sex? Like I'm not really there. Like I'm watching a movie?

In that why I feel so disconnected to what I am doing on the show? Do I feel indifferent? Or do I just not want to get close? To avoid getting hurt or feeling pain when tragedy strikes.

When the star strikes.

In my entire life, I only felt close to three people. My twin, Irene and Sally. Were they aliens? Two of those people are dead and I haven't heard from Irene for years. She could be dead as well.

So many questions and not a single answer.

"Welcome, California, to the Wednesday show of season four! For the first time ever, we are coming to you on a Wednesday night. As the week progresses, the shows will get longer, there will be multiple S'ers and the Capps will get more and more dangerous and impossible. Yes folks, by the time this season is over, you will have seen things that have never been seen before! It will thrill you and, yes, even shock you. Welcome to the special Wednesday edition of *Capping S'ers* season four! It's going to be AWESOME!"

In the audience, I notice a couple caressing each other's neckwear while kissing. Sick. What has California come to?

"We were supposed to have this show outside for the first time, but guess what, it's raining. It never rains in Southern California. So, we are inside. It is tight, but we will manage. This show will be an extended ninety minutes. We are starting thirty minutes early. We are on a different day, and we have, for the very first time, three S'ers. I hope you are tuning in on time and not thirty minutes late. The first S'er's name is Ming-Na Lee. We are going to visit her in her hometown of Los Angeles. The second S'er is Kristy Nathaniel from Arcadia, and the third is Karla Rojas from Baker. We are going to interview them all live here in our studio, and then LIVE we will watch the Capp and see if Ming-Na, Kristy and Karla do commit suicide or not. Stick around. We will be back after the commercial break."

The couple is still caressing each other's neckwear but are not kissing. I don't get it. What is that supposed to mean?

Commercial.

On screen, while playing the *Capping S'ers* theme music, the camera focuses in on a petite twenty-one-year-old Asian girl standing on a sidewalk next to a structure spanning the road with two dragons on top facing each other. She is smiling as she says, "Welcome to Chinatown."

The girl is standing outside Central Plaza. "Opening in 1938, this was one of the first malls. My name is Ming-Na Lee, and I ready to commit suicide."

Ming-Na stands next to a gold statue. She says, "This is Sculpture of Sun Yat-sen, father of Republic of China."

Ming-Na walks up the outside stairs of a brightly painted two-story house. She says, "I live upstairs."

The camera follows Ming-Na through the door. It pans to show the small red and black room. Ming-Na sits on the couch. She says, "I love to walk around the neighborhood. So many pretty sights. Around corner is best chow mein."

"We will get up close and personal with Ming-Na right after these commercial messages."

I adjust the position of the first pole holding a rope. The couple I observed in the audience is talking with their neighbors and showing off their neckwear.

Commercial.

Phil and Ming-Na are seated in chairs slightly facing each other. Ming-Na is wearing shorts and a pale pink blouse.

"Hello, everyone. I am Phil Ebenezer. I have a PhD in clinical psychology. Now Ming-Na, tell me why you want to end your life."

"I have been bullied all my life."

"I see. Tell me more."

"People call me names. Say terrible things. Make me feel hurt all the time. Because they say I don't speak good English."

"Your English sounds fine to me. Ming-Na, what do you do to deal with that hurt?"

"I cut myself."

"Where?"

"Everywhere." She stands and holds out her arms.

The camera zooms in and cut marks can be seen all up and down her arms. She lifts her blouse to reveal her midriff, and the camera sees more cut marks that cross over each other.

"And what do you want to happen now?"

"I want to be in a Capp. I want Ricky to kill me."

"Well, Ricky doesn't kill anyone. She just provides the avenue so you can kill yourself. You can always step away if you change your mind."

"I won't step away."

"All right then. We are going to take a commercial break and be back to meet Kristy Nathaniel."

Commercial.

On screen is an attractive forty-five-year-old woman standing on a sidewalk next to a tree with beautiful pink flowers. She is smiling as she says, "Welcome to the Los Angeles County Arboretum and Botanical Gardens. It is closed now, but we snuck in for this shot."

The woman is standing outside of an empty parking lot with a big blue building in the background. "This was home to the Santa Anita Racetrack, but it is now a homeless camp. My name is Kristy Nathaniel, and I am ready to commit suicide."

Kristy is standing in the middle of a circular lobby. She says, "This is the Huntington Library. We snuck in here also."

Next, Kristy is walking up the sidewalk toward a well maintained older two-story house. She says, "This is where I live."

The camera follows Kristy through the door. She tours the entire house, every single room. She stops in an upstairs bedroom and says, "This was my son's room. He used to play his music too loud and made quite a racket when he had his friends over. My bedroom is directly underneath, and I remember how much I hated the disturbance. I sure would love to be able to hear it now."

"We will get up close and personal with Kristy right after these commercial messages."

I adjust the position of the second pole holding a rope. The couple is still talking with their neighbors and showing off their neckwear.

Commercial.

Kristy is wearing a women's black business suit.

"Hello, everyone. I am Phil Ebenezer. I have a PhD in clinical psychology. Now Kristy, tell me why you want to end your life."

"My son killed himself. Committed suicide. Now I don't want to go on."

"I see. How did he kill himself?"

"Hanged himself in the garage. Attached a rope to one of the rafters while I was out. I came home, hit the button to open the garage door, and there he was, right in front of me."

"I'm so sorry. How has your husband taken this?"

"He's gone, too. Cancer. Six years ago."

Phil holds the 3 X 5 card up against his forehead as he asks, "Kristy, why did your son kill himself?"

"I don't know. He didn't leave a note or anything. Nothing was bothering him that I knew about. I used to get mad at him sometimes, maybe yelled a little. Maybe that was it."

"What did you yell at him about?"

"The normal stuff. Making too much noise. Coming in too late. Not picking up his dirty clothes. Hanging out with the wrong people."

"And how old was he?"

"Twenty-five."

"So, are you ready to do this?"

"Yes."

"All right then. We are going to take a sixty-second break and then be right back with our third S'er. Don't forget to stay tuned after the show for your XCAL 1 evening news, the only official state newscast. Remember folks, if you didn't see it on XCAL 1, it didn't happen."

Commercial.

On screen, a young woman is sitting in a lawn chair next to a vertical structure. She is smiling as she says, "Welcome to Baker, home of the world's tallest thermometer."

The woman is standing alongside a paved two-lane road. "Baker is the gateway to Death Valley National Park. Of course, there are no national parks anymore, but it is still hotter than hell down there. My name is Karla Rojas, and I am ready to commit suicide."

Karla is sitting in a booth with pale blue vinyl seats. She says, "This is the Mad Greek Cafe. I love the pork gyro here, but they are out of pork right now."

Karla walks in the door of a one-story stucco house. She says, "I live here with two roommates, but they aren't home right now."

The camera follows Karla through the living room and into a small bedroom. The bed is unmade, and the floor is cluttered. Karla sits on the bed. She says, "I wish I had air conditioning. These thick old walls keep it pretty cool, but some days it is just too hot."

"We will get up close and personal with Karla right after these commercial messages."

I adjust the position of the third pole holding a rope. The couple are still talking with their neighbors and showing off their neckwear. How long do you need to talk for to describe neckwear? Maybe where they got it and how much they paid for it?

Commercial.

On stage, Karla is wearing shorts, sandals, and a pale blue blouse.

Ming-Na had the same blouse. Just a different color. Interesting. I wonder where they got them. It's a cute blouse. I could use one like it.

"Hello, everyone. I am Phil Ebenezer. I have a PhD in clinical psychology. Now Karla, tell me why you want to end your life."

"It is the only way I know to get off drugs."

"I see. Tell me more."

"I have tried everything. I have been in and out of treatment ten times. Nothing sticks. As soon as I get out of rehab, I start right up again."

Phil refers to a 3 X 5 card that is on a table next to him. He stares at it for a moment before he asks, "Karla, do you like doing drugs?"

"No. I love the feeling when I get high, but they are ruining my life."

"How?"

"I can't afford it. The cost of the drugs and then the cost of the rehab. It is all too much. I wind up doing all sorts of awful things to get them. But I just can't do without."

"And when you get out of rehab, how do you get started back in?"

"Well, my boyfriend is a dealer, so he gives me what I need to start. And after that. Well, I just don't want to talk about what happens then."

"Maybe your boyfriend is the problem. Maybe you need a new boyfriend."

"I can't do that. I love him. And he loves me."

"Obviously. Well, are you ready to end your drug habit once and for all?"

"Yeah."

"All right then. Let's get on with it."

Commercial.

"Welcome back, folks. I forgot this is an extended show. We have about five more minutes to fill. So, Karla, tell me something amazing about yourself."

"I used to be an MMA fighter."

"Wow. That is amazing."

"I had a record of 10-2-0. I fought in the atom weight division."

"Wow. I feel like I should be getting your autograph, or something. So, are you ready for your last big fight?"

"I'm ready."

"Okay. The LIVE Capp follows this."

I direct the stagehands to pick up and carry off-camera the three poles holding rope. The couple is sitting back in their seats counting money while their neighbors are proudly wearing the neckwear that the couple previously wore.

Commercial.

I am standing where the first pole with the rope stood. Brian escorts Ming-Na to where I am standing. I study Ming-Na's neck. I pull back to see Ming-Na's face and her dark brown eyes. I check Ming-Na's position by looking up the line, then down the line. She is going to get blood all over that nice blouse.

I lean in and whisper, "You don't have to do this. Just step away, and the star won't hurt you."

I walk over to where the second pole with the rope stood. Brian escorts Kristy to where I am standing. I study Kristy's neck. I pull back to see her dark blue eyes. I check Kristy's position by looking up the line, then down the line.

I lean in and whisper, "You don't have to do this. Just step away, and the star won't hurt you."

I walk over to where the third pole with the

rope stood. Brian escorts Karla to where I am standing. I study Karla's neck. Her pale blue eyes match her blouse. How did she do that? I can never find clothes that match anything. I can't help it. I touch her blouse to check out the fabric. Karla glares at me like I am about to molest her. Silk. Even better. I wonder if she would tell where she got it if I asked? Judging by the way she is looking at me, probably not.

I lean in and whisper, "You don't have to do this. Just step away, and the star won't hurt you."

I walk to my starting position and cock my arm back. I look over to the snack table. There are three doctors there, leaning forward as if at a starting line. Still just two paramedics, however. Where did Brian get *three* doctors from? I thought they were in short supply these days.

I extend my arm forward and the star flies off. With a *clang* and a spark, the star bounces off the first in-line's neck armor and continues on toward Ming-Na, grazes by her, cutting her neck. She shudders and falls to the ground, blood streaming from her body. The star bounces off the second in-line the same way it did the first. One doctor takes off running.

The star flies on toward Kristy, grazes by her, cutting her neck. She shudders and collapses, blood streaming. The star bounces off the third in-line. Another doctor races off.

The star flies on toward Karla and cuts her neck. She falls, blood pooling around her body. The third doctor takes off.

I stare at the expanding pools of blood as another *clang* is heard, then a *thud*. If they bleed a little more the pools could merge. The line seems crowded now with three S'ers, four in-lines and three doctors. Brian walks over to supervise. Great. Even more crowded now.

The only way I can see anything is to look up at the screen, which is split into three segments, each focused on a different bleeding S'er. One thumbs up. Two. Three.

The theme music starts up. Ming-Na, Kristy and Karla are lying dead on the ground. The crowd is going crazy with shouts and cheers.

The couple's seats are empty while their neighbors are caressing each other's neckwear while kissing.

Commercial.

Four more shows and I am free.

Season Four, Episode Four

CAPPING S'ERS
XCAL - 1
9:30-11:15 pm
New "Tammy Tucker, Dorothy Perry, Leslie Logan & Ronald Maldonado"
S4/EP04, (2019), The Thursday edition of the week-long Season 4 of the show that highlights four individuals who desire to commit suicide. With an assist from thrower Ricky Fordham, the individuals may go through with it or not.

"Welcome, California, to the Thursday show of season four! For the first time ever, we are coming to you on a Thursday night. As the week progresses, the shows will get longer, there will be multiple S'ers, and the Capps will get more and more dangerous. Yes folks, by the time this season is over, you will have seen things that have never been seen before! It will thrill you and, yes, even shock you. Welcome to the special Thursday edition of *Capping S'ers* season four! It will wow you!"

In the audience, a beautiful blonde woman is wearing a replica of my Cat woman suit.

"This Capp, for the first time ever, is being done outside. It is also being done in the dark for the first time ever. There are clear skies and no wind, so it should make for an excellent show. It will be fifteen minutes shy of two hours starting at 9:30 and continuing until 11:15, and we will have a first ever four-S'er Capp. They are Tammy Tucker from San Jose, Dorothy Parker from Anaheim, Leslie Logan from Barstow and Ronald Maldonado from Chino Hills. We are going to interview them all live here in our studio, and then LIVE we will watch the Capp and see if they do commit suicide or not. Stick around. We will be right back after this commercial break."

I stand in the studio looking out at the darkened parking lot. All that can be seen is a spotlight shining on the four poles holding ropes and the final post. The bleachers are dimly lit. Probably so the audience can see where they are going and not trip and fall. All five of the in-line positions are lit up brightly so the audience can see all their beefy bodies. Later, those lights will extinguish, and the in-lines will be in the dark so everyone can see the spark.

The beautiful blonde woman is sitting by one of the lights, so I can easily see her using two fingers and her mouth to produce a loud whistle. Wish I could do that.

Commercial.

The big screen was moved outside and attached to the side of the building. It comes to life while playing the *Capping S'ers* theme music, and the camera fades in on a tired looking forty-five-year-old lady standing outside the Berbeda Place Hotel. Her lips barely move as she says, "I tried to kill myself there."

The woman is standing outside the Sainte Claire Hotel. "I also tried to kill myself there. My name is Tammy Tucker, and I am ready to commit suicide."

Tammy is standing next to a Motel 6. She says, "Yep. There, too."

Next shot is of Tammy walking into a bright white apartment building. She says, "I've tried to kill myself six times here at home."

Tammy walks through the door. It is a small drab apartment. Tammy sits on the couch. She says, "That is why I need your show. To kill myself for good."

"We will get up close and personal with Tammy right after these commercial messages."

I step into the spotlight and adjust the position of the first pole holding a rope. The beautiful blonde woman wearing a replica of my Cat woman suit is shouting and waving. To whom, I wonder.

Commercial.

The stage is also outside for the first time, positioned under the giant TV screen. Phil and Tammy are there. Tammy is wearing blue jeans and cowboy boots.

"Hello, everyone. I am Phil Ebenezer. I have a PhD in clinical psychology. Tammy Tucker on a Thursday. Sounds poetic. Now Tammy, tell me why you want to end your life."

"Well, I've tried so many times, and it hasn't worked out yet."

"I see. Why hasn't it worked out?"

"Because something always happens. Like at the Berbeda Place Hotel. I slit my wrists. I was lying there on the bed waiting to bleed out when the maid knocks on the door. Well, I couldn't very well go and answer it, could I? She thinks the room is empty. Uses her passkey and comes in. Sees me and starts screaming bloody murder."

Phil picks up his 3 X 5 card and seems to be counting before he asks, "Tammy, how many times have you tried to kill yourself?"

"Including last week? Nine times."

"And each time something happens so it doesn't work out?"

Tammy glances from side to side, "Every time."

"And did you ever think that maybe you don't want it to work out?"

"Of course I want it to work out. Why do you think I'm here?"

"That is a very good question. You know, I'm curious. How else did you try killing yourself?"

"Oh, lots of ways."

"Well in your video package, you mentioned that you tried to kill yourself at the Sainte Claire Hotel. Tell me about that one."

"That one. Yeah, that one was funny. I was going to hang myself. I brought the rope with me and everything. Tied it to one of those little sprinklers things in the ceiling and jumped off the bed. What a mess that was. Water everywhere."

"What about at the Motel 6?"

"That time I brought with me a butter knife from home. Stuck it in the electrical socket."

"And then what happened?"

"The shock of that thing blew me clear across the room."

"So why didn't you just try that one at home? Why go to a Motel?"

"I did once. Blew out every fuse in the apartment. Cost me over 100 California dollars. I'm not doing that there again."

"You also said that you made six attempts on your life at home. Was the electrical socket one of them?"

"The electrical? Well no. Make that seven attempts at home. Plus, more elsewhere."

"Tell me about those seven attempts at home. Not counting the electrical socket. We already know about that one."

"Well. I tried drowning myself in the tub once."

"And what happened then?"

"Had to give it up. Couldn't breathe. Then I stuck my head in the oven once. But a neighbor smelled gas and called the fire department. I tried pressing a pillow over my face. Do you know that when you pass out, your arms relax? I tried to blow my head off with a gun, but I couldn't get a permit to buy one."

"Wonder why?"

"I took poison once. Was sick for a week. I guess that's it for the apartment."

"What about outside the home? What have you done there?"

"I jumped in the river once. In January. Thought I could get hypothermia."

"But you didn't?"

"No. It was ninety degrees out. I drove my car into a tree. Airbag worked. I pulled a toy gun on a cop. He just told me to go home. Took a plane ride once, but it didn't crash and wasn't hijacked. Before I wrecked my car, I ran a hose from the tail pipe into the car compartment."

"That usually works. What happened with that one?"

"One of my neighbors came by. Wanted to borrow gasoline for his lawn mower."

"Okay, well, you have certainly been an interesting guest. Are you ready to finally go through with it? Here? On our show?"

"Yes."

"Okay. Good. Don't forget to stay tuned after the show for your XCAL 1 evening news, the only official state newscast. Remember folks, if you didn't see it on XCAL 1, it didn't happen. We will be back with our next S'er right after this."

Commercial.

Next on the big screen is a thirty-something

woman standing outside a train station that says Disneyland. She smiles as she says, "Welcome to what used to be one of the biggest attractions in the world. It's abandoned now, as far as I know."

The same woman is seen standing in Pearson Park. "They used to have some of the biggest and best free summer concerts here. But as you can see now, it is just full of homeless people. My name is Dorothy Perry, and I am ready to commit suicide."

Dorothy stands outside St. John the Baptist Greek Orthodox Church as she says, "I used to love to go to the Greek Festival every year."

Next, Dorothy is walking into a beige apartment building. She says, "I rent a one-bedroom apartment here."

It is a small one-window apartment. Dorothy sits on the couch. She says, "It used to be so nice here in Anaheim. Now, it is all gone. There used to be a firework show that I could watch every night from my window. Now, all I get is nightly gunfire noise."

"We will get up close and personal with Dorothy right after these commercial messages."

I step into the spotlight and adjust the position of the second pole holding a rope. The beautiful blonde woman wearing a replica of my Cat woman suit is still shouting and waving. At me, maybe? I wouldn't mind that.

Commercial.

Phil and Dorothy fidget in their chairs. Dorothy is wearing blue jeans and a black tunic.

"Hello, everyone. I am Phil Ebenezer. I have a PhD in clinical psychology. Now Dorothy, tell me why you want to end your life."

"Well, I'm in constant pain, and nothing I tried can make it stop."

"I see. Have you seen a doctor about it?"

"Yes. Several. They always prescribe something. Some narcotic. I won't take those. I don't want to get hooked."

"Nothing helped?"

"Marijuana did. But you can't get that anymore."

"So, you want to kill yourself because you can't get marijuana anymore?"

"Well, when you put it like that, I guess so."

"Okay, well, so are you ready to go through with it? Here? On our show?"

"Yes. That is the only way I know to stop the pain."

"Okay. Good. Stay tuned, folks. We will be back with our next S'er right after this."

Commercial.

The big screen comes to life and shows a middle-aged woman standing outside the California Welcome Center. She smiles as she says, "Not much need for this anymore since the borders closed."

The woman is standing alongside a highway sign that says Route 66. "This was one of the original multiple state highways. Built in 1926, it ran from Chicago to Santa Monica. Maybe it still does. I wouldn't know. My name is Leslie Logan, and I am ready to commit suicide."

Leslie is standing in the middle of Calico Ghost Town. She says, "This former silver mining town started in 1881 and then became a county park. It is closed now. Pretty quiet here."

Leslie walks into a pink and white apartment building. She says, "I live in a third-floor apartment here."

The camera follows Leslie up the stairs, through the door and into a small but clean apartment. Leslie sits on the couch as she says, "I have been here for three years, and there are still boxes in the bedroom yet to unpack."

"We will get up close and personal with Leslie right after these commercial messages."

I step into the spotlight and adjust the position of the third pole holding a rope. The beautiful blonde woman wearing a replica of my Cat woman suit is still shouting and waving. Maybe she knows one of the in-lines?

Commercial.

Leslie looks cool in blue jeans, a cowboy shirt, and loafers.

"Hello, everyone. I am Phil Ebenezer. I have a PhD in clinical psychology. Now Leslie, tell me why you want to end your life."

"Well, I've tried therapy so many times, and it hasn't worked out."

"I see. And what is this therapy for?"

"My nightmares."

"What are these nightmares like?"

"Well, they vary. Sometimes I dream about all my teeth falling out. When I wake up, my teeth hurt something fierce,"

"What else?"

"Sometimes I dream that I am being chased. And no matter how hard I run; I can't get away. When I wake up, my legs are all cramped up."

"Is that all?"

"No. Sometimes I am in a strange place, and I can't find the toilet. I wander around and around and can never find it. When I wake up, I have to go pee really bad."

"Anything else?"

"Sometimes I dream that I am in the middle of the road totally naked. I try to cover myself but don't have enough hands."

"What about when you wake up?"

"What about it?"

"Never mind. What else are your nightmares about?"

"Well, sometimes I dream that I am taking an exam. Either I am back at school or it is for a job. I don't know any of the answers. None. A complete failure."

"Interesting. Is that all?"

"No. Sometimes I dream that I am in an airplane. Flying. And I hate flying."

"Well, that one doesn't sound so bad. What else?"

"Falling. I am afraid of heights, and I am very high up, and I go over the rail, and I am falling. I always wake up before I hit the ground. But when I do wake up, it seems like I was floating because it feels like I drop a few inches."

"Okay. You must have covered them all by now."

"No. Not yet. There is the dream where I am driving fast down a hill, and I have no brakes."

"You know, I am a clinical psychologist, and all those dreams mean something."

"What do they mean?"

"That you are one screwed up lady. Are you ready to get on with it?"

"No. I'm not done yet. There is the dream where I am late for work. I rush and rush, and the clock keeps going faster and faster, and I can never catch up."

"Speaking of the clock going faster, we are out of time. That's a first. Stay tuned, folks. We will be back with our next S'er right after this."

"Wait, I'm not done yet. I haven't told you about the supernatural parasitic worm that steals your breath as you sleep."

"Yes, you are done. We get it. You have bad dreams. They are ruining your life. Therapy doesn't help. The only way to end your nightmares is to end your life. We get it. You are done."

Commercial.

On the big screen is a forty-five-year-old man standing outside a home. His lips barely move as he says, "Chino Hills saw rapid housing development in the 1980s and 1990s. Of course, most of these homes are burnt down now." The camera pans out to show that the house the man is standing in front of is the only one left on its block.

The same man is standing beside a dirt mountain bike trail. "Chino Hills has numerous parks and trails for its few remaining residents to enjoy. My name is Ronald Maldonado, and I am ready to commit suicide."

Ronald stands next to a sports park and says, "Yep. Chino Hills has these, too."

Ronald walks into the tan, stucco two-story house he was standing in front of before. He says, "I've stayed here even though everyone else was burned out. They may come back for my house at some point, but for now, I think they just moved on and forgot about me."

The camera follows Ronald through the door and pans to show the open concept kitchen and living room. Ronald sits on the couch and says, "The rest of the family is out foraging for food. I sure hope they find something. We haven't eaten in three days."

"We will get up close and personal with Ronald right after these commercial messages."

I step into the spotlight and adjust the position of the fourth pole holding a rope. I go back to the snack table and gaze at the bountiful spread. The beautiful blonde woman wearing a replica of my Cat woman suit is shouting and waving still. Maybe she knows Brian?

Commercial.

Ronald is wearing a dirty, dusty, ill-fitting

suit that looks like he found it in the trash.

"Hello, everyone. I am Phil Ebenezer. I have a PhD in clinical psychology. Now Ronald, tell me why you want to end your life."

"Well, I keep having these panic attacks."

"Let's see. You are living in the sole surviving house on your street. Your family must forage for food. You haven't eaten for days. Is it any wonder you feel anxious from time to time?"

"It isn't just feeling anxious. It is a full-blown attack. Like right now, my heart is racing. I'm feeling weak. My hands are tingling. I'm sweating. My chest hurts. I can't breathe."

"Ronald, you know what? Our other interviews went a little long. I think we get the idea. Let's just go straight to the Capp. Is that okay?"

Ronald's eyes close, "Sure."

"Great. Stay tuned, folks. We will be back right after this."

Hidden in the dark, I direct the stagehands to pick up and carry off-camera all four poles holding a rope. The beautiful blonde woman is pretending to throw a star. I guess she is a fan.

Commercial.

"Ladies and gentlemen, welcome to the LIVE part of the show. I know that we are already fifteen minutes past our scheduled closing time, but I was having so much fun with a couple of those interviews that I just couldn't help myself. Especially that suicide lady. Can you believe her? Anyway, let me introduce you to Ricky Fordham, our Capper."

A spotlight shines on me as I wave to the crowd. It follows me as I walk over to where the first pole with the rope stood. Brian escorts Tammy out of the darkness to where I am standing. I study Tammy's neck. She has dark brown eyes. I lean in and whisper, "You don't have to do this. Just step away, and the star won't hurt you."

I walk over to the second spotlight. Brian escorts Dorothy out of the darkness. I study Dorothy's neck. I pull back to see Dorothy's face and her eyes. I whisper, "You don't have to do this. Just step away, and the star won't hurt you."

I walk over to the third spotlight. Brian escorts Leslie to me. Her eyes are a pale gray. I lean in, "You don't have to do this. Just step away, and the star won't hurt you."

I walk over to the fourth spotlight. Brian escorts Ronald out. His eyes are closed. He seems much calmer now. Almost like he is half asleep. "You don't have to do this. Just step away, and the star won't hurt you."

I walk through the dark to my starting position. It is so quiet that the audience could hear my bare feet walking. They picked up a lot of grit from the asphalt. Maybe I should start wearing sandals? The spotlight blinks on when I get there.

I look at the nine people in line before me; the four S'ers in spotlights and the five in-lines I can barely see in the darkness. Brian is helping Ronald stand straight. By the snack table, are four doctors lined up and ready to go.

I extend my left arm with the mangled hand as I cock my right arm back and throw the star. My spotlight goes out. There is a *clang* and a bright spark.

The star appears in the spotlight shining on Tammy who bends down to tie her shoe. The star flies past, leaving her unharmed. I watch a confused Tammy as there is another *clang* and bright spark.

The star appears in the spotlight shining on Dorothy, grazes past her, cutting her neck. Dorothy's body shudders and collapses as the blood flows out. There is another *clang* and bright spark.

The star appears in the spotlight shining on

Leslie, grazes past her, cutting her neck. Her body collapses as the blood flows. There is another *clang* and bright spark.

The star appears in the spotlight shining on Ronald, Brian is still holding him up. The star cuts his neck. His blood flows and his body falls after Brian releases it. There is another *clang* and bright spark, then a *thud*.

The first doctor looks pissed. Like he is being cheated out of something. The third doctor gives a thumbs up, then the fourth. The second doctor starts yelling that they should have signaled in order. Brian looks to have gotten some blood on himself. Maybe Ronald leaned into him when he fell. The second doctor finally looks down and signals another death.

The *Capping S'ers* theme music starts up. I am still standing where I began, my spotlight back on. The light is shining in my eyes. Maybe I need a hat with those sandals. The in-lines are still in darkness, so I can't see what they are doing. Tammy is being led away by Brian. Dorothy, Leslie and Ronald lie dead on the floor. The star is stuck in the last post. The crowd is mixed. Some are yelling and cheering. Some are silent. Others look upset and are making rude hand gestures at Tammy.

The beautiful blonde woman sits down, her face a perfect picture of rapture.

"Good for you, Tammy," I mutter aloud.

Commercial.

Almost there.

Season Four, Episode Five

CAPPING S'ERS
XCAL - 1
9-11 pm
New "**Connor White, Gordon Holland, Wayne Madison, Paul Dasher & Anthony Crawford**"
S4/EP05, (2019), The Friday edition of the week-long Season 4 of the show that highlights five individuals who desire to commit suicide. With an assist from thrower Ricky Fordham, the individuals may go through with it or not.

"Welcome, California, to the Friday show of season four! For the first time ever, we are coming to you on a Friday night. As the week progresses, the shows will get longer, there will be multiple S'ers, and the Capps will get more and more dangerous. Yes folks, by the time this season is over, you will have seen things that you have never seen before! It will thrill you and, yes, even shock you. Welcome to the special Friday edition of *Capping S'ers* season four!"

In the audience, a man is wearing a blue suit with a *Capping S'ers* tie.

"This is the longest attempted Capp yet. We will see if Ricky can pull it off. We are back outside our studio again. Having eleven people in one arcing line is just too big of a show to be inside. The show will be two hours long. We again moved the time up half of an hour. We are going to stay with a 9:00 pm start time both Saturday and Sunday.

We have five S'ers for you tonight. First up is Connor White from San Diego. Then Gordon Holland from Azusa, Wayne Madison from Brea, Paul Dasher from Carlsbad, and Anthony Crawford from West Covina. Wow, what a line up. We are going to interview them all live here in our studio, and then LIVE we will watch the Capp and see if they do commit suicide or not. Stick around. We will be right back after this commercial break."

I am standing by the final post. The man in the audience with a *Capping S'ers* tie is on his cell phone. Who could he be calling now?

Commercial.

On screen is a short, forty-year-old man standing outside a building that holds a blue sign that says Scripps Mercy Hospital. He sports a huge grin as he says, "I mostly come here for my treatments."

He is standing outside a tuna cannery. "San Diego has been called the Tuna Capital of the World. My name is Connor White, and I am ready to commit suicide."

Connor stands next to a giant wall that stretches off into the distance as he says, "This is the California Mexico border. No more trips to Tijuana this way."

Connor is walking toward a cute tiny home. He says, "This is where I live. Welcome."

The camera follows Connor through a white picket fence, across a small yard, and onto the front porch. The camera pans to show the well-kept home. Connor sits in a recliner. He says as he rocks it back and forth,

"I am tired of living with my condition, and I want to end it."

"We will get up close and personal with Connor right after these commercial messages."

I adjust the position of the first pole holding a rope. The man wearing a *Capping S'ers* tie is standing up watching the show.

Commercial.

Phil and Connor are seated in chairs slightly facing each other. Connor is wearing a neat suit and tie.

"Hello, everyone. I am Phil Ebenezer. I have a PhD in clinical psychology. Now Connor, tell me why you want to end your life."

"Because I can't live a normal life. I have tried and tried. The medications don't seem to help. Sometimes I feel so great that it's 'Why do I need them?' And at other times it is, 'What's the use?'"

"I see. You admit to having bipolar disorder. What is that like?"

"It's hell. I am either euphoric or depressed. There doesn't seem to be any middle ground."

Phil refers to his 3 X 5 card, stares up at the ceiling, then asks, "Connor, do you think that being so very short is part of why you want to kill yourself?"

"No. That has nothing to do with it. Why do you even ask that?"

"Just curious."

Connor shakes his head from side to side, "No. It's all about the bipolar."

"So, you go from euphoric to depressed?"

"Yes."

"Tell me how you feel when you are euphoric?"

"When I am euphoric, I am full of energy. I don't need more than three hours of sleep a night. I can do anything. My mind goes a mile a minute."

"And what about when you are depressed?"

"I am sad. Everything feels hopeless. Time just drags by. I lose interest in doing anything. I don't want to leave the house. I don't want to eat. I lose weight. I sleep all day. I am constantly fatigued. I can't think. I just want to kill myself."

"And how often do you switch from one state to the other?"

"It depends. Sometimes several times a week. Other times I am stuck in one state for weeks."

"How long does it take to switch from one state to the next?"

"That varies also. Sometimes the switch can take a full day, other times the switch can be measured in minutes."

"What does your girlfriend think about this?"

"I can't have a relationship with a woman. I am either too attentive or not attentive enough."

"Are you ready for the Capp?"

"I am."

"I guess I don't need to ask you which state you are in now?"

"No, you don't. I am depressed. If I was manic, I would be the one doing the throw of the Capp."

Phil laughs, "Well, I don't think Ricky would like that too much. She is pretty attached to that star. Stay tuned, folks. We will be back with our next S'er right after this."

Commercial.

I watch as on-screen the camera fades in on a twenty-five-year-old man in a wheelchair outside a log cabin in the woods. He smiles as he says, "Seven years before the big gold rush at Sutter's Mill, a rancher named Francisco Lopez discovered gold here in Placerita Canyon."

The same man is in downtown Azusa. "Because

Azusa lies at the base of the mountains, flash flooding is a frequent occurrence. My name is Gordon Holland, and I am ready to commit suicide."

Gordon is next to a white house. He says, "This is the Durrell House Museum. It was built in 1923 by former mayor M.T. Durrell."

Next is Gordon wheeling up a handicapped ramp into a manufactured home. He says, "This is where I live now. I had to add the ramp."

The camera follows Gordon through the single wide. He says, "I live here alone now."

"We will get up close and personal with Gordon right after these commercial messages."

Commercial.

Gordon is wearing jeans and a t-shirt.

"Hello, everyone. I am Phil Ebenezer. I have a PhD in clinical psychology. Now Gordon, tell me why you want to end your life."

"I have been in this wheelchair for four years now. Ever since the LA riots of 2015. I can't stand it anymore, and I don't see that life is going to get any better."

"I see. What happened to you in those riots?"

"Well, as you know, the riots started in downtown LA after a white cop shot and killed a black businessman. The riots spread into the valleys, and I was in downtown Azusa picking up supplies for my horses when I was shot five times."

Phil looks at his 3 X 5 card and laughs before he asks, "Where were you shot?"

"In the feed store."

"No. Where on your body were you shot?"

"Oh. The spleen, the spine, the skull, the scrotum, and the stomach."

"Wow, all the organs that start with S. And now you want to be an S'er?"

"Yes."

"There must be a witty comment I can make about all that, but I can't think of what it is. Stay tuned, folks. We will be back with our next S'er right after this."

Commercial.

I watch as on-screen the camera fades in on a short, very young-looking man standing next to a sign that says Brea Mall. He smiles as he says, "Starting in 1977, this was an upscale, highly successful mall. It collapsed, as so many others did, when the borders closed."

He is standing under a marquee that says Improv. "I used to perform here at the Comedy Club. I still do when it is open. My name is Wayne Madison, and I am ready to commit suicide."

Wayne stands next to several orange public art statues as he says, "This is the Orange Tree Grove Water Fountain. It is turned off to save on water."

Wayne walks into a 3,900-square-foot house. He says, "This is where I live. With my parents still."

The camera follows Wayne past an elegant entry, and up the winding stairs to a bedroom. The camera pans to show the large room. Wayne sits in a chair by the bay window. He looks out as he says, "I am tired of all the online bullies. Just because I am short is no reason to make fun of me."

"We will get up close and personal with Wayne right after these commercial messages."

Commercial.

Phil paces. Wayne is wearing a very expensive looking black with dark blue pinstriped suit and power red tie.

"Hello, everyone. I am Phil Ebenezer. I have a

PhD in clinical psychology. Now Wayne, tell me why you want to end your life."

"Because of all those online bullies. They won't leave me alone."

"I see. What do these bullies do? They call you names like Shorty and stuff?"

"Yeah, they do that. But they do a lot more than that. They make up lies about me and what I am doing. They take pictures of me naked in the showers at school and make fun of how small my you know what is. But hey, that water is cold. What do they think happens?"

"What else do they do?"

"Well, I can't get a date. As soon as a girl shows any interest in me, they start bullying her also."

"Curious."

"You know, I can take the bullying at school. When I get home, I can play a game and forget all about it. But the cyber bullying just goes on and on. Twenty-four hours a day. Seven days a week. I think they sleep in shifts just so they can bug me."

"Do you know who is doing it?"

"I do, but no one will do anything about it."

"Why don't you just shut your phone off at night?"

"I can't. You see, there is a group of us that support each other. I need to be instantly available if one of them needs me, or else something bad could happen."

"You mean, like they could attempt suicide?"

"Yea, like that."

"Heaven forbid something like that happens. Okay. And you are ready to end your life over this?"

"Well, I am mainly on the show to make people aware. This is a real problem, and it needs to be addressed."

"But you are ready to end your life over this?"

"Oh. Yes, of course."

"Okay. Good. Stay tuned, folks. We will be back

with our next S'er right after this."

Commercial.

On screen is a short, fifty-year-old man standing next to a booth holding up one half of a sign that says Legoland California. He says, "While this opened in 1999, it is closed today. You can see the army tents inside."

The man is standing outside a luxury hotel. "Starting with a simple mineral spring in 1882, Carlsbad quickly became a mecca for luxury spas. My name is Paul Dasher, and I am ready to commit suicide."

Paul is standing on the eighteenth green of the Rancho Carlsbad Golf Course. He says, "Carlsbad also became famous for its fabulous golf courses." He points at some distant figures, "See, people are still playing. Golf lives on. Golf is eternal."

Paul walks toward a drab, brown apartment building. He says, "This is where I live. In apartment 3D."

The camera follows Paul through the front door of the building, up the stairs, and down the corridor to his front door. "I don't think I should let you inside. It is a real mess."

"We will get up close and personal with Paul right after these commercial messages."

Commercial.

Paul is wearing black jeans and a white polo shirt.

"Hello, everyone. I am Phil Ebenezer. I have a PhD in clinical psychology. So you live in Apartment 3D?"

"Yeah."

"That's funny."

"Why?"

"You know. You live in the third dimension."

"I don't get it."

"Never mind. Now Paul, tell me why you want to end your life."

"Because it is in my blood. It is a part of my life. Because I have to."

"Explain, please."

"It is my family's history. My dad killed himself at fifty. So did his dad. And his dad. And his dad. And his dad. All the way back as far as we can trace, every male Dasher committed suicide at fifty years of age."

"And how old are you?"

"I just turned fifty last week."

"And now you feel you have to kill yourself?"

"Yes. It is my destiny."

"Has anyone ever looked into why every male Dasher kills themselves at fifty?"

"No. Why would we do that? It is tradition. This is what we have always done."

"And there is nothing I can say to talk you out of it? Not that I would."

"No."

"Sounds like the dumbest reason to kill yourself I've ever heard of. So, are you ready for the Capp? Ready to give up golf?"

"I am, but I don't play golf."

"Okay. Strange. Stay tuned, folks. We will be back with our last S'er of the night right after this."

Commercial.

I watch as the camera fades in on a short, twenty-nine-year-old man standing by a row of used cars. He has a slight grin as he says, "Because it has been so long since we had any new cars in this state, car dealers now only sell used cars. And those get older every year."

Then he is standing beside a walnut tree. "West Covina used to be full of walnut groves. I think this is the last surviving walnut tree in the city. My name is Anthony Crawford, and I am ready to commit suicide."

Anthony stands beside a sewage plant and says, "West Covina was incorporated as an independent city in 1923 to prevent the city of Covina from building a sewage farm in the area. Then between 1950 and 1960, it became one of the fastest growing cities in the nation with a 1,000 percent increase."

Anthony walks toward the garage of a rambler house. He says, "This is where I live. In the garage."

Anthony rolls up the garage door. The camera shows the small, neat space. Anthony sits on a hard wood chair. "I am tired of living with my parents, and I want to end it."

"We will get up close and personal with Anthony right after these commercial messages."

Commercial.

Phil is glancing at Anthony, who is wearing sneakers, blue jeans, a red shirt and a *Capping S'ers* cap.

"Hello, everyone. I am Phil Ebenezer. I have a PhD in clinical psychology. Now Anthony, tell me why you want to end your life."

"Because of my parents."

"What about your parents?"

"I don't think they love me."

"Why do you think that?"

"Because I am adopted."

"Well, lots of people are adopted. That doesn't mean that they aren't loved. Some people say that adopted children are more loved because they were chosen."

"That's a load of crap. You don't understand. They make me live in the garage."

"Maybe there is no room in the house?"

"It is a three-bedroom house. They have their

bedroom. Then their office. Then the media room."

"How many bathrooms?"

"Two. One for them, and one for me."

"That doesn't sound so bad."

"Then there was Christmas."

"What about Christmas?"

"I got a soap dish."

"A what?"

"A *Capping S'ers* soap dish."

"Well that sounds like a great gift to me."

"Also, this *Capping S'ers* baseball cap and a *Capping S'ers* blanket."

"Wow, now it sounds like a great Christmas."

"I think they were trying to tell me something."

"I wonder what that could be. Are you ready for the Capp?"

"I guess."

Phil laughs, "Not good enough. You must say you are."

"I am."

"Okay. Good. Stay tuned, folks. We will be back with the Capp right after this."

I direct the stagehands to pick up and carry off-camera all the poles with rope. In their place, they come back with a small stand for each spot. Each stand was carefully engineered to a height specific to each S'er. The man with the *Capping S'ers* tie is on his cell phone again. Again? Did the first call not go through?

Commercial.

"Ladies and gentlemen, welcome to the LIVE part of the show. Once again, we are past our scheduled ending time. I apologize. Without further ado, let me introduce you to Ricky Fordham, our Capper."

I step into camera range and wave to the crowd. The crowd is hushed. Why? Too exciting for them?

One by one, Brian escorts all five S'ers over to

where I am as I move down the line. They all step up onto the small stands, except Gordon, who has a ramp. I position them all, double check the heights, and then study their necks. I pull back to see their faces and their eyes. I check their positions by looking up the line, then down the line. This is going to be difficult.

I lean in and whisper to each of them, "You don't have to do this. Just step away, and the star won't hurt you."

I walk to my starting position and cock my arm back. I look over to the snack table. Five doctors. Are there any others left in the state or do we have them all? Maybe they aren't really doctors? They have lab coats on.

I throw the star. It flies straight at the first in-line. With a *clang* and a spark, the star bounces off the first in-line's neck armor and continues.

It flies on toward Connor, grazes by him, cutting his neck in the process. His body shudders. He collapses onto the stand, blood streaming from his body. I stare at the blood as another *clang* is heard, and a spark is seen.

The star flies on toward Gordon in his wheelchair, grazes by him, cutting his neck. He collapses in his chair, blood streaming and dripping from his body. One side of the wheelchair is getting drenched. Another *clang* is heard along with another spark lighting the night.

The star flies on toward Wayne, who steps away. I watch Brian running toward Wayne as there is another *clang* and spark.

The star flies on toward Paul and cuts his neck. He collapses, blood squirting. I stare as there is another *clang* and spark.

The star flies on toward Anthony, who collapses onto his stand. I stare at the ever-increasing pools of blood as another *clang* is heard, then a *thud*.

The 'doctors' do their thing and the *Capping*

S'ers theme music starts up. Connor, Gordon, Paul and Anthony are lying dead, three of them half on the short stage and half on the ground. Brian is escorting Wayne into the studio. Heading for one of the back rooms, I bet. The star is stuck in the last post. The crowd is going crazy with shouts, cheers and jeers.

The man with the *Capping S'ers* tie must have finished his phone calls as his seat is empty. Thanks for giving me the courage to end this, sis.

Commercial

Two more shows, and I am free.

Season Four, Episode Six

CAPPING S'ERS
XCAL - 1
9-11:15 pm
New "Madeline Martinez, Ann Thompson, Connie McDaniel, John Johnson, Raymond Williams & Donna Brown"
S4/EP06, (2019), The Saturday extended edition of the week-long Season 4 of the show that highlights six individuals who desire to commit suicide. With an assist from thrower Ricky Fordham, the individuals may go through with it or not.

With the longest Capp so far, they expanded the seating again.

"Welcome, California, to the Saturday show of season four! For the first time ever, we are coming to you on a Saturday night. We are finally getting down to what you folks have been waiting for. This show is longer, one hundred and thirty-five minutes, there are six S'ers, and the Capp is so much more dangerous with seven in-lines instead of the usual three. The Capp is so long that it could only be done outside. The arc is sharper, and the total distance of the throw is longer than ever. The star must maintain its speed and altitude over the whole entire distance. Can it be done? Yes folks, by the time this season is over, you will have seen things that have never been seen before! It will thrill you and, yes, even shock you. Welcome to the special Saturday edition of *Capping S'ers* season four!"

In the audience is a man wearing a Dodger's cap and looking through binoculars at the in-lines, or maybe just the female one.

Earlier today, the Governor struck again. It was pretty much a repeat of the last time. Dragged out of bed at five in the morning. Why did he have to be such an early riser?

Shuffled out in his limo. Escorted to his library/den. Interfaced with him and a stranger. And another stranger. And another stranger. His disposal team is having a busy day today.

What a mess my life has turned into. All I ever wanted was to be left alone. Just me and my dog. Throwing the star into the woods. Having Irene watch me. Now I am a celebrity with my own TV show who has become a recluse and an interrogator for a madman. This must stop.

"The six S'ers that we have for you tonight are Madeline Martinez, Ann Thompson, Connie McDaniel, John Johnson, Raymond Williams and Donna Brown. Madeline lives in Chula Vista, Ann lives in Orange County, Connie is from Burbank, John came down from Corning, Raymond lives almost as far away in Elk Grove, and Donna hails from Fullerton. We will visit them all in their hometowns. We are then going to interview them here in our studio, and then LIVE we will watch the Capp and see if they do commit suicide or not. We will also see if Ricky has the right stuff to pull off such an extended Capp. Stick around. We will be right back after this commercial break."

I stand in the darkened studio and stare outside at the lineup for this Capp. Thirteen of them make for a very long line. Strangely enough, I am not nervous. Ever since I made my decision on what to do, I feel calm and relaxed. Pissed off at the Governor, otherwise, just grinding out the grind to the final Capp. The man with the binoculars is taking notes. On what? Her breast size? Why doesn't he just record it?

Commercial.

On the big screen on the side of the building the camera fades in on a stark looking twenty-three-year-old Goth attired girl standing on a sidewalk. Over her left shoulder is a span across the road proclaiming Third Avenue with a circular portion that reads Chula Vista Downtown. She is tight-lipped as she says, "This is the Third Avenue entrance to downtown. A lot of the shops are closed now, but the Dollar Store and Goodwill are still open."

Standing by a tall chimney, she says "This is the South Bay Power Plant. It is a 700-megawatt, four boiler plant. It is still operational, run by the state. My name is Madeline Martinez, and I am ready to commit suicide."

Madeline stands outside Chula Vista City Hall while she says, "Chula Vista is San Diego County's second largest city."

Madeline walks into a purple stucco house. She says, "I live here with my parents still."

The camera pans to show the small well-kept home. A woman can be seen in the kitchen, and a lawn mower is heard outside. Madeline sits on the couch. She says, "I can't believe what has happened to California. I am tired of all the fighting and all the deaths. I don't see any reason to continue living in such a state."

"I'm sure Madeline isn't implying anything,"

Phil interjects, "She just seems upset. We will get up close and personal with Madeline right after these commercial messages."

I adjust the position of the first pole holding a rope. The man in the audience is looking through his binoculars at me. Why? I don't have big breasts.

I move further into the shadows.

Commercial.

Seated next to Phil, Madeline is wearing a black dress with black leggings and black shoes.

"Hello, everyone. I am Phil Ebenezer. I have a PhD in clinical psychology. Now Madeline, tell me why you want to end your life."

"Things are not the way they are supposed to be. Things are not the way they used to be. I don't think things will ever get back to how they were ever again, so I have no reason to live. I just want to die."

"I see. And what do you think happened to change things?"

"It was when the federal government collapsed. Or maybe before then, I don't know. Now, we can't go anywhere or do anything. Armed guards on every street corner. Always being asked for your papers."

"And do you think the state is to blame for that?"

"No. Of course not. Everyone knows that Governor Johnson is doing a great job. Everyone knows that it is the federal government that is to blame. Even after California closed its borders and kicked all the feds out, they are still to blame for all the riots here. The lack of food, water and sustained electricity. It is all still their fault."

"Good girl. Just so we are straight on that part. So, are you ready for the Capp?"

"I am."

"Okay. Good. The LIVE Capp is coming up soon,

right after we get up close and personal with the rest of our S'ers. Ann Thompson is up next. Stay tuned, folks. We will be right back after this."

Commercial.

The theme music starts, and the camera fades in on a twenty-five-year-old girl standing next to an orange tree. She says, "There used to be acres and acres of orange orchards here in Orange County. That is how the county got its name."

She is standing on a grassy lawn with an empty air strip visible over her right shoulder. "This used to be a Marine Corps Air Station called El Toro. The Marines all flew off just before the borders closed. I don't know where they are now. My name is Ann Thompson, and I am ready to commit suicide."

Ann points at an asphalt road and says, "This spot is actually part of the old paved track that was Riverside Raceway. My dad said he used to go to the races here all the time. Of course, it is all houses now, although most of those are burned down."

Next shot is of Ann walking into a pink stucco house. She says, "I live here with my parents."

The camera follows Ann through the front door. It is a well-kept home. A woman can be seen in the kitchen, and a woodchipper is heard outside. Ann sits on a couch. She says, "After what happened to my twin sister, I don't see any reason to continue living."

"We will get up close and personal with Ann right after these commercial messages."

Commercial.

Ann is wearing a pale blue dress with blue pumps.

"Hello, everyone. I am Phil Ebenezer. I have a PhD in clinical psychology. Now Ann, tell me why you want to end your life."

"Like I said in my video piece, after what happened to my sister, I don't want to go on living."

"I see. And what happened to your sister?"

"She was murdered. Her throat was cut. It happened right in front of me. I watched it as it happened. Me and one hundred other people."

Phil sighs as he looks at the 3 X 5 card that was on a table next to him, "And what happened to this person who killed your sister?"

"Nothing. As a matter of fact, she is a big TV star now."

"Just goes to show that there is no justice in this world."

"No. There isn't."

"Do you want revenge for your sister's death?"

"I would love it. But I am afraid the killer is untouchable."

"No one is untouchable. Just tell me who it is, and we'll get them on this show and Ricky will take care of them."

"Ricky is the killer."

"No, Ricky doesn't kill anyone. She just provides an avenue for them to take their own life."

"She killed Kathy Lyndhurst! I saw it all!"

"That was ruled an accident."

"Whatever. I said she was untouchable."

"Well, now that we have that settled, are you ready for the Capp?"

"Sure. Whatever."

"Okay. Good. The LIVE Capp is coming up soon. Connie McDaniel is next. Stay tuned, folks. We will be right back after this."

It has been a very long time since I heard that name spoken aloud. Kathy Lyndhurst. Yes, I can see the resemblance now. The same appearance, especially in the eyes. Kathy was the very first person to die by the star, except for my mom of course. I mean the first to die as an S'er. Although that was before there ever were S'ers. The first who wanted death by star. The girl who jumped the barricade and ran into the star's path. The name I can never forget. The girl I had known only five minutes. The person who started it all.

The one who made me what I am today.

Why did Kathy have to die that day? Wasn't there another relative she could have turned to for support? What about Ann? Weren't they close? She said she had a boyfriend. Wouldn't he have fought for her? If he loved her? How about going back to the police and pestering them until they finally did something about the rapes? How about plotting revenge on her stepdad? Catching his next rape attempt on a recording or live broadcast? How about fighting back? Self-defense classes? A gun?

Why did she have to run in front of the star and ruin my life?

I direct two stagehands to pick up and carry off-camera the second pole holding a rope. The man in the audience is sitting back in his seat smiling. What is he smiling about? I remember that guy. He was with the Governor earlier today. What is he doing here? Spying on me?

Commercial.

The camera fades in on a forty-one-year-old woman standing next to a fence. She says, "Behind me is one of the runways of the Burbank Airport. Some people call it the Bob Hope Airport, but that is just silly. There is no hope anymore."

The same woman is standing outside of a massive office building. "This used to be the Warner Bros studio offices. They are all empty now, except for some homeless people who moved in. My name is Connie McDaniel, and I am ready to commit suicide."

Connie is beside an empty fountain. She says, "This is the Burbank City Hall. It was listed on the

National Register of Historic Places. It is lunchtime. See all the people going in and out." The camera pans to the doorway to show two people exiting the building. No one is going in.

Connie enters a plain green with white trim house. She says, "I live here with my husband and two kids."

The camera pans to show the spotless home. Connie sits at a bar stool, sipping a drink. She says, "I like a little pick me up throughout the day."

"We will get up close and personal with Connie right after these commercial messages."

Commercial.

While Phil is dressed as usual, Connie is wearing a pale blue house dress.

"Hello, everyone. I am Phil Ebenezer. I have a PhD in clinical psychology. Now Connie, tell me why you want to end your life."

"I'm bored."

"What?"

"I'm bored. I sit around the house all day watching soap operas. I can only clean so many times a day. I cook the meals and do the dishes. I do the never-ending laundry. I swear my husband throws clean clothes in the hamper just to piss me off. I'm bored."

"Don't you socialize or have a hobby?"

"Who is going to 'socialize' around these parts? You can get your head blown off these days just because someone doesn't like your hair color."

"Well, there must be something you can do to relive your boredom."

"There is. Kill myself."

"Alright then. So, are you ready for the Capp?"

"I am."

"Okay. Good. The LIVE Capp is coming up soon. John Johnson is next. Stay tuned, folks. We will be right back after this."

I direct two stagehands to pick up and carry off-camera the third pole holding a rope. The man in the audience is sitting back in his seat, still smiling. Yes, he was with the Governor today. He's the driver of the Governor's limo! Is the Governor here too?

Commercial.

The camera fades in on a middle-aged man stand-ing next to a highway sign. He says, "Welcome to Corning. The Olive City."

The same man is standing next to a different highway sign. "This is the I-5 freeway. It is the main north-south route through the state. Too bad each city on it turned their parts into toll roads. It now takes five days to drive from one end of the state to the other. If you can find the gas. My name is John Johnson, and I am ready to commit suicide."

John stands next to a casino as he says, "The Paskenta Bank of Indians acquired 2,000 acres here and built the Rolling Hills Casino. In its heyday, it had over 500 employees with a monthly payroll of over $1,000,000. Sadly, like most everything in California, it is closed now."

John is standing outside a green and gray crafts-man style house. He says, "I don't live here anymore. I used to."

"We will get up close and personal with John right after these commercial messages."

I adjust the position of the fourth pole holding a rope. The man in the audience is filming. What is he doing? Making a movie? The Governor knows how a Capp goes. He was here once.

Commercial.

Phil and John are seated in chairs slightly

facing each other. It is a hot night, so John is wearing shorts.

"Hello, everyone. I am Phil Ebenezer. I have a PhD in clinical psychology. Now John, tell me why you want to end your life."

"You saw the house. The one in the video."

"Yeah. You said you don't live there anymore. Well, who lives there now?"

"My family does."

"Well, if your family still lives there, why don't you?"

"I walked out on them. Ten years ago."

"You walked out on them ten years ago. And you haven't gotten over it yet?"

"No. It was the dumbest thing I ever did."

"Well, I imagine that is a pretty long list, too. So, if you walked out on them ten years ago, and you still regret it, why don't you just walk up to that front door, knock and tell them so?"

"I can't."

"Sometimes this job is like pulling teeth. You can't. Why not?"

"Because they already moved on. She has remarried. He adopted the kids. Dumbest thing I ever did."

"Yes, we already established that. We are running out of time, so are we good here? Are you ready for the Capp?"

"I guess."

"Not good enough. You must say yes."

"Alright. Yes."

"All righty then. That is coming up soon. Raymond Williams is next. Stay tuned, folks. We will be right back after this."

I direct two stagehands to pick up and carry off-camera the fourth pole holding a rope. The man in the audience is sitting back in his seat, smiling again. That must be one happy dude. Now he is pointing at me and saying something. He is too far away to hear, and I can't read lips. I walk back into the darkness of the studio.

Commercial.

The camera fades in on a handsome thirty-five-year-old man standing next to wetlands. He says, "This is the Cosumnes River Preserve. It is a 46,000-acre nature preserve."

He is standing next to different wetlands. "This is the Stone Lakes Wildlife Refuge. It covers nearly twenty-eight-square-miles. My name is Raymond Williams, and I am ready to commit suicide."

Raymond is standing in the middle of a pumpkin patch. He says, "I used to so enjoy the pumpkin festivals we had around here. Now, whenever two or more people gather, a fight breaks out."

Walking into a white house with a star on it, he says, "I live here alone."

It is a small and extremely messy home. Raymond pushes aside a pile of junk, then sits on a couch. He says, "After I come home from work, I am just too exhausted to do anything."

"We will get up close and personal with Raymond right after these commercial messages."

Commercial.

Raymond looks shabby next to Phil's dark blue suit and power red tie.

"Hello, everyone. I am Phil Ebenezer. I have a PhD in clinical psychology. Now Raymond, tell me why you want to end your life."

"Like I said in my video piece, after work, I am just too exhausted to do anything."

"And that is why you want to kill yourself?"

"Well, yea. Work is just too hard. Always demanding one thing or another. Deadlines followed by even more deadlines."

"What kind of work do you do?"

"I'm a salesman. The world is going to hell in a hand basket, and I'm supposed to keep selling pens."

"Well, everyone needs a good pen."

"That is the same thing my boss says."

"So, are you ready for the Capp?"

"I am."

"Okay. Good. The LIVE Capp is coming up soon. Donna Brown is next. Don't forget to stay tuned after the show for your XCAL 1 evening news, the only official state newscast. Remember folks, if you didn't see it on XCAL 1, it didn't happen."

Commercial.

On screen is a plain forty-two-year-old woman standing next to a tall building. She says, "There used to be a state university here. Now the dorms are full of displaced citizens, and the buildings are used for rehabilitation."

The same woman is holding a Fender guitar. "Not many people know that the Fender Electric Instrument Manufacturing Company was founded here in Fullerton by Clarence Leonidas "Leo" Fender in 1946. My name is Donna Brown, and I am ready to commit suicide."

Donna is standing by an oil well. She says, "Discovered in 1880, the Brea-Olinda Oil Field is the sixteenth largest in California and was the first of California's fifty largest oil fields to be found."

Donna walks into a yellow stucco house with red trim as she says, "I live here with my husband."

The camera follows Donna through the front door and pans to show the small orange and purple home. A weed eater is heard outside. Donna sits on a couch. She says, "I love my husband and would do anything for him."

"We will get up close and personal with Donna

right after these commercial messages."

Commercial.

In her chair, Donna is wearing an orange and purple dress that matches her hair.

"Hello, everyone. I am Phil Ebenezer. I have a PhD in clinical psychology. Now Donna, tell me why you want to end your life."

"I don't want my husband to leave me."

"What makes you think he might leave you?"

"Because he said he was going to."

Phil notices that the table normally next to him is gone. "And did he say why?"

"No."

"Did you ask him why?"

"No."

"Don't you think that is a good place to start?"

"I don't want to know the answer."

"Why not?"

"I'm afraid the answer might be because of me."

"Why? Have you given him a reason to leave?"

"No."

"Then, what's the problem?"

"I don't know."

"Well, this is getting us nowhere fast. Your husband said he is going to leave you. You don't know why, and you don't want to ask. You think that by killing yourself, he won't leave."

"That's right."

"Well, I fail to see the logic there, but okay. Maybe we should have had him on the show. The LIVE Capp is next. Stay tuned, folks. We will be right back after this."

Commercial.

"Ladies and gentlemen, welcome to the LIVE part

of the show. We are not too bad on time. Maybe a little over. Let me introduce you to Ricky Fordham, our Capper."

A spotlight comes on as I wave to the crowd. Shouts and cheers greet me. I walk over to the first S'er's spot. Brian escorts Madeline over to me. I position Madeline and then study her neck. I pull back to see Madeline's face and her black highlighted eyes. I check Madeline's position by looking up the line, then down the line. I lean in and whisper, "You don't have to do this. Just step away, and the star won't hurt you."

I walk over to the second S'er's spot. Brian escorts Ann over. I study her neck. She has pale green eyes.

As I lean in, Ann whispers, "I know who you are. What you are. You killed Kathy. Who I miss so much I want to die."

I'm silent as I pause, then position Ann again. I check her new position by looking up the line, then down the line. There is so much I want to ask Ann. So much I want to know. But, instead, I move on to the next S'er. Did I tell Ann about stepping away?

Shaken, I mechanically deal with the rest of the S'ers, being sure to warn each one that they can step away.

I move to my mark, barely check the extended line and the four doctors. Four? Which S'er isn't going to get the attention that they need.

I rush my throw. My left hand feels like it is on fire and my right hand won't stop itching. The star flies straight at the first in-line. With a *clang* and a spark, the star bounces off the first in-line's neck armor and continues.

The Capp would have gone off perfectly, but I had promised to muff it up. So, before the show, I moved the final post two inches off mark so that the star would stick at its very edge instead of the center as it always does. I know it is not much of a mess-up. Most people probably won't even notice, but that is the worse I can make it.

The star flies on toward Madeline, grazes by her, cutting her neck in the process. Her body shudders. She falls to the ground, blood streaming. A doctor runs over. The star bounces off the second in-line the same way it did the first.

It flies on toward Ann and passes by her, leaving her unharmed. Ann looks confused. Brian starts running toward her.

Another *clang* and spark.

The star flies on toward Connie, grazes by her. Her body shudders. She falls to the ground, blood pooling. Another doctor takes off. The star bounces off the fourth in-line.

The star flies toward John, cuts his neck deeply. He's dead almost immediately. The star bounces off the fifth in-line.

The star flies toward Raymond. Dead even before the doctor can get there. The star bounces off the sixth in-line.

The star flies toward Donna. Another one gone.

The star bounces off the seventh in-line. All doctors are giving thumbs up. Brian has escorted Ann back into the studio.

I focus on the final post as the star clips it, then sails right past it and into the crowd. It hits one of the new flag poles and flies off on another tangent. The star sails into the parking lot and becomes embedded in a car door with a loud *thunk*.

Kathy had died at my hand. I didn't see any reason for her twin to meet the same fate. Fortunately, the star didn't hit anyone or anything else until it stuck itself in that car door. Brian's car door. He is going to be mad. He loves that old car.

The *Capping S'ers* theme music starts up. I am still standing where I began. The in-lines are starting to leave. Madeline, Connie, John, Raymond, and Donna are all lying dead on the ground. Ann is still alive. She didn't have to die like her sister did. Death by star. The flagpole has a shiny new dent. The star is stuck in Brian's car door. The crowd is confused, going crazy with shouts and cheers but many are totally silent.

"Can you believe it? A failed Capp. The first one ever. How will Ricky ever pull off a seven S'er and eight in-line Capp tomorrow night? Tune in and find out. See you tomorrow, folks."

The seat where the man with the binoculars was is empty.

Commercial.

It all ends tomorrow. Thank God.

Season Four, Episode Seven

CAPPING S'ERS
XCAL - 1
9-11:30 pm
New "Benjamin Clark, Laurie Brown, Molly Brock, Jorge Cardoza, Judith Davis, Dora Wilson & Robin Moore"
S4/EP07, (2019), The Sunday extra-extended final edition of the week-long Season 4 of the show that highlights individuals who desire to commit suicide. With an assist from thrower Ricky Fordham, the individuals may go through with it or not.

Sunday morning, I go to church. I have not been in a church since the days when my mother rolled in the aisles while spouting nonsense. But my thoughts today are not on my mother. I think about my sister and all her years of suffering. I think about all the people who have died by the star. Do I deserve to be punished for all the actions or non-actions that I have done in my life? The people I killed.

Do I deserve to live?

Sunday night, we are assembled outside again. There is a mild breeze, five miles per hour out of the west. The air is Southern-California-night chilly. The in-lines are positioned where I want them. There are seven S'ers, three boys and four girls. All under twenty-five years of age. Why is it mostly young people who want to die? When they have so many exciting adventures waiting for them later in life?

By the stage, one of the girls is shivering. Maybe from the cold, maybe not. While the in-lines stand momentarily in the bright lights, there is a soft spotlight on where each of the S'ers will be. Wouldn't want the viewers to miss the blood spurts. The bleachers are dimly lit. The bleachers are expanded again; every seat filled. The Governor is here with his entourage. Along with every A-list celebrity I can name and several others I can't. They take up a whole section of bleachers. The new VIP section. The wind gusts a bit as I wait for Phil to start the show.

Promptly at 9:00 p.m., the spotlights start weaving back and forth, and I hear Phil say, "Welcome, California, to the final show of season four! This is the show you have been waiting for. This show is longer—two and one-half hours—there are seven S'ers, and the Capp is so much more dangerous with eight in-lines. So many things can go wrong. A Capp this long has never been done before. Ricky confided in me earlier that she couldn't get a successful Capp even in practice. It is so long that this could only be done outside. The arc is almost a full ninety degrees, and the total distance of the throw is greater than the distance of a football field. After the near disaster last night, can Ricky pull off an even more complicated Capp? I doubt it.

Per Ricky's request, this show is being dedicated to Sally Henderson. Don't ask me why. As far as I am concerned, Sally was a two-time loser who got what she deserved. But that is what Ricky wants. And what Ricky wants, she gets. I'm your host, Phil Ebenezer, welcome to the final edition of *Capping S'ers* season four!"

I walk inside the studio to where the coffee

and donuts are set up as Phil continues, "We are back outside, and we are back in the dark! We have seven S'ers for you tonight. Their names are Benjamin Clark from Fremont, Laurie Brown from San Francisco, Molly Brock from San Bernardino, Jorge Cardoza from Los Angeles, Judith Davis from Costa Mesa, Dora Wilson from Fountain Valley and Robin Moore from Garden Grove. We will visit with all of them in their hometowns. We will then interview them all here live on our stage, and then LIVE we will watch the Capp and see how many do commit suicide. We will also see if Ricky has the right stuff to pull off such a challenging Capp. Stick around. We will be right back after this commercial break."

After eating a donut, I take my coffee and head to my trailer as that damn *Capping S'ers* theme music starts. Let the costume bust a seam. I don't care. This is the last time I am wearing it. In my trailer, I pick up a magazine off the couch, then go and sit at the table. I hum loud enough so the sound from the show is muted to where I can't make out the words. To hell with Brian and his rules. What is he going to do? Fire me?

In my ear I hear, "Sixty seconds to commercial." Ear bud works.

I leave the trailer and walk back outside. I go up to where the first S'er will be and move the pole holding a rope two inches to the right.

"In commercial."

I move the pole back to where it was. I walk over to my throw spot and look onstage at the first S'er being interviewed. He is a young-looking man. Seems nicely groomed. Why? WHY? So young. Benjamin talks about how he hates himself. How he is no good. How he will never amount to anything. How his whole life is a waste. He keeps that up until it is time for the first pole to be carted off, and they go to commercial again.

They start up with the theme music again, and on the big screen a girl starts pointing out her favorite spots in her hometown. I walk over to the final post and try to ignore it all. I reach out and lightly touch the post in the spot I expect the star to end up at the end of the Capp.

When it is almost commercial time, I go over to the second pole and rope. I adjust it, then put it back once the commercial starts.

Now the S'er being interviewed is the same young girl. Laurie is the one who was shivering before. She is wearing a thin silk blouse, so she could be cold. Her story is that she is gay and has been rejected by her girlfriend. Is that any reason to end a life? She knows for certain that she will never find love again. How can you know that at such a young age?

Before the commercial, I go over to the second pole with a rope and have it carried back inside for the grips to put in storage. Permanently.

While Phil introduces the next S'er, I go back to the donut table. I have another donut and take another coffee back to my trailer. One hour is over. Thank God.

Just before the next commercial, I go out and do my thing with the third pole.

The next S'er is Molly, who complains of being sad, depressed, and afraid of leaving the house. I find it boring, so I walk over to the final post again. I wonder if I can go through with it.

Just before the commercial, the next pole is carried away. I don't think I could hold down another donut. Maybe just one more coffee. Wish we had something stronger.

Phil introduces the next guest. Jorge Cardoza. He is a doctor, and I am intrigued with why he is on the show. He talks about his favorite places in Los Angeles. A restaurant, the library before it closed, and the David Geffen School of Medicine at UCLA. He goes on to describe why he wants to die. He talks about losing patients who should have survived. He talks about trying to comfort patients and families when he knows that it is hopeless. He talks about the current decline of health care, lack of availability of medicines, the skyrocketing cost, and the falloff of qualified medical providers.

I look over to our four doctors. They look uncomfortable. I don't know what the censors do with all that, but there on that stage, he speaks very passionately and is extremely critical of the state of California. At the end of it, I have the next pole removed. Why do I have butterflies in my stomach? I thought I was calm. My right hand itches, and my left hand is in extreme pain. One hour left to go.

Phil introduces the next guest. Judith Davis. She talks about why she wants to die. She thinks that getting Capped is the only way to get away from all the people stalking her. She isn't famous or anything. She is just a normal person, so I don't know why she thinks anyone would want to stalk her. She doesn't offer any proof that anyone is. She just knows they are. At the end of it, I have the fifth pole removed.

The next guest is Dora Wilson. Dora is a famous rock star and actress. Even I know Dora. She has it all. Guys, money, houses, awards, movie roles. Everyone begs for her autograph everywhere she goes. Why she would want to end her life, I have no idea. She talks about how she isn't perfect. How she isn't deserving of it all. About how everything just happened, and she didn't earn any of it. How she feels guilty and ashamed. About how someday everyone will find out that she is just a fake. Phil calls it maladaptive perfectionism. At the end of it, I have the sixth pole removed. Almost there.

Robin Moore is the last S'er. He wants to die because the world is not happy. I don't get him at all. When was the world ever happy? Between wars, famines, and plagues, I would say never. At the end of it, I have the last pole removed. It is show time.

Phil introduces me, and I walk out in front of the audience bleachers, hide my left hand, and wave. I walk over to the first S'er spot. Brian escorts Benjamin from the stage over to where I am waiting. I make sure his feet are on the mark. I have him stand straight. I check his position between the first in-line and the second. I study his neck to see how deep of a cut I will need. I move him slightly, but now he is leaning. I move him back and have him stand straight again. I study his neck again. I check his position in the line again. I try not to, but I look into his eyes. I see fear. How many S'ers wish they could change their mind after they had told their story? How many S'ers would change their mind if we gave them a week to think about it? I lean into him, place my lips near his ear, and whisper, "You don't have to do this. Just step away, and the star won't hurt you."

Finally, I am satisfied with him, and I move through the dark to the second S'er position. Brian escorts Laurie over. I make sure her feet are on the mark. I have her stand straight. I check her position in the line. I study her neck. I look into her eyes. They are a blue so pale as to appear transparent. Soon I will be free of all those eyes. I lean into her, place my lips near her ear, and whisper, "You don't have to do this. Just step away, and the star won't hurt you." She doesn't respond, so I move to the third S'er's position.

Brian escorts Molly over. I make sure her feet are on the mark. I have her stand straight. I check her position. I study her neck. I look into her eyes. Dark Brown. Sad. Tired. The eyeliner she chose does not go well with her eyes. I lean into her, place my lips near her ear, and whisper, "You don't have to do this. Just step away, and the star won't hurt you." She doesn't respond, so I move to the fourth S'er's position.

Brian brings Doctor Cardoza over. I make sure his feet are on the mark. He is already standing straight. I check his position in the line. I see determination. I see despair. Still looking into his eyes, I say, "You don't have to do this. Just step away, and the star won't hurt you." He holds my gaze, then he looks away before saying in a deep, low voice, "I'm ready."

Judith is next. Feet on the mark. Stand straight. I check her position. I study her neck. I look into eyes which are hazel with green flakes. I say, "You don't have to do this. Just step away, and the star won't hurt you."

Brian escorts Dora over. On the mark. Standing straight. Position. Neck. Eyes. I say, "You don't have to do this. Just step away, and the star won't hurt you."

Robin is last. Feet. Straight. Position. Neck. Eyes. I say, "You don't have to do this. Just step away, and the star won't hurt you."

I walk pass all the S'ers and in-lines. As I pass the in-lines, their spotlights go out. My spotlight comes on. I look down the curving line. Seven S'ers under lights. Eight in-lines in the dark. I glance over to make sure our four doctors are ready. A lot of good they will do. I can't believe this is my last Capp. After all I've been through. All that I have done.

It all comes down to this.

"Sixty seconds."

The wind gusts again. Do I need to take that into account? No. I never have. I stare down the line again. My right hand itches.

"Thirty seconds."

I fully extend my left arm with its aching mangled hand. I cock my right arm. I hold the star in ready position. I look down at my scar and the star. The wind dies down. I look up, and I fling my arm out and let the star fly. My spotlight goes out. A *clang*. The spark is easy to see in the dark. Benjamin stands in the spotlight. The star enters the light, grazes by him, cutting his neck in the process. His body shudders. He falls to the ground, blood streaming from his body. A *clang* and a spark.

The star grazes by Laurie, cutting her neck. Her body shudders. She falls to the ground, blood flowing.

A *clang* and a spark. The star grazes by Molly, cuts her neck. She has her eyes closed until she feels the impact. She screams, shudders, then falls to the ground, blood pooling.

I don't see the next spark because I am running. Despite the sound of my bare feet slapping the asphalt, I hear the star's impact with the fourth-in-line. Doctor Cardoza looks confused. He sees me moving. Is this how it's supposed to go? He backs off just before the star reaches him. Did I just save a life? Am I ready to take my own?

I run over to the final post and place myself in front of it. My exposed neck is in perfect position for where the star will impact if this Capp works as planned.

I hear Brian's voice in my earbud, "What do you think you're doing?"

A new spotlight comes on to highlight the final post. The light is coming from a different angle. I look toward the eighth-in-line, but he is in darkness, and I am blinded by the new spotlight. I didn't expect this. I am afraid that this Capp is taking too long. It's giving me too much time to think. It's giving Brian too much time to react. I should have waited and run over here later.

"You're killing the show!"

Was I? Was I killing the show, or was I killing myself? In either case, I am about to make this the most watched show ever in California television history.

"Get out of there! This instant!"

The fifth-in-line seems about to waiver. Despite the new spotlight, I can see his arms twitch and his body start to turn. He can see Brian running from inside the building toward him. Or maybe toward me. Before the fifth in-line can decide what to do, the star strikes him and moves on.

The star grazes by Judith, cutting her neck in the process. She shudders, then falls to the ground, blood dripping. The cut may not be deep enough. She can be saved if a doctor gets there in time.

Brian is getting closer. The noise from the crowd is deafening.

A *clang* and a spark. The star grazes by Dora, cutting her neck. She shudders, then falls to the ground, the pavement turning red around her body.

Brian is running, but he can't outrun the star. He will never reach me in time.

A *clang* and a spark. Robin acts confused. He stares at me, then at Brian, at me, then at Brian. He steps back just before the star reaches him. A *clang* and a spark.

I know that I can just step away. Isn't that what I have told every S'er? I will die if I don't. But do I deserve to live after all that I have done? All I have to do is step away.

As I stand, waiting before the final post of the Capp, the star, in darkness, speeding toward me, I know it's time to make my decision. I thought I already had. With my back still against the final post, I turn my eyes away from the new spotlight and let my gaze wander over to the stands where the audience is on its feet in hushed silence. I notice a girl with wide open pale green eyes. Just like my sister's. Just like Irene's. So expressive. What are those eyes telling me? Is it terror or excitement that makes her eyes open so wide? Is she afraid for me or does she want to see my blood flow also? Do I really want to kill myself? My sister forgave me. Can I forgive myself?

I step away. I don't want to die.

Maybe my life has not been perfect. Maybe I made

a lot of mistakes. But ending my life because of them is not the answer. Living my life better is. Doing good. Making up for my mistakes. That is the better way to deal with everything. Everything that is troubling me.

The star hits the final post right on the mark. The sound it makes by my ear is deafening and seems to echo forever. Brian, panting, stops beside me. "What were you thinking? You almost gave me a heart attack."

"I'm done. I just gave you the best show ever, but I am done killing people. I am done killing myself, little by little, for this damn TV show."

Epilogue

The Governor immediately had me seized and thrown in jail. There is no trial and later he moved me to a room in the basement of his mansion.

He has possession of the star.

I am kept there for days before anyone talked to me. The Governor finally came in and said that I am working for him now.

I have two bodyguards who are with me 24/7. Bodyguards. More like watchdogs.

At gunpoint, the Governor has me use the star to interface between him, me and someone else. Without me holding onto a point, the star won't let him enter another person's mind. He tried, but he can't get it to work. With me holding a point, the Governor has the freedom to explore a third person completely. But the Governor can also crawl through me. Whatever escape plans I make are revealed and blocked. Whatever guards I am friendly with are replaced.

There is no escape.

He had me do two more seasons of *Capping S'ers*. Season five had longer and longer Capps. We had twen-ty-five S'ers at the max. The problem was, with that many stories to tell, the show became too long, or the stories were cut too short. The audience lost interest.

With season six, they went back to the original format. One S'er. One hour. But after such spectacular shows, the original felt boring, and the audience viewership fell even more. Halfway through the season, they added audience participation. They presented three potential S'ers who told their story, and the audience voted on which one could die. This provided a temporary lift to ratings, but at the end of the season, the show was canceled.

The Governor kept me locked up. He had a never-ending supply of people he needed to interface with. Is this my fate? Am I going to be doing this for the rest of my life? I didn't avoid becoming an S'er for this. To be the Governor's pet? I need to get out of here.

It finally occurs to me that from the first time I bled on the star, it changed. From failing to fly straight to hitting the right trees. To killing my mom. To doing Capps. The star has been under my control this whole time. Maybe not my conscious control but under my control, nonetheless. So, the next time the Governor has me hold onto the star at gunpoint, I keep telling myself, or telling the star, "Don't let him in. Don't let him in."

"How did you do that?" the Governor asks.

"Do what?"

"Block me out like that."

"I didn't do anything."

The Governor laughs. "Right. Well don't think you are getting out of anything. You still cannot escape, and I am still the one with the guns. I can and will get inside of anyone I need to."

He turns to one of the guards and, indicating the third person who held the star, says, "Take him out back and shoot him."

Pointing at the star which I still hold in my

hand, he says, "I'm going to lock that up in my safe now."

One of the guards leaves the room with the other gentleman. The Governor's back is to me as he is spinning the dial on the safe. The other guard is looking at me, his hands at his side.

The Governor coveted the star for its ability to put on a TV show. He coveted it for its ability to enter people's minds. But I remember how it dealt with my mother, so I hurl the star at the last remaining guard.

The star hits him in the throat, and he goes down. The Governor turns and sees me pull the star out of the guard's body. He flees out the nearest door before I can do the same to him.

I look around a minute before I jump out of the window, kill two more guards on the grounds, and escape over the wall. I am done with California. I am heading for Nevada where the Governor's thoughts revealed that everything is legal, even murder.

NOTE FROM THE AUTHOR

Thank you for reading my book. I hope you enjoyed it. If you would like to find out more about me or about the other books in The Star Universe, just go to <u>www. lrkerns.com</u>.

.